Bayou Moon

C. L. Bevill

ST. MARTIN'S MINOTAUR
THOMAS DUNNE BOOKS
NEW YORK

FICTION

www.minotaurbooks.com

Library of Congress Cataloging-in-Publication Data

Bevill, C. L.
    Bayou moon / C. L. Bevill.—1st ed.
        p.   cm.
    ISBN 0-312-28207-9
    1. Women artists—Fiction.   2. Missing persons—Fiction.   3.
Mothers—Death—Fiction.   4. Louisiana—Fiction.   5. Voodooism—
Fiction.   I. Title.

PS3602.E85 B39   2002
813'.6—dc21

                                                            2002069251

First Edition: October 2002

10   9   8   7   6   5   4   3   2   1

To Michelle Gomez, Jennifer Llewellyn, and Violet Urquidez, good friends, all

Acknowledgments

Grateful thanks to Palma Beckett, dedicated reader, Carolyn Chu, committed editor, Ron and Mary Lee Laitsch, inspiring agents, and Woody Bevill, supportive husband.

By the light of a bayou moon,
A ghostly figure wanders there,
Once radiant as sunlight at noon,
Now pale as ice with black eyes that stare.

BAYOU MOON

Prologue

From ghoulies and ghosties and long-leggety beasties
And things that go bump in the night, Good Lord deliver us!

CORNISH PRAYER

FOG ROLLED OFF THE river, obscuring the waning, crescent-shaped moon. All that was left of the heavenly body was the midnight glow that permeated the clouds of moisture flowing effortlessly over the bare earth. It highlighted skeletal fingers of mist grasping for unknown quarry. The mist conspired to keep all of its secrets, from the untenable September chill that had blown down from the north, dropping the temperature below fifty degrees, to the abnormal silence of the night crickets and cicadas.

Indeed, no human seemed to wander this night. The wind tenderly moved the branches of the tallest trees. Only a little debris from pine trees moved restlessly under their full branches. The land was silent. It was as if it prepared itself for what it knew would come, what it knew *must* come.

The sliver of yellowy-silver moon stared unflinchingly down at the St. Michel mansion where it arrogantly sat on a hill in the St. Germaine Parish of northwestern Louisiana. Once all of the land around it belonged to the wealthy St. Michel family. There, slaves had toiled to grow and pick cotton, pecans, and corn. The produce was loaded onto barges that sailed up a river hardly large enough to contain the barge. Then it returned down river, finding passage to bigger rivers and eventually the grand Mississippi and to the city of New Orleans where its cargo was sold. Once, the St. Michels had ruled the parish with an iron fist, in politics, in employment, and in sheer brutality. The St. Michels were a rich, influential family, with similarly powerful relatives in both Washington, D.C., and in Baton Rouge. And the St. Michels were never known to be kind, gentle people, much less benefactors to those who labored for them.

But time had had its way with the St. Michels and their land, and although they were still wealthy, their base of power had faded, leaving them big fish of the little pond called La Valle, Louisiana. The politicians still asked for money, but it was rarely given. The charities still invited the family matriarch, but she came only sporadically.

The land that had been plowed using the blood and sweat of purchased men was sold off piecemeal. Sometimes it was leased to farmers, who continued to grow intermediate crops of pecans and corn. The great St. Michel mansion became another interesting landmark to those who visited the South. It was a plantation house of tremendous Greek-inspired architecture, with fancy, towering columns, and so many rooms that two housekeepers were employed to supervise the cleaning. At one point, there were so many maids that one St. Michel mistress took to calling them all Sally; she could never remember all of the names in the endless rotation of young women who came to work there and then moved on. The house still boasted its bounty of silver, gilt-edged wainscoting, velvet wallpaper, crystal chandeliers, and ornate furniture. An antique dealer would have been joyfully exuberant at the chance to sell such wondrous possessions.

And although the St. Michel empire shrank in size, the wealth did not. One canny forebear discovered that he had a knack for investing money, and bought early into such companies as Ford, General Electric, and even the newest technology, computers. This man, whose name was Pierre St. Michel and who died long before the night of September 3rd, made more money for the St. Michels in a decade than the entire family had made in a century. But the power base that had been theirs never returned. The St. Michel children never again showed an interest in politicking, other than obligatory contributions to a cause. Their lives were spent in modest business pursuits, if that, and the life of what was called "the plantation set." They spent time in Europe, Baton Rouge, they attended the best balls during Mardi Gras, they were known throughout Louisiana, but they also became isolated.

And isolation might have begot that which came to the St. Michels.

Only one housekeeper stayed nights at the St. Michel mansion. The other slept at her home, on the other side of the town. Most of the maids were away, snug in their little homes, many miles away, many of them still in high school, a few in junior high school. Only a few slept in the maids' quarters, behind the mansion. The groundsman slept in the cottage near the maids' quarters and never budged, because he was as deaf as a post, and typically drunk on a pint of Southern Comfort.

In the withering fog that poured across emerald green shrubbery and through cleverly crafted Japanese boxwood mazes a figure clad in white drifted. Her features were vague, and long, red hair streamed across her back, delicately moved by a desolate breeze. She made her way through the gardens and seemed to cast no shadow from the meager, fog-obscured moon.

Inside the mansion a woman stared out the windows so intently that she did not see a man approach her silently from behind. A lean, willowy figure silhouetted against the glowing light outside, her hair was the same color as the sliver of heavenly body above. She clasped the curtain in one hand and pressed herself closely to the glass, fogging the window with her breath.

"Eugenie," said the man. He was her twin in almost every respect. His hair was the same silver-gilt. His eyes were the same midnight blue. His face was square and aristocratic. His figure was that of a whipcord strength. He was a man who worked at maintaining his trim, angular physique in the same manner that the woman did. One needed only to compare the two people for a second to realize that they were siblings.

"I saw her, Geraud," said Eugenie. "She walks again." One of her elegant, well-manicured hands pointed into the weighty fog. "Can't you see the glow in the night? Can't you see?"

Geraud stepped forward, centering himself at the window, framed by luxurious velvet and silk, and gazed into the world of white light refracting off moisture-laden clouds. He stared, looking for whatever it was that his sister saw. For a moment, he straightened up, not believing what had passed so briefly before him. His eyes narrowed as he pressed his face closer to the cold glass in front of him. There was a figure in the mist. A female figure with long red hair, hair the color of burnished bronze, stood at the bottom of the hill, staring at them. Her figure was lost in the whirling clouds of fog. He blinked, and when he opened his eyes again, the figure was gone. *A trick of the imagination*, he thought, almost desperately. *Only a trick. The fog is thick like I've never seen it before, and who knows what could have caused that?*

Geraud stared into the fog until his eyes began to hurt, but there was nothing else. Nothing moved that he could see. *There is no one*, he thought. *There is no one there.*

A hand touched his shoulder, and he spun around. Their mother, Eleanor, stood behind the two of them, observing them with eyes as cool as their own. She stood there, wrapped in a silk robe, her small feet in satin slippers, her hands resting on her abdomen. Her long, white hair was tucked up carefully into a chignon. If Geraud had not heard the bell on the grand-father clock strike two, he might have thought that his mother had not yet been to bed. She looked calm, serene, as if she could handle anything. No vestiges of sleep still remained on her remarkable visage.

"What did you see?" asked Eleanor. Her face was as angular as her children's. There could be no doubt of their lineage. She was their mother in many more respects than merely appearance. But where she was sedate, Geraud's blood raced with anxiety, as if something lay beyond them, in the fog-screened lightlessness, something that was best faced by people who were inside the mansion, rather than without.

Geraud shook his head, not willing to share a midnight fancy, something that was simply shadows out of the darkness, determined that it simply could not be possible. He glanced at his sister and found her looking out the window as if waiting for someone to come home.

Eleanor touched her daughter's shoulder and murmured, "You should go to bed, my dear. It's far too late to be up, staring out into the fog."

Eugenie turned toward her mother and paused before nodding. She wrapped her arms around her slender figure and almost drifted away, her white gown the only thing they could see in the darkness of the mansion.

Later, when Eleanor went to check on Eugenie, Geraud stood and watched from the bedroom door. The dim light from the hallway spilled into the dark room as Eleanor stroked her daughter's hair over and over again, a simple gesture that indicated the depth of love for her child.

"I thought I saw . . . ," started Geraud, and stopped. To admit to his too clever *maman* that he had seen anything would have been a mistake. Inside the house the fog was a distant memory.

"Saw what?" said Eleanor.

"It's stupid."

"You saw her, too." Eleanor's voice was firm, but tranquil, as if ghosts appearing before her children were an everyday occurrence.

"I saw . . . something," he said. He was not willing to put a name to anything, for that would be like accepting the reality of something that could not be proven. "It might very well have been one of those damned tabloid reporters for all I know."

"Did you smell something, too?" Eleanor asked. One of her hands continued stroking Eugenie's hair while the other touched the saint's medal hanging around her neck. "Earlier this evening, after dinner? As if *he* had just been standing there, watching all of us?"

Geraud took a step back from the door. He had smelled something he recalled from the remnants of his childhood, a smell that he could only connect to one person. "It doesn't mean anything."

"I haven't smelled Cuban cigars in twenty-five years." Eleanor put her fingers on her daughter's cheek. Then she finally turned her head to look at her son. "I don't think you have, either."

Geraud's face twisted. "It could be from anyone. Eugenie went out tonight. She went to a bar. She has friends who smoke. It doesn't mean anything." He repeated this litany, as if simple repetition would make it so.

"It's not the first time," said Eleanor. Her eyes were brilliant in the night, the blue so dark, they could have been black. She looked at him with the expressionless face of a Madonna. She might very well have been discussing the weather. "On nights like this, when the fog rolls across the lawn in a wave, it's like he's come home. I could walk into the study, and there he'd sit, waiting for me, waiting for us all."

There was silence between mother and son for a long time.

"It doesn't mean anything," Geraud finally said. "And don't go calling on one of your ripoff psychics to clear this up. It's just Eugenie, making us think that ghosts are walking in the night. She sees these things only in her head. Nothing more. She needs to take her medication. That's all." He spun around and stalked off, his footsteps echoing behind him.

Eleanor looked back at her daughter, who had escaped into the world of dreams, where nothing was real, and everything could be twisted to suit one's purpose. "Who are you trying to convince, Geraud?" she asked herself softly. "Me or you?"

Chapter One

It's like a lion at the door;
And when the door begins to crack,
It's like a stick across your back;
And when your back begins to smart,
It's like a penknife in your heart;
And when your heart begins to bleed,
You're dead, and dead, and dead, indeed.

A MAN OF WORDS AND NOT OF DEEDS

IT WAS A WARM, cloudless, Friday morning when a living ghost walked the streets of La Valle, Louisiana. There were some who actually gasped when they saw her. One old woman turned to her equally elderly companion and whispered of the will-o'-the-wisp, an evil *diable* at work, even in the most powerful magic that was full sunlight. She crossed herself, and spat on the sidewalk where the ghost had trod, vowing to make a protective gris-gris for herself that very night.

Bill Martinez, the pharmacist, dropped his customer's prescription all over the pharmacy's floor, scattering blue and white pills to the four winds. The customer peered curiously over the counter and asked, "Now what in the name of God has gotten into you, Bill?" He laughed. "A ghost walk over your grave?"

Bill stood up straight and banged his head against the bottom of the counter, under which he had been fishing with stubby fingers for a stray pill. "Goddamnit," he muttered. His eyes were level with the counter for a moment. Then he rose up and looked back outside, watching the woman strolling down the main street of La Valle, as if she had stepped out from two decades past. He stuffed the last of the errant pills into the bottle and passed it over to his customer without saying another word. Finally, it occurred to him that his customer was still standing in front of him, staring. "What?" asked Bill.

Jourdain Gastineau, a seasoned and well-connected lawyer on the verge of being appointed Supreme Court Justice, studied the pharmacist with all of the skills he used in politics and in his thriving law practice. He hadn't known Bill to get upset about anything or anyone, much less so flustered that he had dropped pills all over the floor. He had known the pharmacist for nigh on thirty years, since they were in high school together, playing football in a mud-splattered field behind the school's main building, not a mile from where they now stood. "You want me to pay for that, Bill?" he said. "I 'spect you might like to get a little return on your investment."

Bill studied Jourdain in return, regaining his composure and most of his good humor. The woman had stopped to look at the pharmacy's window display, inadvertently centering herself in the large opening. She stood behind Jourdain, just through the plate glass window, looking intently at a display of cameras that Bill had gotten in a few days before. "You want to look out my front window, Jourdain? Then we'll speak of the money for your prescription. Though I'd think a fella like yourself wouldn't need a sedative. Being such a cold-blooded lawyer and all."

Jourdain laughed easily. "My wife is having trouble sleeping, Bill. Not that it's any of your business." He was not a tall man, nor short. His hair had turned gray, and he wasn't one to use some fancy hair dye to keep it the color it should have been. But his figure and face belied his fifty-odd years, and his clear brown eyes often sparkled with a vigor that Bill knew other men of their age had long since lost. Most of the time Jourdain's humor was easygoing, except when it took place in the courtroom or at a mediator's table. He was a well-regarded man in the small town of La Valle, a man who spent more of his time in Baton Rouge, where the true political struggles happened, and a man who was going to move up soon, if the rumors held any truth. But there had always been that hint of ruthlessness that Bill and others of his ilk had known about. Bill had discovered it on the playing fields of their youth, and suspected that other men had discovered it on the playing fields of the legal system. Furthermore, Bill knew perfectly well that it was Jourdain Gastineau's name on the prescription bottle, not his wife's.

Jourdain was still laughing when he turned and saw what Bill had already seen. His laugh was abruptly cut off by a loud wheezing noise.

Bill rubbed the bump on the top of his head with grim satisfaction. "Talk about something walking over your grave," he said.

Jourdain was wondering if he were having a heart attack, because he couldn't move. All he could do was stare. Blood roared in his ears. His vision was tunneled at the woman standing almost directly in front of him, as if she were presenting herself to him. It *was* her. Her fine, beautiful features were the same. That color of hair, burnished bronze, shining brilliantly in the sunshine, was so patently hers. He could remember it vividly. That was her well-shaped figure encased in a little gray business suit. A sensible suit, but curve-hugging all the same, accentuating her long legs.

Quite suddenly she looked up, and her green eyes, the color of glass that has sat in the sun for a long time, contemplated Jourdain without a hint of recognition. It seemed like time stretched out forever as their eyes locked on each other. Finally, she turned away and continued her stroll down the avenue, as if she didn't have a care in the world. She touched a bag of pecans from a stand outside the produce store and passed it by. She bent down to smell Mrs. Regret's flowers on the corner. She sauntered down the street, as if she were taunting all of those people who were watching her.

With his mouth gaping wide, Jourdain watched her, too.

"I would have known her anywhere," Bill said.

Jourdain shook himself. He turned to look at Bill. "What do you mean?" he croaked, and winced when he heard himself. He sounded like he had years ago when he was a first-year graduate fresh out of Harvard. In an instant, he had been transported back to the days when his tongue tied at the tip of a hat, and the jewels of merciless wit that now sprang forth readily escaped him.

The other man screwed up his face. "Well, goodness, Jourdain. They run off together, come . . . oh . . . twenty-five years ago. She was raised here. She still has cousins here. You know the Dubeauxs over to Provencal, don't you? Or maybe you don't. They're not the type to hire such a fancy-pants lawyer as yourself, and you've spent so many of the last years down to Baton Rouge. Surely, some of the St. Michels had to expect that one or t'other would be back one day. It wasn't like they fell off the face of the earth."

Jourdain stared at Bill, not seeing the man at all. His mind was working like a computer, calculating what her presence meant. *It's true, all of it. But that woman . . . she. . . .* "Isn't her," he said positively, finally, determined that it should be so.

Bill snorted. "What do you mean? I saw her, too. So did half the townspeople, by the look of the people peeking out their windows. I ain't seen so many people on Main Street at nine in the morning since the Pecan Festival in July. You'd think the woman was prancing down the middle of the street

wearing nothing but a smile and a how-d'you-do?" He smiled
at the mental picture that popped into his mind.

"Think!" Jourdain raised his prescription bottle and shook
it in front of the pharmacist, blue and white pills rattling like
a maraca. "Did that look like a woman in her early fifties?"

The other man chewed on his lower lip. He took a moment
to answer. *Damned if she couldn't be her twin sister, back
from years ago, and that is the point Jourdain's getting at, that
it was a whole lotta years ago.* But there was only one expla-
nation to be found here, the most obvious one, the one that
hadn't immediately occurred to Bill. He said at last, "No, it's
got to be the other one."

Jourdain nodded and left the pharmacy abruptly. He left so
quickly that he didn't pay his bill, and Bill didn't think to ask
for it until much later. Jourdain went to his Mercedes Benz
and almost ran over the postman's cat, who wandered too
much to suit Jourdain or the postman. He left the town of La
Valle, driving north.

There were many others who noticed the woman. Her auburn hair, her green eyes, and her clean-limbed figure were all
pleasing to the eye. Even women responded to her welcoming
smile and throaty voice. She stopped several places in the
course of the morning, and many people saw her. She browsed
through the hardware store. She bought a bouquet of autumn
mums. She chatted with two teenage boys on the corner of
Main and Jacques Streets, both of whom were obviously playing hooky from school, and couldn't keep their young eyes off
her legs and breasts. Before long, many more people were talking about her. The murmurs moved faster along the main
street than she did. She heard the mutters a few times. There
were a few people who out and out stared, but no one asked.
No one had the courage, because they weren't sure if they
wanted to hear the answers she might give. Nor did they care
to understand why her presence coincided so closely with the

return of the St. Michels, and the return of an onslaught of rumors.

It was the realtor, Vincent Grase, who confirmed her identity. She stepped into his office with a brilliant smile. He had only lived in St. Germaine Parish for fifteen years, and although he had heard the hearsay before, he didn't put it together with his first client of the day.

"Good morning," said the red-haired woman. Vincent was instantly entranced. He was in his forties, married to a shrew of a woman, and had two shrewish children who didn't care to follow their father in the real estate business; he was always looking for future Mrs. Grases, whether the female in mind was interested or not.

"Good morning," he responded enthusiastically, rising up from behind his large oak desk. He even took the time to suck in his not inconsiderable stomach for effect. He offered his hand. She took it. There was a quick shake and release, just as Vincent liked his handshakes to be.

"I'm looking for a place," said the beauty.

"To rent or to purchase?" asked Vincent. *Please let it be a home to buy. Maybe one of those six-figure babies on the south side of town. Hello, Christmas bonus. Maybe ask me over for a brandy one night. . . .*

"A rental to begin with," she answered, waving a hand at one of the chairs in front of his desk. "May I?"

"Of course," Vincent agreed. He even came around the side of the desk to help her be seated, which was, of course, unnecessary. After she had brushed his wandering hands off her body, he asked, "Coffee?"

"Yes, please."

"How do you take it?"

"Black as sin." Her throaty voice was almost sinful to listen to, as she gazed up at the realtor with those pale green eyes.

Focusing on her answer, and not its implications, Vincent

appeared surprised. "Most young woman, such as yourself, seem to care for a bit of sugar, a bit of milk. Something to take the edge off the bitterness." He busied himself at the table beside his desk, which contained a full coffee pot and all of the essentials. Cups clanked together as he made himself useful.

"Isn't life a little bitter?" she asked, folding her hands across her stomach.

Vincent handed her a cup of coffee and watched her full lips take a sip of the steaming brew. He thought that he knew women pretty well, and when the lovely young woman gave him a certain look, he knew that he didn't have a snowball's chance in hell of making any moves on her. Inwardly he sighed. His stomach abruptly expanded itself again in abject resignation.

"You mean you drink your coffee black to remind you that life isn't all peaches and cream?" he asked.

"That's a very accurate way of putting it. Sometimes a person has to remind oneself that life isn't always sweet and tasteful." Then she laughed. "Or perhaps it's just that I simply care for my coffee black."

Vincent looked at her for a moment. He stood propped against the front of his desk, not three feet away from one of the most beautiful women he had seen in years. Finally, he shook himself out of his reverie, and asked, "Do you have a price range for a rental, Miss . . . ah . . . ?"

"Price isn't an object," she replied smoothly, ignoring his attempt to produce her name. "I would like to be comfortable. In a place that has at least one room with a lot of light, and nothing near a freeway. Older properties are just as acceptable as newer ones. Later, I will be looking to purchase certain properties in the area, and naturally I shall require a realtor, such as yourself."

"Naturally," said Vincent, totting up dollar signs. She wore an expensive suit, a Donna Karan, if he wasn't mistaken. Her shoes were Ferragamo's. Her purse was Dooney & Burke. The scent of money poured off her just as her exquisite perfume did. It was the kind of fragrance that Vincent was positive he couldn't buy his wife in any store around these parts, and one that he was not altogether sure he could afford even if it was available. "Do you mind me asking what kind of business you're in, ma'am?"

"Oh, I'm an artist." She took another sip. "Just an artist."

Chapter Two

The Queen of Hearts,
She made some tarts,
All on a summer's day;
The Knave of Hearts,
He stole the tarts,
And took them clean away.

THE QUEEN OF HEARTS

"HER NAME IS MIGNON Thibeaux," said Vincent Grase in a little café, three doors down from his office. "She's an artist from New York City. She was born here."

Mrs. Regret, whose first name was unknown to most of the population of La Valle, and who owned the flower shop and a bed and breakfast, looked at Vincent the way she might have looked at some creature that had crawled up on her doorstep. The red-haired woman had left his office at half past eleven, walked back to her rental car, and driven away. After she left, Vincent had stepped out of his office, intent on lunch. Mrs. Regret and three other business owners had followed Vincent like a pack of voracious hyenas. Now they sat at the counter on stools, looking at each other and at Vincent in turn.

Even the waitress at the café horned in on the conversation. She said, "She looks just like her mama."

Mrs. Regret turned her withering gaze on the waitress. "Eloise, you weren't even born when Garlande Thibeaux left La Valle."

"Of course I was," protested the waitress vehemently, rubbing her hands on a dish cloth. "I was three years old."

"Garlande Thibeaux," repeated Vincent thoughtfully, trying to mentally scrounge up the connection to his present-day client of the same last name. "Now where have I heard that name?"

"It was the biggest scandal since that Jew fella up and shot Huey Long," someone three stools down the counter called out.

"I've only been in these parts since the middle eighties, you know," said Vincent. "Give me a cup of your coffee, Eloise. Mine tastes like battery acid. Don't know how that young woman drank three cups of it."

"So what's she doing back here?" asked Mrs. Regret, irritated that the conversation had veered away from her, and away from the subject she most wanted to hear about: the presence of Miss Mignon Thibeaux in the town from which she had been absent for over two decades.

People all along the counter squirmed and wriggled to look at each other.

"Looking for a place to live, of course," said Vincent. "Why else would you go to a real estate office? Can't tell you any more. It's confidential." He sounded as if he had signed and sworn a solemn oath of office before the President of the United States. He even pulled back his shoulders and stuck out his chin in a manner that might have put people off asking the question again.

Mrs. Regret and Eloise both stared at Vincent. Neither was impressed. Finally, Mrs. Regret said, "You ain't a medical doctor, Vincent. Nor, the last I heard, are you a psychiatrist. So I don't think that's rightly correct."

Vincent looked at his cup of coffee. Upon discovering that the presence of Mignon Thibeaux had caused some sort of brouhaha, he was not about to admit that he hadn't pumped the woman for as much information as he could about her appearance in La Valle. Since she wasn't about to flirt with him, he had concentrated on finding a listing for her that was suitable. She had filled out a bit of paperwork about her preferences, told him she would check into a bed and breakfast nearby, and would be in touch. In fact, her last name had sounded familiar, but in north-central Louisiana there were dozens of French names like Thibeaux. There were Cheres, Thibodouxs, Regrets, Roques, St. Michels, and others too many to name. It had been filed away in Vincent's mind as merely a coincidence.

In any case, if he had known that Mignon Thibeaux was someone everyone was wondering about, then he surely would not have allowed her to leave his office until he had connived to get everything he could out of her. "She's an artist," he repeated, weakly. "Said she'd published a book of her paintings. Watercolors and oils, I think."

"Uh-huh," responded Mrs. Regret.

Nearby sat the postman, who happened to be the only man who knew Mrs. Regret's first name and why no one else was permitted to know it. It had been her mother's name and just as hideous a name as the postman had ever heard. He said, "I think I heard of her. She won some awards and such. You remember, Eloise. There was an article in the *Shreveport Herald*. Goes by just her first name, like Cher or Madonna. But no one said she was born here, and I ain't put two and two together to realize it was the very same gal."

Eloise shrugged. She was more interested in hearing about scandals and such. Like all of the hubbub up at the St. Michel mansion about ghosts walking the halls there, looking for God knows what. Some of the young women who worked there as maids refused to go there after dark, and even the speculation on just who the ghost was supposed to be was heated. A St. Michel had died in the Civil War protecting the family's silver.

A slave had been beaten to death by an owner in the nine-teenth century. Or perhaps it was the infamous white lady, who visited the St. Michels when some type of catastrophe was about to pass. There were even a few who intimated that the ghost was Luc St. Michel himself, though there was not a bit of proof that Eleanor St. Michel's husband was dead, and even Eloise knew that story. Finally, she answered, "I don't remember."

The postman went on, " 'Cause she was an orphan and all. Of course, no one really knows if she's that, because her mama's probably still alive. I remember way back when that Ruff Thibeaux died over to Dallas. Suppose the child went into the foster care system, because the mother did abandon her. Anyway, that article said she managed to get herself some scholarships, lives in both New York and California. She even studied in Europe. One of her paintings sold for over one hun-dred thousand dollars. Although I think it was a Japanese fella who bought it. Imagine that. A Thibeaux selling a picture worth one hundred thousand dollars."

"One painting," repeated Vincent. He had visions of a won-derful listing being sold to Mignon Thibeaux. *Maybe a quarter of a million dollars. Hell, a half a million dollars, with a seven percent cut for me. Yee-haw.* He was so busy thinking about it that he almost drooled in his coffee.

"I can see exactly what's on your mind," Mrs. Regret sneered.

Vincent was nothing if not willing and able to change the subject at an opportune time. "So what's the big scandal?"

"It involves the St. Michels," said Eloise. Then she glanced crossly at a customer who had gone from waving his hand at her to flailing his arms about in an effort to gain her attention. "Hold on to your horses, *mon ami.* I'm a'coming."

Mrs. Regret frowned at her bowl of gumbo. She never liked eating here since the owner had hired a new cook from Yankee

Land who didn't even know how to make a proper bowl of the Louisiana staple. "You know Eleanor St. Michel?" she asked Vincent, moving the bowl to the side.

"Sure." Sometimes the matriarch of the St. Michels would put a listing with Vincent. It was usually a farm lease of some sort, considering the vast amounts of farmland that the St. Michels owned in the area. It was either Eleanor or her oldest child, Geraud, when he was about.

They were not the friendliest sort of folks around, but Vincent chalked it up to them being rich and uppity plantation people. Their forefathers could be traced back to the French-Acadian influx in the eighteenth century and so forth, and the Grases were only Johnny-come-lately's to Louisiana in comparison. It wasn't an unusual situation in the area; there were many poor families who could trace their roots back a century before the St. Michels, if they were so inclined. But those kind of people didn't have the cash in the bank, nor the antebellum home to show for it.

"Her husband up and ran off with his mistress back in the seventies," continued Mrs. Regret.

"Not only that," the postman interrupted.

Mrs. Regret nodded. "Not only that but his mistress was married and had a child. She up and left her husband and child for Luc St. Michel. He left Eleanor in the lurch with two children of their own, although they sure weren't hurting for money or support."

Vincent wasn't exactly impressed. Men did that, upon occasion. So did women. He'd do it, given the opportunity. *Say, if Mignon Thibeaux looked at me longingly with those pale green eyes, and asked pretty please with sugar on it, I'd be there just like that.* He mentally snapped his fingers. Then he snapped them again. *Maybe quicker.*

"That woman was Garlande Thibeaux," finished Mrs. Regret, ever anticipatory of a good ending to a story.

Vincent opened his eyes up wide. "And Garlande is Mignon's mother," he finished.

Mrs. Regret smiled slowly. "Just so. The very spitting image."

"Imagine that," sighed Eloise, eyes heavenward. "True lovers running off to be together, forever."

Vincent couldn't imagine that. But what the heck, if Garlande Thibeaux ran off with her wealthy lover, who might blame her? He thought about that and answered it himself, thinking of the cold, collected woman who came to his office upon occasion. A woman who carefully compiled each piece of paperwork, and made sure she had copies in triplicate, might blame the woman who had stolen her husband away. *Eleanor St. Michel might do just that. There is a woman who would hold a grudge.*

Dismissing the thought, he wondered about Mignon Thibeaux and what exactly had brought her back to this town.

Mrs. Regret smiled to herself. "They say that he died someplace, Luc St. Michel. That he came back to torment the St. Michels because of the way the daughter of his mistress was treated." Her voice trailed off, and her eyes focused on the man who had been sitting in a back booth listening to the conversation. He stood up to his full height of over six feet and carefully put his hat on his head. "Oh, hey, John Henry," she stuttered. "I sure didn't see you there."

The man in the Stetson and the khaki uniform dumped a handful of bills on the table, and nodded vaguely at Mrs. Regret and the others. His neatly pinned sheriff's badge glittered in the fluorescent light as he turned. The active murmurs died away until he stepped outside and got into his official white Ford Bronco.

———

THE WOMAN WHO was the focus of so much discussion, in part because of her successful occupation and in part because of the deeds of her mother, stood beside her rental car, which was parked in the middle of a rough, single-lane road that led through the pines to a little house. It was spitting distance from the Kisatchie National Forest, and on each side of the tiny road sweet gum, pine, birch, cypress, and fir trees stood thickly, reflecting its long uncut and unharvested status. Beyond the thickly forested lane lay a swampy bayou where she had once watched beavers build great mountains of wood in the algae-covered water and where the cypress trees dripped with moss and jasmine.

Mignon Thibeaux hadn't been sure if she would remember the way, but she had. It had been many years, after all, since she had been here. Her last memory of this place was peering out the back window of her father's old Chevy truck with the tree branches from the pines scraping the roof of the truck as they always did, and her father cursing under his breath as they drove away.

The road wasn't blocked, but the parallel tracks seemed overgrown as if no one came down this way much anymore. The trees that bordered the road were taller and the shrubs thicker from years of being left alone, leaving a dimly lit path to the house. She had once trod the path daily, skipping her way down the road after the schoolbus dropped her off on the highway. Then, there hadn't been that utter darkness of the massed trees that now seemed to block out the light from above.

She threaded her way through the woods, careful to stay in the ruts of the road, because she knew that there were snakes here, including some lethal varieties common in the area. Her shoes weren't made for walking down a road like this, but she managed slowly and carefully. She would rather break a heel than damage the rental car she had driven here by testing its worthiness on a road with some holes that were knee-deep.

After a few minutes of picking her way down the furrowed path, she saw the house. It was a small place, not visible from the main highway. A single story, which included three rooms with a wraparound porch that curved around the front of the house and across the main bedroom. The kitchen and living room were one room. One bedroom lay off to the right of the kitchen. On the other side was another tiny bedroom, where Mignon had slept in a single bed that almost filled the room. She never understood until later that it wasn't a bedroom at all, but a pantry; her father had removed the shelves in order to provide a place for his only child to sleep.

The house dated back perhaps a hundred and fifty years. If one crawled into the attic, the rough-hewn logs that were used for the frame could be seen. The house had existed when the Civil War was at its peak, when both Union and Confederate armies rode by La Valle in pursuit of each other. It had seen generations of people living within it, even born within it, although the Thibeauxs had come only recently.

Mignon stood in the front yard, which was overgrown with fledgling pine trees and brush, leaving little grass. The windows were whole and intact, but the house seemed to be sinking in the middle, as if some great giant had stepped on it and forced it to bow downward, on the edge of being precarious. She abruptly realized that probably no one had lived in this house since the last time she had stepped off the front porch, when she and her father had fled in shame. The outside was almost as rough as the interior logs that supported the house itself. The wood was worn gray in places. The incised tin sheeting on the tops of the walls near the roof had turned black with age, and only the rounded patterns were left shining in the light that reached this small clearing in the middle of all of these trees.

She stood in front of the house she hadn't seen in so long. Upon discussion of her plans, her friend Terri, back in New York, had said, "Miggy, it's a bad idea. You go back, but it's never the same. Your home looks like a shack. Your neighbors don't recognize you, or don't care if they did. It just reminds you of how shitty it all was. It's a bad idea."

It was just like the old saying, "You can't go home again." Well, here she was, and she didn't think of it as home. She had never thought of it as home. This was merely the place where she had been born, in that one back bedroom, with her mother on a four-poster bed. This was a place where she had learned how to talk, how to walk, how to run laughing to that tall, beautiful woman she called, "Mama."

She walked around the house, studying its imperfections. The house did appear tiny, just as her friend had suggested. But the answer was that she had been five years old when she had last seen it, and now she was thirty, and had an apartment in New York City with a living room bigger than the entire house.

Around the back of the house about fifty feet was the out-house. This was another reminder of how rural the area was. She had no doubt that other homes still depended on out-houses, or if not that, septic tanks. This house had no sewage system and no running water. In fact, Mignon had a very dis-tinct memory of the house's only source of water. She glanced back at the house and studied what was left of the gutter sys-tem along the eaves. It was designed to collect rain water into a tank mostly hidden by the brush at the side of the house. This tank was periodically emptied into a cistern somewhere behind the house.

Mignon glanced down. She could be standing over it right now. A large cistern made of cement, designed to hold water for the use of farming, bathing, cooking, for those areas that could not afford to dig a well.

She had a vivid memory of her father standing over her, near that very place. He had been tall, red-haired, brown-eyed, rough-hewn like the timbers in the attic. He had been a farmer, a laborer, like his father had been; a man with broad shoulders and large, callused hands. He had stood over her, shaking her tiny shoulders, saying loudly, "I told you, no playing near that cistern, Mignon. You might fall right in and break your little skinny neck. You hear me, child?" And there had been another shake of her tiny shoulders to emphasize the urgency of his command. "You hear me?"

Once, the cistern had been covered by a cement slab. The slab obviously was long lost in the shrubs and weeds growing rampantly in the area that was the backyard of the house. Try as she might, Mignon couldn't see where it was, and she only had a vague recollection of where it was once located.

Then there was the old oak tree towering over the backyard, where she had once played endlessly. Her father had even carved her initials into the tree for her, with a heart surrounding it. "It's your tree," he had said, his Louisiana accent thick. "This here is Mignon's very own oak."

Her long fingers traced the *M* and the *T* as if she had never seen them before. The tree had grown. It was so thick around, she knew she couldn't span it with her arms. As a child, it was the perfect size, small enough to climb, but tall enough so that a child pretending to be the queen of the world felt she looked down on her kingdom.

Or, she considered, *the queen of her world for at least a little while.* It had felt good to be in control of her little world then, even if had been for only a short time.

Another memory came to her, a vision of her father long before he had descended into the alcoholic stupor in which he lived out his last years, a man who had patiently taught his daughter the fine art of snapping flies with whatever piece of string or chain was available. He would flick his strong wrist,

snapping the fly or mosquito with the end of the length of
string and laugh like it had been the funniest joke of all. With
the quiet tolerance of a loving parent, he had shown little Mignon how to hold her hand and how to whip her wrist about
to aim for insects that dared too close. It was one of few memories that his daughter found pleasing to remember.

Finally, Mignon faced the house. She wasn't concerned that
she was trespassing. She hadn't seen any posted signs, but
there were a few shotgun holes in the outhouse. Hunters were
discouraged from wandering through here. This property belonged to Miner Poteet, the man who had rented the property
to her father years before. She remembered that Mr. Poteet
was a kind soul, who had never complained when Ruff Thibeaux had been late with the rent, and sometimes took the
price in trade, work performed by Ruff or sewing by Garlande.
She even remembered that Mrs. Poteet had often brought the
leftovers from some dish or other that she had made, ever
wanting to be the good neighbor. Both had been good-natured
sorts, even at the bitter end. Mr. Poteet wouldn't mind if Mignon wandered this property.

The back door had been broken long before, as if someone
had pried it away from its wooden frame. It opened with a
creak. She stepped inside the small house and walked through
a door in time, where her mother made red beans and rice in
the small kitchen, and the smell of baking cornbread was
heavy and redolent in the air.

In the present it smelled like mildew, rot, and decay. It was
a place where no man lived, and few ever visited. Her heels
clicked on the wood floors, and she touched the walls for support where the floor began its precarious dip downward.

The old Ben Franklin stove remained in the living room-
cum-kitchen, although it appeared as though someone had
dragged it halfway across the floor in an attempt to steal it.
The bottom was lined with bricks; Mignon had watched her

father do this, in order to make the stove more heat-conductive. Consequently, it probably weighed a ton, causing would-be thieves to abandon their theft in mid-backbreaking attempt. There was an ancient refrigerator, and Mignon recalled that although the house had been wired for electricity, the Thibeaux family often used gas lanterns because the bill hadn't been paid. In the main bedroom, there was a pile of wood and some newspapers on the floor. In the pantry that had been her bedroom, a hole in the floor indicated that rodents had taken up residence in this place where no humans would.

An old, cheap metal chair sat near a window by the stove. Mignon decided that it wasn't too filthy, and it would hold her weight. She brushed off spiderwebs and sat carefully, gazing out the dirty window. She was vaguely surprised that hunters and children hadn't broken out all of the windows. In fact, she was surprised that the house still stood, considering its age and the reputation of those who had last inhabited it.

Mignon was lost in her reverie of the past and all the memories that the house evoked until she felt a hand on her shoulder.

Chapter Three

A man of words and not of deeds
Is like a garden full of weeds.

A MAN OF WORDS AND NOT OF DEEDS

MIGNON BOLTED UP AND scrambled to one side, knocking the rusted metal chair onto its back. Two steps later, struggling to break into the bright light outside the blackened house, she tripped over something unidentifiable, tumbling onto the hard wooden floor amidst the debris and rubble that littered the place. A calm voice and gentle arm pulling her to her feet enabled her to regain a modicum of composure.

"You're Mignon Thibeaux," said a man in a sheriff's uniform, looking altogether too official for this rural setting.

Mignon folded her arms across her chest and tried to look as formidable as she could. One moment she had been lost in a world of memories. The next moment a hand was on her shoulder, startling her out of her daydream in a way that had caused her heart to pound as furiously as an innocent man would hurl his fists against jailhouse walls.

Mignon looked at the man and saw that he was studying her from behind dark sunglasses. She glanced downward and swore as she surveyed the damage. Her knee was bleeding, her hose had run, there was soil on her skirt, and trash stuck to her suit jacket. She brushed her scraped hands together to shake off the dirt and debris, ignoring the fact that she was trembling. She carefully shook the edge of her skirt, taking the opportunity to pluck off a stubborn pine needle. Each gesture was calculated to give her a few more moments to gather her wits.

The sheriff didn't object, as they stood just inside the back door of the house where the light poured in and she could see what she was doing. Mignon brushed herself off more vigorously than necessary and finally faced him. He was camouflaged under his glasses, but she saw very quickly that he was observing the length of her legs in a very masculine manner. This was something she was used to, that men found her pleasing and looked at her in that way. It was something she could hang onto in her mind to regain control. She saw that her seemingly quick return to full equanimity had surprised him, and took a moment to look at him in turn. He would never know about the tremor in her knees or the butterflies in her stomach.

She noted his crisp tan uniform and his name on the badge, as well as the polished black utility belt with holstered weapon and handcuffs. *John Henry Roque, the sheriff of St. Germaine Parish,* she thought, with a bitter taste in her mouth. *They didn't waste any time sending a lackey to kick my ass out of town, right out of the parish. Terri told me I couldn't go home, for all kinds of reasons. And here's one, standing right in front of me.*

John Henry was a tall man, standing perhaps a half foot above her, a few inches above six feet. In his early forties, she ticked off in her mind. Brown hair, brown eyes, square jaw. *A cop's jaw,* she added to herself. Broad in the shoulders, narrow in the waist and hips. He looked like a man who enjoyed a good run in the morning, all lean muscles and sinewy lines, a man with a few calluses on his hands, a man who wasn't afraid of hard work.

At last Mignon decided that offense was the best defense. "You scared me half to death!" she said.

John Henry took off his sunglasses and put them in the front pocket of his shirt. He regarded her steadily with those brown eyes. *Brown eyes that were the color of warm sherry,* she thought, *a hint of ocher with a touch of gold.* "I'm real sorry about that, ma'am. You were miles away."

"You're here to escort me someplace?" Mignon couldn't hold back her sarcasm.

To her surprise, John Henry looked confused. "Where is it that I would want to take you, Miss Thibeaux?"

Mignon raised her chin up proudly, acknowledging that he already knew her name. "You must know the history. I understand the St. Michels are still pretty powerful around here."

John Henry's jaw tightened as he put a meaning to her words, and found it distasteful. "My name is John Henry Roque," he said, using that same Louisiana drawl she associated with memories of her father's voice. But there the resemblance ended. John Henry's voice was a deep sound, full of character and individuality, qualities that escaped her memories of her father. "I'm the sheriff of St. Germaine Parish. I saw your car out at the road, and Mr. Poteet isn't one to let hunters back here in these woods, or teenagers with nothing better to do. Not to mention that not many people know about the old place back here, nor the bayou and the quicksand to the south. I don't care to have to put out a fire by hand because the fire trucks can't get back here because of the bad road. Nor to rescue some fool who wandered off the road."

Mignon stared at him, searching unsuccessfully for a hidden meaning behind his words. "I used to live here," she finally said. "With my parents. Mr. Poteet used to rent this place to my father. I didn't think he'd mind."

John Henry's face softened a bit. He gestured at the house.

"It's not in the best condition, as you can see. I didn't care to think of a lady back here in the woods with no one to help her . . . in case something happened."

Something? Mignon's mind snapped back to the present and to the reason she was here. *What could happen to me?*

She knew that the St. Michels had their hands in the sheriff's pockets. It was an elected position, and the man who could garner support from the richest family in the parish was almost certainly the winner of the position, like another sheriff had been when she was a little girl. Parts of Louisiana were as crooked as they could come, and Mignon was well aware of the present political system now.

In her mind she could hear the icy, condemning words of Eleanor St. Michel: "Find out why she's back here. Find out what she knows. Find out what she wants."

"I appreciate that you stopped to check on me, but I'm fine, as you can see."

John Henry sighed, recognizing a stubborn woman when he saw one. "You're bleeding."

Mignon shrugged. "Just a scratch."

"Look, you obviously don't think highly of the sheriff's department, but I just wanted to make sure you were all right," he said. "If you'll come with me back to my truck, I'll fix that knee right up. I've got a first aid kit in the cab."

She had a sudden vision of his hands on her legs and shivered. Somehow, Mignon didn't care to have his hands touching her legs, not someone who would have a loyalty to the St. Michels. But if she didn't, then he might think she had something to hide.

She nodded quickly.

To her surprise, John Henry offered her his arm, holding it out like a Southern gentleman asking a lady to dance at a ball. She took it, her fingers grasping the breadth of his biceps, sensitive to the heat of his flesh under the tan cloth. "Work out, do you?" She almost winced at her words, but it was the first thing that popped into her head. He guided her out of the house, and they began the walk back toward the highway.

John Henry grinned. Out of the corner of her eye she saw a flash of white teeth in a full smile. Laughter lines radiated out from his eyes. He said, "Sure. Got to catch the bad guys. Every day." He glanced at her, taking in her five-foot six-inch frame, lingering on the curvature of her thigh, the bend of her knee. He couldn't see many flabby muscles on her and he was really looking. "So do you."

"I run." *For all kinds of reasons.*

"Me, too. A couple miles every day. Sometimes longer on the weekend." He glanced at her knee again. "Although you might not be running for a few days. Looks like you bruised your knee cap."

Why couldn't the sheriff be a fat, pot-bellied man who chews tobacco and spits it out at my feet, like the one who was here when I was a child? A man who would leer at my legs and breasts, and think about nothing more than how to get me in bed? Mignon chewed on her lower lip in frustration. She hadn't counted on this man. He showed a little ingenuity, a little intelligence, and perhaps a little too much individuality for her needs.

"Why did you come back here?" he asked.

"Why do you think?" This was Mignon's cardinal rule; when in doubt, always ask a question. She kept her voice neutral and non-accusatory, as if she didn't have a care in the world.

"You think the St. Michels called me up and said, 'Hey, John Henry, go run that gal out of town because she's the daughter of the woman who ran off with Luc. We're inclined to think that little lady's up to no damn good.' " John Henry glanced at her again. "Is that what you think?"

Mignon avoided his gaze. "I think that Louisiana politics can be a dangerous thing."

John Henry knew that he wouldn't be getting anything out of this woman except with a rubber hose, and maybe not even then. Finally, he said, "They didn't call me. Hell, woman, it's been two decades and change. You think Eleanor St. Michel gives a good goddamn whether Luc St. Michel comes crawling back here, much less the daughter of the woman he ran off with back when Gerald Ford was falling down boarding ramps? She controls his money. Has for all these years. She's got her hands in the kitty, but good. She doesn't give a damn about you, or your mother. And for your information, she ain't one to give to politicians' campaign funds. At least, not anymore, not to anyone but the Governor of Louisiana, and maybe not even him."

Just then a deer exploded out of the vegetation in front of them, giving them both a startled look before leaping gracefully into the woods on the other side of the road, vanishing forever into the green jungle-like forest.

It was a long moment before Mignon said, "It's hard to say what Eleanor St. Michel would think, much less do." But in her mind was the vision of an article Terri had brought to her months before, from a newspaper Mignon wouldn't line the bottom of a birdcage with. HAUNTED PLANTATION IN LOUISIANA, screamed the headline. A GHOST WALKS THE HALLS! Terri had known about her past; she was one of the few people that Mignon had ever spoken to about that subject. The article had transfixed her, putting together all of her feelings of confusion and dread in a way that gave her life a new purpose. Then there had been the anonymous letter, some months later. A cryptic letter which had told her that things were happening at the St. Michel mansion that would interest her.

She abruptly changed the subject. "I haven't seen a deer in years, perhaps decades."

"You'll see more here," John Henry said. "This ain't the city. You never know what's going to jump out of the shadows."

When they got to her rental car, Mignon could see the four-wheel-drive Bronco parked behind it with its rack of lights and parish emblem emblazoned on the side. "They call you John Henry, not John." It was not quite a question.

"A few do," he said. He opened her car door and handed her inside it, in a way that made her feel a little special. "My mother named me John Henry, not John. Though I like to get to know people before I invite them to call me John Henry."

One of her eyebrows rose eloquently, wondering if he was intentionally flirting just then. "I wouldn't think otherwise."

John Henry retrieved a small first aid kit from his vehicle, and took a few minutes to tend to her injury, completing the action by putting a large Band-Aid across the scrape. The warmth of his fingers touching her flesh made her shiver, and she bit her lip until he finished. When he was done, he stood up and tucked the kit under one arm. Then he leaned down into her open door and stared at her with his piercing brown eyes, trying to figure out what her motives were for being in this place.

Mignon thought about drawing his face on a blank canvas, glorying in the strong lines, embracing the clean delineation of his cheekbones, the curve of his forehead. It was such an interesting face. He smiled at her, and the smile changed his features, showing her the charm that he must have innately possessed because of the very nature of being a politician.

He said, deliberately, "I don't work for the St. Michels. I work for the parish. The St. Michels don't have nearly the influence over the area they did a decade before."

"And now you'd like to know why I'm here. Just out of normal curiosity, I suppose . . . ," She trailed off, drawing her legs up into the cab of her rental car. She closed the door, forcing him to withdraw, and spoke to him through the open window. "Because I'd like to learn a little about my heritage, that's all."

Mignon started the car and carefully backed out and around the Bronco, leaving John Henry staring after her. He rubbed his chin thoughtfully, and put his sunglasses back on. *You never know when one of those pesky skeletons wants to come popping on out of the closet. Damn fine looking skeleton, that.*

A few moments later, Mignon forced herself to stop shivering. She had expected a lawman to visit her, just not that quickly, not within hours of her setting foot in the town. Either he had an idea who she was and had stumbled upon her at the old Poteet place—and therefore was innocent of being an ally of the St. Michels—or he had been informed of her presence immediately through the grapevine and had been conducting a little reconnaissance to find out what Mignon Thibeaux was doing in town. Either way, he had demonstrated the suspicious nature of a longtime peace officer and was accordingly dangerous to her.

She hadn't counted on the instant recognition. In her memories, Garlande Thibeaux was a tall, beautiful woman with long auburn hair, pale green eyes, and an infectious laugh that invited one and all to participate with her in laughing even more. Garlande couldn't have been the exact image of her one and only daughter, except that the tiny town of La Valle seemed to think she was just that.

Mignon could barely remember her mother's face. Almost every personal possession she'd had was lost in the challenging system that sheltered abandoned children. Every move she made, things disappeared, got left behind, or other foster children stole or destroyed for reasons Mignon never understood. Consequently, there wasn't even a photograph of Garlande left for her to look at, much less for her to compare their remarkable similarity.

But Mignon knew that they were similar, and she had heard some of the mutterings in the town very clearly. A few people thought she was Garlande Thibeaux, back from distant places to haunt La Valle with insidious rumors and taunts about how she'd spent the last quarter of a century. The reasoning was ironic because Garlande would be in her early fifties now, and surely showing some of that age, whereas Mignon was only thirty years old, and sometimes looked twenty.

She had to laugh. She'd believed most of her naïveté had left her long ago when a foster parent tried to feel her up in a walk-in pantry. The remainder of her naïveté had disappeared when the foster system administrator didn't believe that she had been trying to protect herself when she smashed the man across the head with a can of baked beans, leaving him with a cut that required six stitches. *Imagine that*, she told herself. *I have a little naïveté left, after all.*

Chapter Four

FRIDAY, SEPTEMBER 10

Rain, rain, go away.
Come again another day.

RAIN, RAIN

THE STEEL-GRAY MERCEDES BENZ entered the gates of the St.
Michel mansion only fifteen minutes after it had left La Valle.
Jourdain Gastineau sat in his car and stared at the rows of
pale Grecian pillars lined up before the generous doors that
guarded the interior and all of the St. Michels who dwelled
within. He stared as he thought about what he had seen.

Moments later he was admitted by a maid and shown to
the back patio, fitted with red flagstones a St. Michel ancestor
had brought from the Texas hill country by wagon and barge
a century before. The patio was a wide expanse overlooking
elaborate gardens filled with boxwood that framed arrangements of roses in every shade conceivable. The huge area was
lined with oaks blanketed with Spanish moss and honeysuckle,
and the delicate aroma overflowed Jourdain's nostrils.

Eleanor St. Michel was taking in a bit of sun with Eugenie
at her side, both sitting at a glass table on intricate wrought-
iron chairs. Jourdain smiled when he saw Eleanor, admiring
her trim figure, the fine length of her neck, and the sheen of
her hair as a fall breeze gently teased it. Dressed in casual
cotton and twill, both women looked like they might have
come from a walk in the nearby woods, and were now taking

in glasses of iced tea with a sprig of mint and a slice of lemon to cool the perspiration from simple excess.

Eugenie saw Jourdain first, but he didn't bother to look at her. If he had, he might have seen the dark smudges beneath her eyes, similar to the ones under his own, and pondered the meaning of that.

Eleanor finally turned around and smiled brilliantly at Jourdain, a flash of white in a mouth outlined flawlessly in lipstick purchased at an exclusive New Orleans boutique. "Why, Jourdain, we've not seen you so much in a month of Sundays." One hand graciously touched her daughter's arm. "As I'm sure Eugenie could tell you."

Jourdain nodded at Eugenie and said, "And we haven't seen Eugenie in, oh, goodness, it's been years since you've come home. How does it feel to be back at the home front after all this time?"

Eugenie shrugged carelessly. "After the divorce, Cannes wasn't the same. I needed a change."

"And the mansion was the change you needed."

"Mother insisted I come home. It was time for me to return. And it's been so long . . ." Her voice trailed off.

Jourdain turned to Eleanor. "I wanted to be the first one to tell you," he said.

Eleanor took a sip of iced tea. "So dreadfully intent, my dear. Why not sit and take a glass of tea? Sally makes a lovely mint tea that delightfully quenches one's—"

"Eleanor," he interrupted. "The girl is back."

The St. Michel matriarch studied Jourdain thoughtfully. Eugenie's hand shook as comprehension flowed through her body. Eleanor put down her glass as her eyes flickered toward the distant trees in the direction of the old farmhouse where the Thibeauxs had once lived. "What of it, Jourdain?"

"I think you know," he answered.

Eugenie murmured, "I told you. *She's* come back." She

shivered despite a warm breeze and rose in a smooth motion, disappearing into the depths of the house within seconds, leaving the glass of iced tea on the table, beads of sweat rippling down the sides.

Eleanor was still staring into the black horizon of oak and pine in the distance, immersed in the domain of her own mind as Jourdain stepped closer. His hand reached out to touch a curl of silvery hair that had escaped her chignon, wrapping it around a finger. Her hair was as it ever was. Soft and silky, beckoning to him to run his hands through it, and then to touch her satiny flesh. *How could Luc have wanted to leave this woman?* he thought with disgust.

"I went to the old witch-woman last night," she said.

Jourdain closed his eyes for a moment and took a deep, cleansing breath. The curl slipped from his fingers and his hand retreated to safety at his side. Finally he said, "Is that old woman still alive? It seems that she was a thousand years old when we were children. She tolerated us as though she were an autocratic queen and we merely peons."

That same enigmatic smile passed over Eleanor's finely wrought features. She might have been just forty years old, ever palely refined, ever coolly enthralling. "She cast the bones for me and said that secrets are about to be revealed."

"What does that mean?" Jourdain asked.

Eleanor's dark blue eyes moved away from the forest and back to Jourdain. "I believe it means that life is ironic."

Chapter Five

Goosey goosey gander,
Whither shall I wander?
Upstairs and downstairs,
And in my lady's chamber;
There I met an old man who wouldn't say his prayers;
I took him by the left leg
And threw him down the stairs.

GOOSEY GOOSEY GANDER

AFTER JOURDAIN LEFT, ELEANOR met with the witch-woman
again. She parked her Lexus next to a tin and wood shack
deep in the woods ten miles from her own home, and gracefully exited the car, careful to adjust her skirt as she stood up.
The sun cast the shadows of late afternoon and Eleanor knew
that the old woman would probably be expecting her. She
didn't know how the woman knew, but she never seemed to
be surprised.

The old woman opened the ragged hanging door and beckoned at Eleanor with wizened fingers stained with nicotine and
her hands showing liver spots as large as quarters. Eleanor
paused for a moment, carefully sorting her turbulent thoughts
into neat little compartments which she could open at will.
She wanted to know what needed to be done. She wanted
answers that only the witch-woman could provide. But she

didn't dare lose her composure. After all, she was a lady and a St. Michel.

The inside of the shack was neat and clean, even more than was usual. Everything seemed to have its place and was appropriately free of grime and dust. The woman herself was clad in old, patched, but clean clothing, from the cotton print blouse that did not match the striped skirt to neatly mended stockings. Even her steel-gray hair was fiercely scraped back into a bun at the back of her head.

Her family name was Poulet, and sometimes she was called *Maman* Poulet by the people in La Valle. But to Eleanor she had always been the witch-woman, to whom girls had gone for sage advice and surreptitious readings. Sometimes Eleanor saw young women hurrying away from the shack, intent on whatever they had been told. Whispers of the woman carried on the wind, and the next generation would soon be knocking at her door.

Inside the tiny dwelling only a few items indicated the witch-woman's profession. Candles burned along one wall, emitting odd smoke and musky aromas. A set of bones, dry and tiny, polished to a shiny gleam from repeated handling, lay in a brass bowl near the candles. Little bottles of unidentified substances were scattered along the crudely made shelves of another wall, their contents as mysterious as their purpose. All of these things hinted at the old woman's vocation, but it was the shrewd, knowledgeable face that showed it in the most undisguised fashion.

"You don't normally come back so soon, madam. Yest'day only hours before. Dem bones, they cause you some concern, no?"

Eleanor withdrew two crisp hundred dollar bills from a calfskin pocketbook. "I have a question."

The woman sat at a card table and motioned for Eleanor to take the opposite seat, a rattling aluminum chair that was probably older than both of her children. She passed the bills to the witch-woman and waited.

The old woman withdrew a pack of tarot cards, well used and weathered with age. It was not a standard Rider deck but something that had been passed down through generations of Poulet women, the figures on the cards primitive and earthy. In years of using psychic readers and fortune-tellers Eleanor had never seen another deck like it. "Think you of your question, madam, and de cards, dey answer you." She set the deck before Eleanor and tapped the top. "Cut thrice, each to de west, so the sun's gracious light will shine on de cards."

Eleanor cut the deck, carefully placing them in the direction indicated, and the witch-woman then laid out the cards in a cross formation.

The first card the witch-woman revealed was the hanged man. The old woman studied the card and pronounced, "Dis man hanging. He tell of trials to come. He say dat you must be full of wisdom to overcome, dat sacrifice must be made." She flipped over the second card with her yellow, gnarled fingers and withdrew her hand quickly.

The card was the tower, a crude drawing of a wooden structure with lightning striking it, indicating destruction. The old woman said, "You have ter'ble obstacles, madam, oh, *oui*. De tower speak of misery. Devastation. Wretchedness to come."

Eleanor wanted to reach out and touch the cards that were displayed on the small table but her hands seemed to be frozen in place as the old woman turned over the third card and carefully positioned it at the bottom of the first two. "Dis card," she said. "Dis is you. De high priestess." The card showed a delicately framed woman sitting in between two marble columns. She stared forward as if nothing could touch her and the world only passed her by. The old woman tapped the card once. "Dis shows dat dere are secrets here. Many secrets and secrets sometimes as bad for dose who keep dem as for dose who wish to reveal dem."

The fourth card went at the head of the other three. It was the moon card. The yellow sliver of a moon with a crooked face stared down upon two wild dogs baying up at it from inside a dark forest, black tendrils curling and reaching for nothing at all. The old woman let out her breath. "Dere is danger here. Danger for you. Danger for your own. Dere are enemies hidden from your eyes. Not dose who you t'ink are your enemies but dose around you. You must act. You must bring forth someone you ain't never t'ought to bring forth before. A stranger, but not a stranger to your family."

The fifth card went to the right of the pile, a standard cross appearing before Eleanor's eyes. "De judgement card," the old woman murmured. The card showed an angel from heaven blowing his horn of adjudication, as woebegone mortals supplicated him from below, expressions of abject terror on their faces. "Dis say dat t'ings will change. T'ings *must* change. Dere is no choice here. Only warning to de one who may prepare herself."

Eleanor stared at the cards, trying to discern the old woman's meaning. "And the last card?"

The old woman flipped it over. Eleanor held her breath for a moment. She'd expected a severe card, such as the devil or death, showing the dire state of affairs, but instead it was the magician. A man in a robe looked down upon a table filled with mysterious items that provoked one's thoughts, a goblet, a sword, a pentagram, and a staff. The witch woman studied it carefully. Finally she said, "What will come, dis is up to you. You must take de first step to salvation. Your salvation. Your family's salvation."

———

MIGNON CHECKED INTO a bed and breakfast in Natchitoches, a full ten miles outside of La Valle, well across the parish line.

Natchitoches was the oldest city in Louisiana, a city full of French and Spanish influence, and streets that transported one back a century or two. Its character was rich, well nourished, and enchanting, and felt to Mignon like taking a stroll in a place that shouldn't exist. It was also a place where people didn't burn holes in her back staring, whispering things that she could almost hear, that she could imagine all too well. In Natchitoches she could pretend she was a normal young woman who was more than successful in her given career and was only taking some time off to visit the place where she was born.

She changed her clothing into something more comfortable, re-dressed her throbbing knee, took a dose of Motrin, and even took some time to extract a sketch pad from the trunk of the rental car. It was in her nature to draw, and draw she did. She sketched some charcoal studies of the Cane River, a portion of the Red River that had changed its course after a massive logjam a century before. Now it was a lake, with lakeside homes that dated back to the Civil War and before. Many of the streets in the downtown area of Natchitoches were cobbled, and even in September tourists flocked to the ancient city and the starting point of the historic Spanish Trail which led to Mexico City.

The rustic streets were crowded with people on a Friday night, and horse-drawn carriages passed her as she walked, her pad tucked under her arm. There were paddleboats on the river, and people congregated on every corner. She almost had to fight to return to her bed and breakfast. She took a minute to brush her hair, reapply her lipstick and drove back to La Valle, where she ate at a little restaurant on the edge of the town.

Bertrand's wasn't a fancy place, but was frequented by

working class people. Sturdy booths and wooden tables supported the dozens of people who wandered through to eat on
a daily basis. Most of the patrons seemed to be farmers, but
a few catered to the tourist industry. Mignon wasn't familiar
with that aspect of the area, but she heard people all around
her planning events that would put money in their pockets by
virtue of selling tourist items such as T-shirts, and trinkets, or
participating in historic tours. Many worked in Natchitoches
or at Northwest State University. They ate with their families,
enjoying the odd night out, and most didn't stare at Mignon
as if she were a woman no one ever expected to return.

"Do I know you?" asked the waitress softly when she
served Mignon her meal.

"I used to live here, a long time ago," answered Mignon
just as softly. The rest of the restaurant was caught up in their
own conversations, in eating, and in pursuing their lives. She
studied her jambalaya.

"That must be it," murmured the waitress. "Maybe I knew
one of your sisters, no?"

"Maybe."

Mignon dug into the jambalaya, relishing the spicy taste of
the Louisianan dish, sopping up the remains with a bit of
crusty bread. When she was done, she realized that there were
others in the restaurant who were looking at her oddly. Most
of them were probably old enough to remember another
woman who had lived here until she left at the age of twenty-
five. They gazed at her with a certain trepidation, as if something might happen as the result of her presence.

Mignon smiled brightly at some of them, and nodded politely to the waitress, leaving a good tip. The service had been
fine, and the food delicious.

When she was outside she returned to her rental car and
drove away. Darkness had fallen over St. Germaine Parish,
leaving the land bleak and forlorn.

Before long Mignon found herself on the farm road that ran past the overgrown track that led to the house where she had been born. With a lump in her throat, she parked the car on the side of the road and dug through her purse for the small flashlight she had deliberately placed there.

There was something about the old farmhouse that drew her inexplicably. Something that sat on her chest, pushing against her, even while she tried to shove off its dreadful weight.

The night was silent as she shut the door to her car, and Mignon stood still for a moment, letting her eyes adjust to the dim light that the stars provided. The crickets started up again, with the rattling screech of a locust searching for its own set of answers. The wind began to caress the trees, moving the branches like diaphanous fans in the sultry breeze, sending currents of cooling twilight over her body. For a long minute it was only the night whispering into her ear like a mischievous prophet of doom.

Mignon stepped away from the car and slowly began to pick her way into the blackness that was the edge of the Kisatchie National Forest. She felt like an apprehensive burglar, intent on creeping onto another's private property to steal some precious item, at any moment to be discovered. But the truth was that she was alone in the night, with perhaps only an armadillo or a skunk to keep her company.

The path decomposed into complete darkness as the trees closed over her head. She clicked the button on the mini-mag flashlight and the light abruptly came on. The nighttime noise ceased for a full ten seconds and then began to flow back over her as the animals and insects adjusted to the latest intruder.

Minutes later Mignon emerged from the arms of the forest and stood in front of the old house once more. It stared at her, windows filled with blackness, and even the hardiest insects ceased their endless efforts to feed and mate. The wind whipped around her and cast her hair across her eyes. The light seemed to be intrusive, so she turned the flashlight off and brushed curling tendrils away from her eyes.

She stepped into the porch, listening to the creaking wood, and her stomach clenched in indecision. Memories of evenings spent sitting on this porch or playing in the front yard while her parents enjoyed the shade of the porch came to her in a rush of nostalgia, assuaging the dread that threatened to engulf her. She touched the rough wood support and felt its coarse surface. Then she froze.

Someone was humming. It was a faint noise that flowed from the interior of the old house, a sad melody that sounded familiar to Mignon. It filled the air and whirled about her like a vexing wind. The front door was wide open, allowing the sound through, and Mignon knew that when she and John Henry left earlier, it had been closed.

Steeling herself, Mignon took another step. She had never believed the rumors. There was reality and there was hard terra firma. She was grounded in both, no simpering miss here.

The dim light spilled in from the windows and rested on a pale figure sitting in the kitchen. Mignon gasped and the humming died away. With more strength than she knew she possessed, she brought the tiny flashlight up and turned it on again. The narrow beam forced the shadows away and illuminated most of the small room.

No one was there.

For a moment she had forgotten to breathe. Her tortured lungs took in air with great relief and her pounding heart began to slow. She was alone in the darkness with only shadows for companions and the silence of the night to soothe her anxiety.

The light cast about the room and found it more threatening than in the daytime. The darkness seemed to leap out at her, jumping as she inadvertently moved the tiny flashlight about. But the room seemed so familiar.

Mignon moved into the main bedroom, looking at the rotting wood floor and seeing only the bed in her mind's eye, a brass bed that had belonged to her great grandmother, one of the few possessions Garlande had truly been proud of, a bed that was left behind that night, as well.

Suddenly, she had a vision of that same bed, its white coverlet stained with blood, and she wasn't sure if the whimper of pain that emanated forth came from her or from the echoes of her mind. *Someone is dying*, she thought urgently. Someone was dying. She could see the figure in the forefront of her mind, daylight spilling into the room from the windows at the sides, yellow light showing bright red blood splattered on the walls, on the floor, on the white bedspread, and. . . .

"Oh, God," she muttered, looking down to see blood dripping from the white frock she was wearing, which didn't seem white at all anymore.

She dropped the flashlight with a gasp and stepped backward, closing her eyes and discovering that the vision would not leave her head. It was there and stayed there as if permanently implanted in her brain.

Then she opened her eyes and it was gone. The flashlight spun lazily to a halt on the floor, and there were only oddly shaped shadows moving in time with the motion of the mini-mag. Almost stumbling, Mignon reached for the flashlight and fled the little house in the forest, almost as quickly as she had earlier, but with no one at her heels except strange dreams.

WHEN MIGNON RETURNED to her motel and got out of her car, a man stepped out of the shadows. He had silvery blonde hair and eyes that were nearly black in the night. "I'm Geraud St. Michel," he said and held out his hand.

She hesitated before taking it. He shook it with an iron grip, an air of arrogance surrounding him.

"My mother would like to speak with you," he said, his voice icy, his tone reserved. "The chauffeur will bring you back once you've completed your . . . discussion." He said no more, and Mignon wasn't in a mood to draw him into a conversation, although she insisted on driving her own vehicle, which he conceded with barely concealed irritation.

In a very real way it was like being escorted to the royal court, but Mignon knew she would not refuse. As exhausted as she was, she knew that this was the opportunity she had waited for and it could not be passed up. She wondered why Eleanor had summoned her and how she had found her location so quickly. The area had limited facilities, and Mignon supposed that people with money could use it to their own benefit, such as quickly locating one troublesome mischief-maker.

Eleanor met them at the door of the mansion, her blue eyes set like stones in her face. She was still an attractive woman, dressed in an Yves St. Laurent suit, smelling of Chanel, appearing as though she was going to some exclusive dinner. She approached Mignon and offered a delicate hand. "I'm Eleanor St. Michel."

Mignon studied the hand for a moment. Eleanor didn't wear much jewelry, just a Dior watch encrusted with diamonds. At last she took the hand. "I'm Mignon Thibeaux," she said, and she couldn't quite help it, her chin went up.

Eleanor smiled at the movement. *The little chit has some moxie in her.* It was a calculating smile. "You have the most amazing resemblance to your mother, my dear." With that recognition came the innate knowledge that she might be able to use the young woman to her own advantage. "Come in. Let me show you the mansion."

"More properly, it's a plantation house," Eleanor corrected herself as they stood in the grand foyer, a great round room with black and white marble tiles running across the floor underneath one of the biggest crystal chandeliers Mignon had ever seen. A flower arrangement made of a dozen varieties of hothouse blossoms sat on an Italian marble table in the exact center of the room. The walls were antique white and the many doors around the curve of the room hinted at more elaborate detail inside each of their realms.

They stood there alone. Geraud had vanished upstairs after glaring at Mignon. A maid had asked Mignon if she desired a beverage and then disappeared.

Eleanor went on. "Louis St. Michel, the builder of the house, preferred that it be called a mansion. A deliberate play on the power that simple words can provide." Mignon couldn't help but notice the rich tone of her voice. Educated Southern was what her friend Terri called that kind of voice, with only a hint of its Louisiana origins. "We open the house in the spring and the fall for a week to tourists, who come see the antebellum homes in this area. You recall all of those homes, Beau Fort, Magnolia, and Melrose?"

Mignon stood beside Eleanor, dressed in a white silk shirt and khaki pants which had been perfect for a casual dinner in La Valle, but now made her feel somewhat intimidated. She tried hard to suppress the feeling. She had been to dinner with the richest and most prominent people in both California and New York. She had met the President of the United States. Her manners and dress were as refined as anything Eleanor St. Michel could come up with, but still, being back in this place brought back waves of insecurity that she stamped down ruthlessly. She smiled her best nonchalant smile, and replied, "My family wasn't the type to sightsee when I lived here, Mrs. St. Michel. I'm sure you understand."

Eleanor turned to study the younger woman and found that the little waif had more than moxie, she had pride. But then she was also a well-known artist. Eleanor had a houseful of works gathered by herself and a previous St. Michel wife, resulting in an eclectic and valuable collection of fine art. There was even a Mignon painting in one of the small drawing rooms, a watercolor study of lights on the French Mediterranean. *It is,* she thought, *a work that examines both the light and dark nature of the frivolous and iniquitous ocean-side play area for the idle rich.* It was also a piece that appealed to Eleanor's own varied nature.

It was ironic that she herself had purchased the painting several years ago in a New York City gallery, never realizing just who Mignon was. Mignon Thibeaux signed her works with only her first name, and that was how she was advertised. Eleanor had never made the connection between the famous artist and the gangling red-haired daughter of her husband's mistress. She wouldn't have gotten rid of the piece if she had known, however. It was a fine investment worth ten times what she had paid for it.

"Of course, I understand," Eleanor said. "I think in a very serious way, we are connected by that event. Your mother and my husband both left us. We understand each other completely. Do we not?"

There was, recognized Mignon, another message there in her words. *A warning, perhaps?* It wasn't completely clear to Mignon, so she took the words for granted, and nodded. "An event I prefer to ignore, when I can," she stated, very truthfully.

Eleanor nodded as well. The Thibeaux girl had done well by herself. She had brought herself up to a level that few could hope to attain from humble Louisiana beginnings. She had once played in the dirt around a shanty while her father worked in the fields and her mother had offered her wares to other women's husbands. But Mignon had risen above all of that. Eleanor could respect that, even if she had not been able to accept it years before. But there was more to it than that. The witch-woman had told her that she must appease the spirits haunting the St. Michel mansion and that Mignon Thibeaux could very well be the key. It was possible she could reach them in a way that all of the psychics could not. "I would like very much to invite you to dinner tomorrow night, Mignon."

Mignon raised an eyebrow. It was the oddest invitation she had ever received, but she would play along. This woman had her own private agenda, one that would probably benefit the St. Michels, or perhaps only Eleanor. "And I would like very much to come."

"Cocktails at seven, dinner at eight, and who knows what might come after that?" Eleanor smiled, pleased that the younger woman had acquiesced so easily. But that was hardly a surprise, as she suspected that Mignon Thibeaux had her own order of business, as well. "I have some magnificent artwork to show you. I even have a Diego Rivera I recently acquired. A wonderful piece. His detail and caricature are marvelous. There's a Pollock in the study, and a Poussin in the living room. Exquisite use of color and brush strokes. I know that you'll enjoy viewing these as an artist. But we'll have more than ample opportunity to discuss artwork tomorrow."

With that Mignon was politely escorted to the front door. When she drove out of the gate, she saw John Henry's large Bronco waiting under the trees a mile down the road Mignon had to travel. She jerked a little when she realized who it was, but the vehicle didn't move as she passed and his head didn't even turn. She slowly relaxed and drove as far as she could away from the St. Michel property.

By the time she reached the bed and breakfast in Natchitoches, Mignon was beginning to feel the excess of adrenalin drain out of her body like water falling over a cliff. She stopped for a beer at a local tavern, forgetting that Natchitoches was a college town, and fought her way to the bar. She returned to her room and found the door slightly ajar.

Mignon wasn't particularly surprised. She pushed the door open and looked in the room, the light from a streetlight dimly illuminating the area. There was no one there, and drawers had been half pulled from the country-style dresser. Her suitcase was unsecured and the lid left open. Clothing hung crookedly on hangers in the closet, which was also wide-open. Nothing seemed to be missing or damaged, but everything was askew and out of joint. But whoever had been there had come and gone, and she was alone.

However, when the phone rang she still jumped. It was her adopted father, Nehemiah Trent.

"My dear," he said. "You've no idea how worried we all are about you."

"Yes," she said. "I know. I should have called earlier. But I was invited to the house and I just got back."

"They've invited you already?" he said doubtfully. "But you've only just arrived."

"It's a small town, Nehemiah. It's so very small." She looked around a room that had been systematically searched by someone in the hours she had been gone, and knew that if she told him about that he would demand that she pack up and leave immediately. "They have an intelligence system here that would put the CIA to shame."

He sighed. "That doesn't sound reassuring."

"Everything will be all right. I know you're anxious, but I just want to find out what happened to my mother. I *need* to find out. We can do that, if we just follow the plan."

Chapter Six

Taffy was a Welshman, Taffy was a thief;
Taffy came to my house and stole a piece of beef.
I went to Taffy's house, Taffy wasn't in;
Taffy came to my house and stole a marrow-bone.

TAFFY WAS A WELSHMAN

THE FOLLOWING EVENING, MIGNON was escorted into the front parlor by none other than a man she knew as Judge Gabriel Laurier. She was dressed in an iridescent black sheath that exemplified the natural grace and shape of her sculptured figure. It was one of her favorite dresses because it was simple, smart, elegant, and she could wear it anywhere, from a formal dinner to a regatta. Matching black, high-heeled shoes enhanced her well-shaped legs, and only a simple strand of black pearls was worn for effect. A black designer purse was her only accouterment.

The judge, also dressed formally, wore a dark, distinguished suit. The lines were strong and just as graceful as her own sheath. He was a polished man from the cut of his white hair to the shine of his shoes. As a valet took the keys to her rental car, the judge greeted her with an official tone in his voice, waiting for her at the stairs that led up to the veranda and the front door of the St. Michel mansion. He had been standing there waiting for her as surely as if he had known the exact time she had left her bed and breakfast and would drive through the elaborately embellished, wrought-iron gate.

Mignon noticed on her way into the house that there were several other cars. Clearly she wasn't the only guest, and she forced a smile on her face when the tall, striking judge offered his arm to her in much the same way that the sheriff had the day before.

"My dear Miss Thibeaux," he drawled. His pale blue eyes were agleam in the waning light of day's end. Like many Louisianians, his voice was full of character and appeal, that wonderful accent as charming as any Mignon had heard in her many travels. It was plainly an asset that the judge took advantage of on a daily basis. "You look delicious. If you don't mind an old man saying such a thing to a young woman."

Mignon smiled at the man who was a full forty years older than she was. In her mind she was thinking of the time when they last faced each other, remembering it as vividly as any incident in her life. She suspected that the judge remembered it just as well as she did. He might be seventy years old but his mind was a steel trap of memory, catching everything and releasing nothing. Her voice was rich and throaty as she replied, "Of course not. What woman dislikes hearing a compliment like that?"

"I am Gabriel Laurier, Miss Thibeaux, a retired judge around these parts." He patted her hand as she took his arm. "Perhaps you recollect our meeting when you were just a small child?"

"Have we met?" Mignon pretended to be surprised as she turned her head to gaze fully at his face, studying it carefully, not daring to tear her eyes away, as if she were searching for something to jog her memory. "I'm sorry, sir. I don't remember much about living here as a child. There are only a few pictures in my mind. Woods, humidity, playing out behind our house, and the like." She paused and offered another innocent smile, silently congratulating herself on an acting ability that she hadn't known she possessed. "I would like to think I would remember a man like yourself."

Gabriel chuckled. He patted her arm again and was seemingly satisfied. "Well, you have the opportunity now, Miss Thibeaux."

"Call me Mignon," she invited as they went into the front parlor.

There stood several other people. It seemed an odd group to Mignon. The judge, of course, was an old and valued friend to the St. Michels and his presence was not surprising. Sheriff John Henry Roque was present once again, and Mignon found that unexpected, although having the local law in one's pocket probably had proved valuable to the St. Michels time and time again.

Gabriel presented her to the group standing around a fireplace, drinking amber colored liquor from crystal glasses. "This, my friends, is Miss Mignon Thibeaux, who was flirting with me shamelessly on the way in, and I've decided that she shall become my fourth wife, if I can persuade her." His hand tickled the top of hers, and Mignon almost jumped out of her skin. His voice denoted a playful joke on his part, but perhaps there was a bit of truth in his statement. He found her an attractive young woman and wouldn't mind in the least if she decided to have a go at the much older man for his money.

The problem was that Mignon did mind, and she had to suppress the urge to brush off his hand and wash the place where it had touched hers. She smiled brightly at him. "Oh, Gabriel," she gushed. "I bet you already have a few ladies stashed away."

Gabriel beamed down at Mignon, his hair as pale as salt in the dim light of the parlor. Mignon glanced away and saw John Henry's handsome face regarding her with an expression of distinct mistrust, and perhaps a hint of disgust at the way she was portraying herself. But in an instant that expression melted away, leaving only a neutral mask instead. He said, "I met Miss Thibeaux yesterday. Hope that knee is all right." And his eyes flowed down her body in a similar manner to the judge's. She didn't care for it from the magistrate and she didn't like it any better coming from the sheriff.

The sheath covered her knee, which was black and blue, and Mignon shrugged lightly. "When I went to see the old family house, I got a little too enthusiastic and tripped," she explained to several sets of curious eyes. She turned to another member of the group she did not know, and stated pleasantly, "I don't believe we've met before."

That man was a compact individual with brown eyes, gray hair, and an almost nut-brown complexion that indicated he liked to be outside when he could. Mignon silently guessed that he was a golfer, perhaps a man who wheeled and dealed on the putting green. She listed a few more things in her mind: another distinguished man, a man who was accustomed to power, a man who was interested in her because of the way he was looking at her, and the man who had been staring at her open-mouthed from inside the pharmacy yesterday. He was someone who had known Garlande and clearly recognized Mignon for who she was. *He's dangerous, like the sheriff is, like the judge is, and perhaps like Eleanor St. Michel is,* she thought.

"My name is Jourdain Gastineau." He held out a hand.

Mignon took it steadily and studied him with her pale green eyes. "A pleasure," she said. She knew about him already, of course. Jourdain Gastineau, the St. Michels' old family lawyer and future Louisiana Supreme Court Justice, if the newspapers were correct in their suppositions.

"This"—he indicated the woman beside him—"is my wife, Alexandrine."

She was a similar size, with gray-shot black hair and gray-shot blue eyes. Her tan was interchangeable with her husband's, and her slim figure appeared as though it regularly enjoyed an eighteen-hole romp across a golf course at the local country club. She didn't seem to know Mignon, or her past, or that of her mother and her mother's lover.

Alexandrine offered her hand to Mignon with a pleasant smile. "I've seen some of your work, Mignon, if you don't mind me calling you that. Some wonderful works. I particularly like your series of watercolors of Paris at night. A dark series, but at the same time, it shows the hint of light, like hope shining in the night, where there might not otherwise be."

"You're very astute," she responded honestly, always savoring praise of the work she favored herself. "That series seems to touch various people in unique ways. I'm glad you enjoy them."

The conversation followed along the lines of the art world for some minutes, with Eleanor St. Michel entering a while later, kissing cheeks and making polite conversation. She was dressed in a severely cut blue cocktail dress that worked well with Eleanor's own strong lines. She bussed Mignon lightly on the cheek as if she were her oldest friend in the world, and said, "How glad I am that you came. Dinner will be served shortly. Oh, and don't you look delightfully dark with that sheath so dramatically juxtaposed against your pale skin?" She gave Mignon a frosty smile before disappearing into the main hallway, presumably to check on the progress of the dinner.

Mignon sipped some Drambuie and eventually found herself standing next to John Henry, a few steps away from everyone else. "Well," she said cheerfully, but taking care to modulate her voice. "If it isn't the sheriff of St. Germaine Parish."

John Henry stared down at her, his sherry-brown eyes intent. "And if it isn't Miss Mignon Thibeaux, who hasn't been in these parts for nigh on a decade or two. And damned if she isn't invited to dinner with the wife of the man her own mother ran off with."

Mignon's lips twitched with suppressed amusement. It was interesting to recognize that she had gotten under his skin, just as he had under hers. "I didn't show up and invite myself."

The sheriff's eyes narrowed a bit, examining every detail of her features.

She took the time to study him. He cleaned up very nicely. The suit wasn't designer, but it wasn't off the rack either. It was dark blue, worn with a white silk shirt and a crisp, blue tie a shade lighter than the suit. She said, "You look nice. Not at all like a lawman who probably doesn't even have a bachelor's degree from a public school."

"Oh, Miss Thibeaux, that was a low blow, coming from someone like you," he answered, and she could have sworn there was amusement in his voice. "You're not exactly someone who was bred to be the Queen of France herself."

"We make do, don't we, Sheriff?"

"Call me John Henry," he invited, his voice a little rough. His lips curved ever so slightly upward.

"I thought that was only for people who are your friends," she said, too quickly to bite it back. "And I know I'm not your friend."

He smiled at her, a masculine smile full of challenge. "I think I'll make an exception for you, Miss Thibeaux."

"I thought you didn't work for the St. Michels." Mignon spoke softly, just loud enough for John Henry to hear. "Funny how you've gotten invited to one of their . . . shindigs."

"Shindig?" he said. "I've come upon occasion. I wouldn't have called it a shindig, though."

"I thought it fit," said Mignon. " 'Politics'," she quoted, " 'makes strange bedfellows.' "

"I see you've met our most eligible bachelor," interrupted

a voice. They both turned to see a woman dressed in red silk standing in the doorway of the parlor, looking as though she had stepped off a Paris catwalk. She was every inch the European sophisticate. Her hair was cleverly coifed into a coil at the nape of her neck. Her makeup was applied to make her eyes seem luminous and larger than normal. Her lips were the exact, alluring crimson shade of her dress and her fingernails. Finally, her dress hugged her figure, but also had the devious appearance of being something she had simply thrown on.

"I'm Eugenie St. Michel," she said to Mignon.

Mignon nodded politely. There was a feeling of uneasiness about the other woman that Mignon couldn't shake. Something about Eugenie was decidedly wrong, but she couldn't put her finger on it.

Eugenie analyzed her, rapt with interest. "You have the most phenomenal resemblance to your mother. I would have known you anywhere."

Mignon nodded and said, "I've been told that many times in the past two days." Her chin went up as she looked at the other woman. There was a fey quality about her, as if the world didn't quite reach her. Mignon knew that she liked to spend time abroad and that this was the first time she'd been back in La Valle for years. The tabloids said that her mother and her brother, Geraud, were tired of funding her permanent vacation. Some of the gossip columnists proclaimed that stress from her numerous divorces had sent her running back to her ancestral home.

She placed a hand on Mignon's arm and steered her away from John Henry with a regretful smile. "My brother had some very interesting things to say about you. I believe he was unhappy about *Maman's* order that he bring you forth to the mansion and swiftly, upon wings of shining silver. He must have treated you shabbily because he was like a bear with a sore head last night." She leaned down to whisper into Mignon's ear, "He worries entirely too much about his business. How things look in the papers and such."

Mignon shrugged. "Don't worry about it." Geraud had spoken a dearth of words to her even while he did his mother's bidding, and she had followed in the rental car, aware that he sat stiffly in the back of the Mercedes while the chauffeur expertly negotiated the roads back to La Valle.

Outside the parlor, Geraud was chatting with his mother and his wife. Eugenie interrupted, saying, "Geraud, here is Mignon, Mother's special guest. Do apologize for being so nasty to her last night."

Geraud's eyes betrayed him for just the shortest of instants. He was irritated with his sister, and irritated with his mother for inviting Mignon. He smiled at his sister and then turned to Mignon with his hand held out. She took it and he squeezed gently, looking into her eyes. "I apologize, Miss Thibeaux, if I was too unceremonious."

Does everyone here cater to Eleanor St. Michel's wishes like good little toadies? Mignon knew that Eleanor held most of the purse strings as Luc St. Michel's proxy of choice. Even Geraud only possessed his own meager holdings and did not command the majority of the wealth. She smiled at Geraud and thought her jaws were going to hurt with all of the fake smiling she was doing this evening. "It doesn't matter," she reassured him, and prayed that it came out as sincere.

"This," he said, still holding her hand, while Eleanor looked on approvingly, "is my wife, Leya." He indicated the woman next to him with the briefest of nods.

Leya St. Michel was in every way Geraud's opposite. She was dark while he was fair. Her skin was olive while his was the aged color of a lightly pink ivory. Her eyes were black and his were that curious midnight blue. When Geraud finally released Mignon's hand, Leya took it, and her face arced into a smile. "You're a very sensitive woman, aren't you?"

Geraud snickered. "Don't try any of your crap with her, Leya." Then, to Mignon, he said, "She fancies herself a psychic, Mignon. Don't pay any attention to her. Between her and my mother, it's a wonder we don't have every prognosticator and soothsayer on the Gulf Coast staying here."

"But she is sensitive," insisted Leya, still holding onto Mignon's hand in a grip she almost found painful, staring into Mignon's eyes earnestly. "She knows about things that happen to other people. Sometimes she has dreams about things that have happened. Isn't that true, Mignon?"

Mignon looked into the depths of Leya St. Michel's eyes and said, "I do . . . dream."

"The future or the past?" Leya asked.

"The past," she answered softly. There was a weighty pause as these words were digested.

Geraud laughed again, but it wasn't quite as hard as before. "My mother, my wife, and now you, Mignon. This should prove to be a most interesting evening."

As they stood there, the conversation turned to less controversial subjects. Mignon was unaware that Eleanor and Jourdain were watching her as she participated in the dynamics of the little group of people.

"It might very well provide the impetus that we needed," Eleanor said.

Jourdain didn't look at Eleanor but kept his eyes on the stunning red-haired woman. "What do you mean?"

"What better way to please a ghost than to bring someone back to the place where they belong?"

Jourdain looked at her then. "Have you lost your mind, Eleanor? How could you possibly . . ."

"Shush," said Eleanor, studying Mignon with all the cunning and perception she possessed. "Perhaps this is what we so desperately needed here in this place."

"God, Eleanor, first those obstinate reporters and their silly stories of ghosts drag me back from the capital, and now this *woman*. Who knows what she's up to . . ."

As IT TURNED out, ten had been invited to dinner. One man was obviously Eugenie's date, but Mignon never got past his first name, David. David looked pretty, didn't speak much, and wore a suit as if it were a straightjacket. He didn't seem like much of a date, and Mignon had to wonder if he was something more than just that.

John Henry offered his arm to Mignon before the judge could manage it, and Eleanor smiled at the judge as if she thought him indeed the silliest of old fools. Mignon glanced up at John Henry and said, "I suspect by the way you answered before that maybe you do have a college education, perhaps somewhere Ivy League after all."

John Henry's lips twitched knowingly. Mignon smiled to herself. She knew about him, as well. John Henry Roque had been educated via the Army method. He had attended West Point and graduated second in his class. He had served six years in the Army as part of the military police, and left to join the New Orleans Police Department. He had married and divorced while he worked in New Orleans, and left there to take a position in the St. Germaine Sheriff's Department some ten years before. Consequently, he had run for parish sheriff two years before and won it, with a remarkable career bolstering him.

Mignon suspected that John Henry would run a records check on her, as well, but all he would find would be the misdeeds of youth, an article in the *New York Times* that had made many national papers, and nothing more. No husbands, no children, no looming secrets to be discovered by looking at computer records. She would have liked to be able to see his face when he came up with the fact that she didn't even have a speeding ticket on her record for the last seven years. It would have been worth it.

"Ivy League?" he repeated. "Not this old country boy." Then he put her into her seat and found his own across from her. Geraud was on her left, and Jourdain was on her right. John Henry sat between Leya and Alexandrine.

Dinner was served in courses, but Mignon paid little attention to exactly what was served. It could have been roasted monkey brains, for all she knew. She took a few bites of everything, and tried to pay attention to several conversations going on at once, all while conducting her own. Both Geraud and Jourdain treated her as though she were a thinly disguised spy and spoke a dearth of words to her.

Her saving grace was Eleanor, who engaged her in conversation until some of the ice had melted and the dinner conversation flowed smoothly. After dinner the group retired to one of the three living rooms for cocktails.

Eleanor took Mignon's arm lightly and escorted her through the lower aspects of the St. Michel mansion. There were numerous rooms on the lower level, from the grand ballroom to three parlors, and the kitchens on one side. The drawing room on the east side had approximately twenty paintings hung carefully on the walls. Mignon studied the collection with an expert eye. She said at last, "A viable collection, Eleanor, the envy of any serious collector. I particularly enjoy your Cézanne."

The St. Michel matriarch nodded agreeably, pleased with Mignon's analysis of the pieces in the room. In truth, Mignon was pleased as well. It was rare to see some of the artists included outside of a museum, and to be able to approach and even touch some of the pieces was like touching the hand of God. She took a step toward the Cézanne, then looked back over her shoulder at Eleanor. "May I?"

Eleanor nodded approvingly. "If one cannot touch them, feel them, they certainly don't seem real."

It was all too easy to run her fingers over the brush strokes, marveling in the French master's domination of color and shapes. It was an early piece, perhaps not so valuable as some of his more famous works, but still a wonder to behold. A pastoral scene filled with bright hues, and a use of composition that had led art historians to call Cézanne "the father of modern art."

"I even have one of your works in the small drawing room," said Eleanor. "I purchased it a few years ago."

Lost in texture and style, Mignon couldn't take her eyes off the Cézanne. "You didn't know it was me," she said, referring to her parentage.

Eleanor's voice was unrevealing, "No, dear. I didn't. But I would have bought it for the very same reason you can't take your fingers off that piece. To look at the shapes and feel what you must have felt deeply in your heart transferred by a simple process of paint to paper and canvas."

Jerking her fingers away like a child caught with her hand in the cookie jar, Mignon turned toward the other woman. They stared at each other for a long moment.

Finally Eleanor said, "I think we should have a discernment. It is, after all, almost the witching hour."

"What's a discernment?" Mignon asked innocently, knowing full well what it was.

"A fancy way of saying a séance, my dear."

Chapter Seven

"Who killed Cock Robin?"
"I," said the sparrow,
"With my bow and arrow,
I killed Cock Robin."
"Who saw him die?"
"I," said the fly,
"With my little eye,
I saw him die."

WHO KILLED COCK ROBIN?

IT WAS A DARK room, one of the small parlors Mignon had passed through earlier, with the lights deliberately muted and the drapes across the windows closed. In the dim light one could not appreciate the burnished wood paneling and the intricate wainscoting that circled the room, the plush, red velvet fainting couch to one side, or even the elaborately woven Persian rug underfoot.

Seven people sat around a round table that had been brought in specifically for the séance. The judge had left earlier, pleading that he was a tired old man and staying up past midnight cost him far more than simple sleep. The close-mouthed David had muttered something about needing a stiff brandy and a cigarette, and Alexandrine had murmured apologetically that such a thing did not appeal to her.

"I'm not sure why you believe in all this nonsense," she said.

Eleanor cast a frozen glance at her. "Having an open mind to the world beyond our world presents different . . . orientations, Alexandrine."

Alexandrine shrugged carelessly and turned to her husband. "If I take the car, how will you get home?" Jourdain was gazing at Eleanor and did not hear her. Alexandrine raised her voice. "Jourdain?"

Geraud said, "I'll have the chauffeur give him a lift."

Alexandrine gave her husband one last resentful stare before sweeping regally from the room.

"Seven," murmured Leya. "It's the perfect number for a discernment."

"And just after the new moon," Eleanor added. "We might have some success."

Mignon was seated between John Henry and Eugenie. "And whose ghost are we divining?" John Henry asked with a laugh.

"It's not a specific ghost, John Henry. But rather we're seeking enlightenment," Eleanor said. "It's a way of opening your mind to other . . . possibilities."

Mignon waited until Eleanor's attention was occupied with rearranging some candles on the table before saying to John Henry, "See? Open your mind up a little."

His knee bumped hers underneath the table deliberately.

Geraud sneered at his wife and his mother, leaning back in his chair with a snifter of cognac in one hand. "This is all very amusing, ladies, but you know what I think of all of this."

"It doesn't matter," Leya reassured him. "We need seven people and you can't leave. Besides, you might become a believer." Her husband had drunk enough cognac already that he was pliable and not inclined to spoil his wife's or his mother's fun, so he remained, an irked expression on his face.

Jourdain sat directly across from Mignon, and was again staring at her from under gray eyebrows with such an odd look that she was transfixed when she caught it. Immediately she knew he was thinking of her mother, Garlande. "I'm nothing like her," she said to him. It happened so quickly, without thought, that a moment after she spoke she wondered if she had said it aloud or merely thought it.

Jourdain was taken aback. He was sorry that what was on his mind was so readily apparent to her, especially *her*. "I'm sorry," he said at last. "You do resemble her."

Even Geraud turned his attention upon Mignon. "I remember her with long red hair," he mused. "God, what a beautiful woman. Hair streaming down to her waist, a figure with full. . . . Well, her face is unmistakably the same." He didn't notice his mother's face twitching in irritation.

"I never knew that until I came here," Mignon said. "I've never even seen a picture of her."

"Yes," said Geraud, the slightest slur in his voice. "We never got to that particular subject. Why did you come back here, Miss Thibeaux?"

Mignon folded her hands across her lap. She kept her expression serene and calm. "An interest in my past, perhaps. My family is just about as Louisianian as they come. Everyone likes to know about their heritage."

"And you're not interested in stirring up things?" Jourdain said carefully.

Shrugging, Mignon was aware that all other conversation had ceased and everyone had focused squarely on her. "Stirring up what? I had no control over what happened. I have no interest in raking up the coals."

John Henry said, "Yes, what would be to gain?" But he wasn't being rhetorical, and he was looking directly at Mignon.

Eugenie interrupted with a short laugh. "What difference does it make if she's here? She's a Thibeaux, and Thibeauxs have lived in St. Germaine Parish for two hundred years, just as long as the St. Michels, when it wasn't even a parish. If you were alone, like she is, wouldn't you be curious about your heritage, your upbringing? I know I would be."

"And that's the most she's said all night," Geraud said. "Miss Thibeaux, we stand corrected."

Leya glanced at her watch. "It's almost midnight."

"The saints preserve us," Geraud said dryly.

Mignon couldn't blame him for his skepticism. It all seemed overboard and silly to her, as well.

Leya dimmed the remaining lights and the room was black. Everyone stopped talking. Suddenly, Eleanor gasped. "Stop that, Geraud."

"It wasn't me, Mother. Perhaps an amorous spirit?"

"Quiet," said Leya. "I hear the chimes of the grandfather clock."

Geraud snorted but he didn't say anything else.

"Quickly, hold each other's hands," Leya went on.

There was a brief fumble in the darkness while hands searched for one another. On Mignon's left side, the sheriff's hand was large and warm, holding hers lightly. On her right, Eugenie had a cold grasp, as if her circulation wasn't quite as healthy as it should be.

Leya's voice cut through the darkness again. "Concentrate. Open your minds. Open your hearts and concentrate."

Mignon had thought that her eyes should have adjusted by now, but the dark was as black as a crypt. She closed her eyes as she sat there and relaxed. The chimes of the grandfather clock had stopped in the distance and the house was quiet but for the wind moving along the trees outside.

Again Leya's voice insinuated itself into the gloom, less intrusively now, instead hypnotically working its way into the minds of the people who sat at the round table. Mignon couldn't help a little shiver of apprehension as Leya intoned, "Come, spirits of the midnight hour. Come and speak to us. Share with us your wisdom."

On her left, Mignon felt John Henry's hand twitch in time

with the laughter he was suppressing in his big body. She smiled.

The round table, fully seven feet in diameter, moved with a loud clunk. Everyone jumped.

"What the hell was that?" demanded Geraud.

"The table moved," said Eugenie.

"It did move," said Jourdain. "Someone must have kicked it."

"Turn on the goddamn lights," insisted Geraud.

Leya flicked on the table light behind her and everyone blinked. After a moment it was clear that the table was sedentary and no one was confessing to the deed. Every face appeared surprised, even startled.

Mignon glanced around her apprehensively. Even John Henry seemed to have lost his amusement at the situation. "Thinking about what your constituents would think if they could see you now?" Although she phrased it as a question, it was not.

John Henry glared at Mignon and let go of her hand. Mignon put both of her hands under the table.

There was silence again. They waited and looked at each other for a long minute. Leya slowly reached behind her and turned off the single light again. Blackness descended. "Hold hands again. We mustn't let this opportunity pass."

Arms and hands moved. Finally, John Henry murmured, "Mignon? Your hand?"

Mignon offered her hands to John Henry and Eugenie. "Good God," John Henry exclaimed. "Your hand is like ice."

"Are you all right, Mignon?" asked Eugenie.

"Yes," muttered Mignon. "I'm just a little cold, that's all."

Leya's voice came again, "Do you want to continue, Mignon?"

"Yes," said Mignon. "I'm fine."

"Good," John Henry said. "Perhaps if we rest our right foot on the top of the left foot of the person to our right, we could clear up the table movement issue without ado."

Geraud chuckled in the darkness, inordinately pleased with this method of preventing someone from playing jokes. "A good idea, John Henry."

Feet moved gingerly in the darkness. "Can you put your foot just on my toe, John Henry?" asked Mignon. He complied without answering her.

Eleanor snapped at Geraud, "Rest on top of it, Geraud, not smash it."

"Sorry," her son offered lamely.

At last Leya repeated her entreaty for the spirits to join the circle. Again there was abject silence and again the table suddenly moved, banging heavily on the floor.

"Jesus Christ," whispered Geraud. There wasn't another word in the room. Everyone had been hushed effectively and immediately.

The table heaved again and then was still.

Mignon shivered again.

Leya called, "Spirits? Are you with us?" Her voice was full of apprehension and anticipation at the same time.

It was as though a switch of another kind had been pulled. The atmosphere changed. Each person became silent and anxious, as a black fear seeped through the room. They were present and so was something else that affected each one of them. Long, curling tendrils of dread tangled with the strings of their very souls.

"Isn't it cold in here?" asked Mignon. She couldn't seem to help the way her body quaked. She let go of Eugenie's hand and pulled at the front of her dress almost frantically. "And it's hard to breathe. There's no air in here. *It's like I'm buried alive!*"

"Oh, my God," cried Eugenie and leapt to her feet, crashing into a wall as her chair tumbled to the floor on its back.

"Turn on the light!" said John Henry.

Leya scrambled for the switch and when the light came on,

they all saw that Mignon was staring down at the table, the only person still in the same position she'd assumed when they'd begun the second time. Eugenie had found her way to the parlor door and stopped with her hand on the latch. She gazed back over her shoulder, horror straining her fine features. Her moonstruck blonde hair had escaped its confines and she seemed the picture of a woman on the verge of a breakdown. Eleanor was half out of her seat, staring at Mignon with an open mouth. Geraud had pulled his chair away from the table and clutched at the lapel of his suit as if it were a life preserver. Jourdain had both hands flat on the table as he stared at Mignon.

"Mignon?" whispered John Henry. He leaned toward her.

Mignon slowly looked up. Her eyes were pale green and huge in her pale face. They were lost in another world, focused on nothing at all. John Henry rubbed her hands with his. "God, her hands are like ice."

The others stared at her in hushed trepidation of what might be coming.

"It's so black here," Mignon said softly, but everyone could hear her as clear as a bell. Her voice was a tone deeper, throatier. She stared into nothingness as if she were looking at some other place. "There isn't any air here. I can feel things crawling across my feet. Oh, God," she cried out. "*Where am I?*"

"Mignon!" John Henry yelled, grabbing her by the shoulders and shaking her. Her eyes suddenly closed. He yelled again, "Mignon!"

Mignon's eyes snapped open and she demanded, "What the hell are you doing, John Henry?" The demand was issued in such a normal, slightly curious, slightly outraged tone of voice that the sheriff was taken aback.

John Henry let go of Mignon as if he had been holding a rattlesnake by the tail. There was a collective sigh in the room.

Leya looked at Mignon in awe. "That never happened before."

Even Geraud had lost his sarcasm. "Let's call it a night."

Eleanor still sat in her chair, a blank look on her face. Across from her, Jourdain stared at the table as if it held all of the answers he needed to know.

"What?" asked Mignon, craning her neck around looking at the people who stared at her. "Do I have something on my face?"

"You mean you don't remember what you said?" asked Eugenie, behind her.

"I didn't say anything," stated Mignon. "Leya was asking the spirits to come, and my hands were cold, and then John Henry here was shaking me."

"How very odd," said Eleanor. "You said something about the darkness."

"About not being able to breathe," added John Henry.

"And things . . . crawling over your feet," said Eugenie, her hand still on the door frame. "It was very frightening. Tell us, Mignon, were you playing with us? Was it all a game?"

Eleanor looked at Mignon with a steady expression that the other woman found difficult to read. "Of course it was all in fun, Eugenie," her mother answered, shaking her head slightly at Mignon. "Why don't you go on upstairs. You look very tired, dear."

Eugenie stared at her mother. Finally she opened the door and said, "I am very tired. Thank you for a lovely evening. Especially you, Mignon. Perhaps you might come again." She slid out the door, all crimson silk and platinum blonde waves of hair trailing behind her.

If I'm ever invited, Mignon thought to herself. There had been a risk here. One that she wasn't sure she had managed to overcome, since the remainder of the people in the room were staring at her as if she had suddenly gone insane. *What happened here?*

At last Eleanor said, "Thank you, Mignon. We all know that what just happened was quite real. But Eugenie needs a bit of subterfuge upon occasion. She's not been herself of late. You understand, my dear."

Mignon nodded slowly. She glanced at the other faces in the room. Leya was still staring at her. Jourdain had a blank look on his face. Geraud held onto his snifter of cognac, with perhaps a little tremor in his hand. Finally, John Henry stood up.

"I've got to go, Eleanor," said John Henry, shooting Mignon a glance. He added, "Not that it hasn't been a most interesting evening, but the parish is a seven day a week kind of job."

"Ma'am." He nodded at Leya, and then at Geraud and Jourdain. "Gentlemen." Then he looked very simply at Mignon and his lips tightened. "Miss Thibeaux."

Mignon rose. Her knees were still shaking, but she managed to stand without giving anything away. She wanted to run off so that her heart would stop thundering in her chest as if it might explode at any second. "I need to go, as well."

Eleanor looked at Mignon for a long moment. "Why don't you come back some evening, my dear? I'm sure we might be able to scare up some better entertainment than a séance."

Mignon smiled at the older woman's deliberate turn of phrase. "Perhaps I will." She said her goodbyes to the others, made a brief visit to the bathroom to splash water on her face, and was escorted to the door by Jourdain, who signaled the valet to bring her rental car.

While the two of them stood alone in the chilly night air, he remarked, "You aren't staying here very long." It wasn't a question, and Mignon was sure it was a veiled threat. She took it in the most innocent way she could.

"I'm not sure how long I'm staying," she said brightly as the valet opened her car door for her. Jourdain kept a carefully empty expression on his face as he watched her drive away.

The valet went back to his post near the bottom of the stairs, pulling his jacket together to ward off the cold. Geraud came up behind Jourdain and said, "Isn't it interesting?"

"What?" asked Jourdain, thinking that the sooner he was out of the St. Michel mansion, the better. He never liked to come to this place at night anymore. Too many strange things seemed to happen.

"That she should be the daughter of the whore my father ran off with, and here she is invited to dinner so many years later."

Jourdain smiled, thinking about how life really held no surprises. "Interesting, yes. But, perhaps a little too coincidental."

Geraud looked surprised. "You think she's come back deliberately, in order to accomplish something? Christ, as if the tabloids need any more ammunition. My business is suffering enough as it is."

"Why else would she be here?"

"But for what? Her mother's long gone to God knows where. My father probably dumped her years ago. And what did we ever do to her?"

Jourdain didn't respond. Finally Geraud said, "I'll have my man drive you home, old man."

"Thanks, Geraud. Thanks for an evening I won't forget anytime soon." His tone of voice was far from grateful.

Geraud muttered under his breath as he went back up the stairs to the front door. He was praying that Eugenie didn't have another one of her episodes, triggered by his mother's insane need to participate in these silly little "discernments." Especially after what happened tonight. *What did happen tonight?* he asked himself silently.

MIGNON WAS ASKING herself the same question not very far down the road. After she had passed through a dark and silent La Valle, she realized that she was being followed. Try as she might, she couldn't see enough of the vehicle behind her to tell what kind of make and model it was, except that the headlights seemed as big as moons and never wavered in their pursuit of her. She had never dreamed that returning to this place would cause such an uproar, but it had. Someone felt threatened enough not only to search her room at the bed and breakfast, but to follow her down a dark road.

It was, recognized Mignon, a very dark road indeed. She hadn't passed anyone, and no one would see what might happen to her.

Red and blue lights began to flash behind her, and Mignon realized that it was John Henry tailing her. She wasn't sure about the feelings that coursed through her body. She knew that whoever ransacked her room had wanted her to take it as a warning. After all, why should they kill her if they could simply scare her off first?

She pulled her car over to the side of the road, leaving the engine and lights on. She even reached down and turned on the emergency lights. Then her hand reached to the side of the seat and found the canister of pepper spray she had put there for this very reason. One finger released the safety catch.

The police vehicle pulled up behind her, and the door opened. She watched from the side view mirror as John Henry approached her car with his hands at his sides.

He leaned down to her partially open window and said, "Turn off your engine, please."

Mignon stared at him. He was still wearing his suit and tie and his carefully neutral expression. His hands were clearly visible at his sides; no threatening weapon was held there. She was glad the door was locked and the window wasn't open wide enough for him to stick a hand inside. "Are you arresting me, John Henry?

He stared at her. She was getting quite used to people staring at her, but his was a discerning gaze, full of mechanisms working in his head, figuring out exactly what she was about. Finally he sighed. "Just turn off the engine and your lights and get out of the car, Mignon."

There was that fire between them. He didn't seem like someone who wanted to drag her off to the bayou and throw her dead body into it. But then, that's what they had said about Ted Bundy. John Henry's whole demeanor was that of reluctant obligation. He was doing something that he didn't care to be doing, but it wasn't going to be something illegal.

She turned off the engine, but left the emergency lights on. Then she took her seat belt off, opened her car door, and gracefully stood up, one hand carefully concealing the little canister of pepper spray. He motioned to his side, where he could watch her. "Stand right here."

Mignon stepped to that position, warily keeping her eyes on him. He went to her car and started rummaging through her purse, all the while keeping her in the corner of his eye. Then he looked under her seats, in the glove box, and in the back seat. Finally, he took the keys and looked in the trunk. He lifted up her large leather portfolio and thumbed through a stack of unframed canvases with a blank look on his face. With another sigh, he turned to her and said, "Where is it?"

Pretending to be puzzled, Mignon asked, "Where is . . . what?"

"The ice pack in your purse?" John Henry questioned. "I don't know how you bumped the table, but you had to have something in your purse to make your hands cold, and it's got to be here, because you didn't stop on your way from the St. Michel mansion."

"You think I did those things? That I faked being cold somehow? That I made the table raise up and drop?" Mignon couldn't help it. She laughed. Then she laughed harder. "And I thought you were pulling me over to kill me." All the while she laughed, she thanked God that she had punctured the bag of blue ice and flushed the plastic down the toilet at the St. Michel mansion before she had left.

Chapter Eight

Ladybug, ladybug, fly away home,
Your house is on fire, and children will burn.

LADYBUG, LADYBUG

JOHN HENRY STARED AT the sight of Mignon laughing for a long moment and couldn't help a brief smile from curling across his lips, even while he silently questioned what exactly was so funny. Finally he asked, "Why don't we have a little talk?" but it really wasn't a question.

Mignon dabbed at the corners of her eyes with the back of her fingers to wipe away the tears, and asked, "So you can ask more about my nefarious past? About the time I robbed the crown jewels from the Tower of London? Or perhaps when I assassinated JFK in Dallas?"

John Henry smiled again and motioned to his truck. He turned off her emergency lights and courteously handed her her purse and keys. Then he helped her into his truck and drove away, pausing only to turn off the flashing lights.

Mignon taunted him about his choice of automobile. "You have cop lights in your personal truck?" She laughed again, the same way she had when he suggested that she had faked her performance at the séance. "You must be a little anal retentive," she decided aloud, a hollow note of bravado coloring her words.

That made John Henry laugh, because it was actually true. He liked things done a certain way, and he was like a hound with a particularly tasty bone who wasn't going to let go just because someone much bigger started to pull on the other side. His ex-wife had called him that, and he had often replied that if a cop wasn't that sort of person, then they wouldn't be a cop very long. Furthermore, his years at West Point had taught him to dot every "i" and cross every "t." It was the way he was, and it was suddenly funny that someone he had met only the day before could pinpoint that in him straightaway.

Mignon hadn't said much, except to comment that the police lights didn't do much for the truck and she hadn't seen such a combination before. After a lengthy pause she asked, "You're taking me to the bayous now, John Henry? I think you should have brought the Bronco, because if you get this baby in the mud, you'll have to have a tow truck get it out. It doesn't even have four-wheel drive."

"We're going to the cemetery," he responded with a quick grin, and that was exactly what he did. It wasn't far away. It was off the main road where no one would see them.

Despite what it really was, the La Valle cemetery was a lovely place with a small, red-bricked church with arching, stained glass windows on one side of the rusted wrought-iron-enclosed graveyard. Cypress, willows, and pine trickled with moss gave the church and the cemetery an almost neglected appearance, despite the neatly trimmed graves and the gleam of the polished stained glass windows. Some of the graves dated back to the 1700s, and some of the families represented still lived in the area.

"Wonder if there are any Thibeauxs there?" murmured Mignon, her hands in her lap, carefully concealing the pepper spray. Then she shook her head. "Too rich for their blood. They're probably at the pauper's hill. I think you've taken me to the wrong graveyard, John Henry."

John Henry shrugged. "I'm not exactly from the richest lines myself. My father did me the incongruous favor of being heroic on D-Day in 1944, right on Normandy Beach." He paused to look at her in the darkness of the car. His voice and tone was matter of fact. This was something he hadn't spoken of much, but it seemed important for Mignon to understand that he wasn't in the St. Michels' class. "When he came back from France, he married and had three children, and I was the youngest. Since he got a certain medal, I got a free ticket to a military academy. And I went."

"Your father was awarded the Congressional Medal of Honor?" said Mignon in surprise. That hadn't been in the summary from the private detective she'd hired.

"Only a couple of ways to go to West Point," he replied. "That was one of them. Of course, he lost one of his arms in the process, but he used to joke about college costing an arm and a leg."

"Used to?" repeated Mignon. She had often wondered what it must have been like to have had a loving father, one who would joke about such things as the cost of college and why she hadn't produced grandchildren yet. This man had such a family, and a tinge of jealousy always struck her when other people spoke of their parents. "He's dead?"

John Henry nodded. "About twelve years ago. My mother not too long afterward, as well. Otherwise I might have stayed in New Orleans and fought for custody over my daughter. The ex and the kid live in Shreveport."

"You're divorced?" she asked unnecessarily.

"Yep. It didn't say anything about you being divorced in your records."

The easy mood between them was suddenly lost and Mignon came back to the fact that he was very much suspicious of her. It hadn't been anything she wasn't expecting, but it was an abrupt reminder of whose truck she was sitting in, and whom she was speaking with. "You spend a little time today looking into my past?"

He nodded again, a dark figure sitting in a dark place with no one watching.

She said, "You know, it seems like there are about a million cemeteries in Louisiana. You can't drive a mile without passing some small plot with headstones."

John Henry didn't say a word.

Mignon went on, "This is a nice one, though. I've never been here before. My father wasn't one to win any kind of awards. Neither, for that matter, was my mother. I guess you know that by now. They didn't have a lot of money. Period. My mother used to make some of my clothes out of sackcloth. They'd get some of their flour in these burlap sacks, you don't see them much anymore, and my mother would stitch them together in these ragged shirts and skirts. She managed to get better cloth for the clothing she made for me when I started school, but there wasn't much. I bet you never met someone who had a dress made out of sackcloth."

"I know that you were in foster homes in Texas and California, that you were adopted by a man named Nehemiah Trent in 1985, because no one else would have you. It seems you have a juvenile record in California, but it's sealed and I don't have the authority to find out why you were arrested and convicted. I know that you made in the neighborhood of a half-million last year, because tax records are public property, and you don't have any dependents. You paid a shitload of taxes and your deductions were minimal, like maybe you didn't want the IRS to get too curious. You have an apartment in New York City, and you apparently stay with your adopted father when you're in California, or perhaps with friends. You have enough money not to fuck around a podunk place like La Valle with a bunch of arrogant blue bloods like the St. Michels, but here you are, all the same. But what I don't know"—his voice lowered and he looked at her again, no hint of amusement or kindness there—"is what in the name of God you're doing, in this place, here and now. And I don't know why everyone is so damned sure that Luc St. Michel is dead and haunting the mansion. Jourdain and Geraud seem to think that you're nothing but a con artist out to rip Eleanor off. I don't know that I agree with that, but I intend to find out."

"I've never been married and I don't have any children," Mignon confirmed, staring at the cemetery in front of them. Nothing lived around here but the wail of the wind and the grass which covered the dead forever. She suppressed her anger at his accusation. Eleanor wasn't the victim in this scenario. She never had been. "The juvenile charges spring from being a runaway. Spend any time in foster homes as a teenage girl and you'd know exactly why. I think they call it 'incorrigible.' I'm here because I'm curious about my parents and the place they were born."

"I think you need to leave La Valle," he said, low and urgently. "Before something . . . happens to you."

"Are you threatening me, Sheriff?" she almost yelled the question at him, not quite able to curb her temper anymore, not liking being subtly threatened and being brought to this place as a not-so-subtle message which wouldn't be misunderstood by an imbecile. "You don't know what bad is. You don't know what it's like being labeled a troublemaker because you didn't care to be fondled or molested or raped. You don't know what it's like being shuffled from home to home to home. I know this isn't my home. But it was my parents' once. It meant something to them. They were born here and they stayed here until 1975. My father only left because he was forced to leave, taking only what he could carry in his truck and me. We left many things behind, including relatives who died later without ever seeing us again, because my father didn't dare come back to this place."

Mignon stopped and took a deep breath. She knew that she needed to take control of herself and relax her tense muscles before she exploded. The things she was telling the sheriff had simmered within her for years until she had the time and the money to follow up on them. Then she asked, "Did you ever dream about something that came true?"

"No," he said shortly. John Henry was digesting her words, trying to ferret out the truth.

"I dreamed about my mother and my mother's lover. I dreamed I found them. And I wanted desperately to find them. So I decided to look for them." Her voice trailed off into the darkness. There was so much more to the story. Things she didn't know if she could share with this man, because she didn't know if she could trust him. The townspeople assumed that Garlande Thibeaux and Luc St. Michel ran off to a better life with each other. However, Mignon had discovered that there was no trace of them in the modern world. Nothing had led her to her mother's current whereabouts. Their social security numbers had never been used again. No driver's licenses had been issued in their names in any of the fifty states. It was as if they had fallen into a black hole. *Or as if they disappeared that very day.*

John Henry finally asked, "And did you find them?"

"No, I haven't. But it's only a matter of time, I think," Mignon said. "I'm tired, John Henry. If you don't have any more threats to toss at me, or you're not really planning on planting my corpse in that cemetery"—she waved at the garden of gravestones in front of them—"then I'd like to go back to my car so I can go back to the hotel."

John Henry continued to look at her in the darkness. He hadn't gotten what he'd wanted out of Mignon Thibeaux. He wasn't sure what there was to get. Either she had had some kind of psychic event at the St. Michels' or she was a fraud. His stringent, unrelenting nature told him that her being a fraud was infinitely more likely than the former. But there was something about this attractive young woman who had such strong will and who had survived untold horrors that drew him ever closer. Whatever she went through had made her a fierce, self-determining creature who had carved her own success from the hardest form of granite there was, and he couldn't help but admire her for that. He couldn't help that any more than he could help the attraction between them. He wanted to reach out and stroke her cheek, just to see if the granite had seeped into her flesh, even knowing that her cheek would be smooth and soft. He wanted to do it, but he did not.

What John Henry did do, however, was take her back to her car and watch her drive away, wondering if she had put that little canister of pepper spray away yet.

Actually, it was long after Mignon parked in the tiny lot of the bed and breakfast before she forced her chilled, aching fingers to let go of the pepper spray. She sat there for a long time. It was after two A.M. and she was exhausted. Pasting on a false smile, listening to every nuance, pretending to be something she was not, took more energy out of her than she was prepared to give.

Inside her room, she found that the little red light on the telephone beside the bed was blinking. She didn't even need to check to know who had left her voice mail. She made a call to Nehemiah Trent. He was anxious. "Good God, child. I believe that my heart was failing. I thought certainly I would have heard from you before this. I had a mental image of them tossing your bound and gagged body into the bayou."

It was a little too close to what she had envisioned. So she ignored his apprehension and said, "It worked out pretty much the way we planned it. Your niece was right about the table, and I was able to get rid of the blue ice." She wasn't going to tell him about the sheriff pulling her over in the middle of the night and dragging her off to a cemetery to "chat" with her. "Eleanor believed me. So did Leya, and Eugenie was so afraid, she almost ran from the room. I just need to wait until the next invitation to throw on a little more show." Mignon wanted to give someone a push. A push that would shove that person right over the edge.

"How can you be so certain of Eleanor's guilt, my dear?" asked Nehemiah, careful to keep his voice neutral. "Why would she invite you into her home, if that was the case?"

"Curiosity about her husband's mistress's daughter? Trying to find out information? Trying to find out what I could possibly know?" Mignon hesitated. "Who else had a motive? Perhaps Eleanor had simply been too embarrassed by Luc sneaking around behind her back and lost her temper. Lost it in a murderous rampage."

"I'm simply saying that you've come back to find the truth, and whether you like it or not, she might not be the one who killed them. And furthermore, you may never find out what really happened."

Mignon didn't reply and Nehemiah judiciously changed the subject.

After a few more minutes, they mutually hung up and Mignon started to get ready for bed. However, her mind was on what had happened that night and what had happened all those years before.

There had been something else odd about the séance. Although Mignon had planned what she was going to say, and how she was going to act, the words about being in the darkness with things crawling over her feet had come easily to her. She didn't want to think about it, but it was as if something had been impelling her, forming the words in her mouth, helping her in a way that was unforeseeable and, frankly, hair-raising.

———

JOHN HENRY SPENT the following morning looking at his computer. He had asked Mignon the same questions, but he decided that he needed to answer them himself. *Why is everyone so sure that Luc St. Michel is dead? Why is Mignon Thibeaux back in the parish and why did she mess around with the séance?*

What he found did not please him particularly. Being the sheriff of a parish was a political job and one at which he excelled. Being an Army officer was being similarly disposed. He had predominated in that arena. He had found that it was a game to walk the fine line between not antagonizing the rich individuals who lived in the parish and upholding the principles which he held almost sacred. Most of the time it wasn't a problem. This time it was.

AT ABOUT THE same time, the housekeeper woke Mignon up by tapping on the door.

She sat up in the wooden four-poster bed and looked around the room. It was done in white lace and old country style. Homespun details dotted the walls and the tables. Sun poured in through a window framed by crackled white shutters on the inside of the room. There was no television, and only a white and brass electric fan on the ceiling to deflect the sultry Louisiana heat. It was nice, but it wasn't to her taste, and when she woke up her mind was muzzy enough that she didn't immediately realize where she was. After a moment she understood that someone was knocking at the door. She called, "Yes?"

"Housekeeping, ma'am," came the reply. The owner of the bed and breakfast was older than God and did all of the work, including cleaning. She was at the door, ready to take care of the bathroom and the sheets.

Mignon shook her head foggily. "Just give me a few

minutes." She looked at her travel clock and discovered it was after ten o'clock. She groaned and rolled out of bed.

About an hour later she was dressed in working clothing: jeans, a polo shirt, and high-tops. Her hair was a reddish mop on the top of her head. With the humidity in the area, she couldn't do a thing with it. She went to the local library in Natchitoches and found it closed, reminding her it was Sunday in a small, rural town in Louisiana.

However, Mignon considered, there was always the University. Natchitoches was a university town besides being a tourist spot. She found the library without incident and discovered that all of the old newspapers were on microfiche.

"Microfiche," repeated Mignon doubtfully, looking at the librarian's aide, who was pointing to a specific area of the library.

"Microfiche," affirmed the aide, encouraging her. "It's easy. You'll have it down pat in five minutes flat."

Mignon did have it down in five minutes flat. But she got a headache in about fifteen minutes from studying the microfiche screen. She knew that she and her father had left in the fall. She had been in school for only a few weeks when her mother had gone away with Luc St. Michel. Mignon started from January of 1975 and began methodically shifting over the sections of the newspaper that covered Natchitoches, Winn, and St. Germaine Parishes.

Almost immediately she found out something about Luc St. Michel that she hadn't known before. The St. Michel family owned a few paper mills in Northern Louisiana and Arkansas. There had been a strike in one in January of 1975. Mignon mused over this as she studied the pages on the screen. A union difficulty wasn't an issue she had considered relevant, but union activism had been at a peak in the seventies, and the St. Michels weren't angels of propriety. Thanks to the papers dated a few weeks later, she discovered that she could dismiss this theory. The strike had been settled amicably between a negotiator and Luc St. Michel, leaving the plant workers with less hours and a bit more pay, and Luc with a working paper mill.

There was another mention of the January 1975 strike in April, because of union problems in New Orleans and Baton Rouge. This included an almost congratulatory note to Luc St. Michel for successfully ending the North Louisiana plant's strike without loss of job or revenue.

The spring opening of the St. Michel mansion was described in a late April 1975 paper by a loquacious entertainment reporter as being, "Marvelous, ancient, and awe-inspiring with the quality of *je ne sais quoi.*" The St. Michels were mentioned, but only as the owners and descendants of the original builder.

In June 1975, Geraud St. Michel, the fifteen-year-old son of Luc and Eleanor, became an Eagle Scout. Mignon wondered if Luc had been the Scout leader of the troop for Geraud to attain that status so young.

In September 1975, the ten-year-old daughter of Luc and Eleanor, Eugenie, was hospitalized in Baton Rouge for an unmentioned childhood illness. Mignon sat up and almost pressed her nose to the screen of the monitor. The article alluded to German measles. The child was expected to make a full recovery. And Mignon thought, *How many children get mentioned in the newspaper with some kind of undisclosed illness and have been sent away for a while to a city distant enough that no one will follow up?*

She thought more about it. It must have been after Luc and Garlande vanished. The little girl, always unstable, had become seriously ill after losing her father to his mistress. Apparently the very act of giving up one's family for one's mistress had devastated the entire St. Michel family. In the same way that it had devastated the Thibeaux family.

Mignon looked through the remainder of the seventies and found brief references to the St. Michels. A reference to the spring and autumn openings of the St. Michel mansion, a contribution to this or that, Geraud St. Michel accepted at Princeton at age seventeen, and Eugenie off to Europe for six months in 1980. The youngest St. Michel apparently hadn't returned to the mansion for years. There were brief mentions of her in the gossip columns. Eugenie was in Paris. Eugenie was in New York City. Eugenie married in France. Eugenie at a sophisticated film opening in Europe. But there was no mention of her returning to Louisiana, even for visits, and Mignon thought this might be the first time in over two decades that Eugenie had come back to La Valle.

From the early eighties on, there were increasing references to the St. Michel mansion as a possible site for ghost watchers. These articles came from Halloween-inspired references and treated the rumors as humorous jests, but the rumors must have had some seed of truth.

There wasn't anything else. Even the references to the paper mills ceased after the middle eighties because they were sold to bigger companies. The St. Michels' power base decreased, and as a result people weren't interested in them anymore. They faded from the public eye faster than a pop star with a solitary hit on the music charts.

Mignon stopped for fast food while driving back to La Valle. She ate on her way and found herself sitting at the dirt road entrance to her old home. There was something here to be learned, she had decided. She kept returning in her mind to the house that sat at the end of the single-lane dirt road.

Then it came to her lips unbidden, as if put there by an unknown force. The words seemed to issue out, unwanted, and from what depths of her memory, Mignon did not know, but she whispered, "High diddle diddle, the cat and the fiddle, the cow jumped over the moon; the little dog laughed . . . to see such craft, and the dish ran away with the spoon . . ." Her voice trailed off doubtfully, unsure if she had gotten all the words correct. She sat in her rental car, looking down the shadowy path to the place she had been born.

Where had this nursery rhyme come from? She hadn't thought of a nursery rhyme in twenty years and here was one at the tip of her tongue.

Garlande Thibeaux had loved nursery rhymes. The memory came to Mignon abruptly, with all of the force of a bullet in the night. Her mother had been forever teaching Mignon a new one, until Mignon could repeat it by rote. In her mind she could see her father laughing at her mother's actions, saying, "What will the girl get out of remembering nursery rhymes, woman? There's no money in that." And her mother had laughed, urging Mignon to recite another one. "Do the one about the black sheep, Mignon, *ma chère*. Show your father what a fine mind you have, my little precious child," she had instructed. Mignon had done just that, happily, willfully, with a childlike boastfulness that only a five-year-old could show to her father.

Garlande had learned dozens of the nursery rhymes from her own mother, a tradition she happened to enjoy passing onto her own child. Garlande had only a minimal education at best, and gloried in Mignon's quick intelligence and perspicacity.

Mignon abruptly realized something else. Garlande Thibeaux had loved her child. *She loved me. She really loved me.* There had been kindness in her touch and a joy when she saw Mignon coming home from the school bus. There had been pride in making Mignon even the sackcloth clothing. There had been honest love.

And she would have never left me behind. Never.

Chapter Nine

The man in the wilderness asked of me
How many strawberries grew in the sea.
I answered him as I thought good,
"As many as red herrings grow in the wood."

THE MAN IN THE WILDERNESS

MINER POTEET WAS THE man Mignon knew she had to talk with next. So she drove the half mile to the Poteet home. The house was located at the other end of the Poteet land, down another dirt road, which was regularly leveled and laid with gravel in order to prevent rutting from fog, mist, and rain. The house itself was as small as the shack where Mignon had lived, but kept up with a fresh coat of butter yellow paint and a neat garden along the side of the house. There was no bowing floor, no rotting wood, nor the smell of neglect and decay heavy in the air.

As she parked her car next to a seventies-era Dodge pickup with a camper shell, she noticed an old man plucking at plants with a hoe in the garden. She hadn't been sure if she would remember Miner Poteet, but as soon as his pleasant face turned toward her in the full sunlight, curiously inquisitive, she knew it was him. He had always been a kind man, eternally old to her, especially when she had been a child.

When she stepped out of her car and approached him, he stood up as straight as the slight curve in his spine allowed, dressed in denim farmer's overalls and holding a well-used hoe in his right hand. His eyes were bright blue, the blue of a morning sky, the blue that existed in dreams, and his hair, what was left of it, was as colorless as light. Liver spots ran from the curve of his forehead down his cheeks, and were reproduced in large groups on his hands. All of this showed that he was no longer just the amicable old man of her child-hood memories, but a man who had worked hard in his life to get to his seventies. A man who displayed his badges of honor proudly. He regarded her with a half smile on his face, and then the smile slipped away as he realized who he was looking at. "My God," he muttered.

"Mr. Poteet," she said.

"My God," he repeated. Then he sighed deeply as under-standing set in. "No, you ain't her. You're Mignon." An un-certain smile returned. "I would have known you anywheres, child. You the picture of your mama. You the *picture* of your mama."

"I would have known you anywhere, Mr. Poteet," she an-swered truthfully. "You don't look all that much different to me, either."

"Bless you, child." He waved at his garden. It was obvious he was cleaning out the debris from his summer harvest. All that was left were dying plants. "I should have gone to church today, but I just couldn't stand to let all this mess go. That minister over to the church has been trying to save me. He says I'm off to see the devil if I don't repent and go to church more regular like. But I think he just wants more money in the collection plate."

Mignon grinned. Mr. Poteet even sounded like the same man.

He went on. "Why don't we go sit on the porch and I'll have my granddaughter fix us up some coffee?" He settled the hoe against a fence and led the way, glancing at Mignon once.

In that single look she knew that he hadn't lost any of his mental capacities. He had sized her up in a moment with an instant scrutiny of her features and bearing.

Mignon followed the old man around to the front of the house, and listened while he called inside. After he told his granddaughter that they had company, he said to Mignon, "She's my daughter's gal, twenty years old, and goes to college over to Natchitoches. Can you believe that? She's taking courses in *bi*-ology. Tells me to use organic whatsits on my garden. Good gal, that. Stays with me while she's going to school to save her parents from spending the money to put her in an apartment or a dormitory. The daughter and her husband live over to Alexandria." He lowered his voice to a whisper. "My daughter, she ask my granddaughter about me, then she ask me about her daughter. She one clever woman, my daughter, no?"

He waved her to a swinging porch chair and settled himself into a rocking chair, seeming every inch a man well into his seventies. "You know about Mrs. Poteet?"

Mignon knew that his wife had died of cancer ten years before, and was buried in the same graveyard John Henry had taken Mignon to that very day. A section in the back, walled off with Poteet inscribed in stone in front, dated from the days the Poteet family had been more prosperous. "I'm sorry, Mr. Poteet. She always brought things to us, when we lived here. She was a charitable woman."

"That she was. She would have made me go to church, too. I miss that old girl. Had a sassy mouth and a big butt, but she was the finest woman I ever met." Mr. Poteet's eyes focused on something past Mignon's shoulder. "I'm glad to see you. Always wanted to know what had happened to you. Then we heard your pa up and died in Dallas."

Mignon had heard that, too. But she didn't know it for a fact. One of her foster families had broken the news to her when she was twelve. She hadn't really cared at that time. Ruff Thibeaux had abandoned her in Texas when she was eight years old. She hadn't been surprised to hear of his death. He had taken to drinking even before he had left Louisiana and it had worsened after his wife quit him for another man. She nodded at the older man, intent on the present conversation, dismissing that particular bit of her past with only a tinge of regret.

He went on. "That news came through, but nothing about you. It was like you up and vanished. The missus and I wanted to go to Dallas and find you. We had the minister call, but those officials over to Texas wouldn't even tell us if you was there. Said we wasn't family and we didn't have no right to know such a thing. Wanted you to know that."

Mignon's mouth opened a little. Her throat tightened. She had never known that. She might never have known that about the Poteets if she hadn't come back here. Someone had cared about her. Someone had wanted her. For the briefest of moments she was lost in the realization. She muttered, "I-I don't know what to say."

Mr. Poteet waved impatiently. "It didn't do you no good, no how. So no point in getting misty-eyed about it, girl. Mrs. Poteet thought a lot of you. Thought a lot of your parents right up until . . . well . . . until your ma left."

Mignon digested this carefully. She would have wiped away the bit of moisture at her eye, but she didn't want Miner Poteet to see her doing it. "Do you know what happened to my mother, Mr. Poteet?"

Miner examined the tips of his fingers carefully, then glanced up at Mignon. "I know what the rumors say. She ran off with that Luc St. Michel. Some said they was together for a long time. It wasn't a surprise to me, exactly."

"What do you mean?" she asked cautiously.

"I'd see his car come this way once too often, child. But

what was I going to do, tell your pa that your mother wasn't being faithful to him?" He shook his head sadly. "I was working for the St. Michels at the time. Bringing in a good salary for a wife and three children. Had the rent from your folks. The missus was determined to send our oldest boy to college. I couldn't afford to jump up and say boo."

"You know what I want to ask about," said Mignon. She sat in the swinging chair, holding one foot on the wooden porch floor to keep the chair from swaying as she stared at the older man. She had had her suspicions about the anonymous letter, and Miner Poteet seemed the most obvious suspect. He and his wife had been people of the earth, rooted in superstition like many of the locals in the area. He knew as well as anyone, and better than most, that Garlande would never have abandoned Mignon, and he undoubtedly knew what that meant. That one news article had gone national, and if someone had seen it they might have told him. Miner might have been the one to send the letter, insisting she know that something odd was happening. "You have to know."

"You want to know why you was kicked out that same night," Miner affirmed. "I know. It was the sheriff. Sheriff Ruelle Fanchon. You know the man. He came to me that night and said that Ruff Thibeaux had to leave. Ruff had to leave and take you with him, with just what he could carry. He told me this before he went over to the old house. And he said if I interfered then he would go by the high school and find some drugs in my boy's locker. And my boy would go over to Angola, even though he was just a teenager. And did I know what those bastards at Angola did to young men like my boy?" His eyes burned bright with indignity and rage at what had been done to him and the Thibeauxs. "He said Ruff had done something wrong and had to go. But I knew. Ruff didn't do nothing wrong except to be married to the woman who ran off with Luc St. Michel."

"The sheriff was working for the St. Michels," she commented. Memories came rushing back, the words and sights and smells of an event which had troubled a young girl's dreams for years. "You will leave the parish, Thibeaux," Judge Gabriel Laurier had told her father, his voice as rich and as Southern then as it had been the night before, at Eleanor's dinner party. The sheriff stood at his side, glowering forcefully. "Leave and don't you ever come back."

"Come on, child." Ruff had grasped his five-year-old daughter by the arm, the smell of alcohol heavy on his breath, no fight left in him. "We got to go now."

"But Mama," protested Mignon. "Where's Mama?"

"Your mama done chose some other way t'go, Mignon. Get in the goddamned truck!"

The present forced its way back into Mignon's mind. She looked at Miner Poteet and he confirmed her suspicion. "Paid off by them, by Eleanor. Nothing no one could prove, mind you. But Eleanor was and still is a cold woman. She didn't want no reminders of no Thibeaux around here. So you and your pa had to go."

"We left because he threatened us," she concluded. She could see the scene in her mind, like a fogged, distant dream in which she was a reluctant witness. "The sheriff and the judge, both of them looming over my father, whispering in his ear, in the front yard. I didn't hear most of what they said, but only saw how they frightened my father. They'd already piled our clothing and a few other things on the front porch. They wouldn't even let us go into the house. It didn't take him ten minutes to load up everything, and another five before we were driving out of La Valle forever." That had been her very first meeting with Judge Gabriel Laurier. After he had muttered threats in her father's ear, he had walked over to look Mignon up and down, like she was a piece of worthless lint he would flick off the collar of his suit.

Miner nodded. "I thought maybe they'd change their minds after a few years, let you come back to your grandparents or to us, but Eleanor St. Michel never wavered. The sheriff warned us both the year your father died. Came out and sat right where you're sitting right now, that chawbacon son of a bitch. Said she didn't want to see that 'little red-haired whore's daughter' running around here." He had the good grace to look ashamed. "The sheriff's words, not mine, child."

"What happened then?" Mignon asked as she stared at Miner Poteet.

Miner appeared almost surprised at the question. "Why, nothing much. Life went on. Ruelle Fanchon retired after some time. Don't recall exactly when that was. But he didn't care to stay in this place, with all these people he'd screwed over one time or another for an extra dollar in his pocket. Suppose he was a mite afraid someone would come and burn down his house while he was asleep in his bed. So he moved down to Baton Rouge. Last I ever seen of his sorry hide, I ain't ashamed to say, and I hear tell about him having problems with the law hisself down to the capital. The St. Michels went on the way they always did. I stopped working for the family in '87, and ain't been happier. They keep to their big house and their fancy functions, and I do my business around here. The two don't meet."

Mignon had gotten something here, some kind of vindication. Her childhood memories and adult nightmares hadn't led her astray. Questionable actions had been taken that night such a long time ago.

Then Miner said, "The old farmhouse ain't been lived in since."

She looked at him again. "I was down there Friday. I hope you don't mind."

"No, it ain't that. But if you go again, mind you don't step through the floor. The wood's rotten as a fish market in Denmark. I wouldn't want you breaking an ankle down on the farm, with no one to hear for miles around." Miner trailed off, lost in his own thoughts. "But maybe you don't want to go down there at night."

Mignon was silent for a moment. "Why not?" She already knew the answer, because she had done just that, and she knew what was down there at night.

He didn't answer for a moment, as if he were afraid. "I tried to rent the place out time to time. People would come, stay a week or two, and then leave. That was back in the seventies. They said there was noises at night. Noises like they ain't never heard before." Miner went back to studying his fingers.

"I'm not sure I understand you . . ."

His bright blue eyes caught hers. "You understand me, child. I think you understand me just fine. Even the school kids don't go down there. They don't go down there because they afraid to. *I* don't go down there after dark. I say to you, you go down after dark and you find out things you don't want to know." He crossed himself quickly and Mignon thought that he probably wasn't aware that he had made the religious gesture.

Finally, he shrugged. "I'm saying that place ain't what it used to be, that's all." He looked crossly around him. "Where is that girl with that coffee? Mary Catherine!"

The screen door of the house opened and a young woman dressed much like Mignon came out with two large, steaming mugs. "Hold on to your britches, Grandpa. I've got three chapters left of organic chemistry, and man, you don't want to know what that's all about."

Her grandfather guffawed. "Organic chemistry? What for you got to take a class like that? Don't they offer stuff like history no more? This here is Mignon Thibeaux, Mary Catherine. Her folks and she used to live down at the old homestead, so many years ago I cain't recall."

Mary Catherine was a vivacious twenty-year-old with black hair and her grandfather's blue eyes. She was wand-slim, and held out the mug to Mignon with an apologetic look. "I didn't know how you take it." There was something in the younger woman's eyes that told Mignon Mary Catherine knew who she was. There wasn't anger or mistrust there, but simple knowledge, and Mignon wondered if she knew a bit more than she was telling.

"Black is perfect," Mignon said and, took a sip. "Thank you." It was a strong brew heady with chicory. Try as she might, she wouldn't get another word about Garlande Thibeaux or Luc St. Michel out of Miner Poteet with his granddaughter standing there. However, she had a good idea that he had told her most of what she wanted to know, most of what he knew. She thought he wouldn't answer her about the letter, so she didn't ask.

But there was one last thing she had decided to try before she let go of this thread. "Mr. Poteet, I wonder if there's something you would consider."

Miner listened to her, and finally he nodded. He had his own conditions, but those didn't matter to Mignon so she readily agreed.

It was almost an hour later that Mignon found herself in front of the old house again. She made a mental list of things she would have to accomplish, and was happy to walk back to her car where it sat alone and silent on the side of the highway. She would have to speak with the realtor again, what was his name?

Vincent Grase, that was it. He could finish off the contract between Miner and herself. Mignon smiled. It wouldn't take long before the news had spread and someone would come to nibble at the bait.

She opened the trunk of her rental car, lifted up the spare tire, and removed a black carrying case about the size of a small doctor's bag. Keeping her hands in the trunk, away from outside view, she unzipped the case and removed the gun inside. It was a Beretta nine-millimeter, a gun favored by police departments and the United States Army military police. It carried a clip of nine rounds, with room for one in the chamber. She could shoot until the cows came home if she were so inclined. She had purchased it in California and was registered there as owning it. She didn't have a clue whether it was legal to have it in the state of Louisiana, but she would keep it at her side until she had the answers she sought. Chambering a round, she carefully brought the gun up so that it would be hidden from view. From now on she would keep it within grabbing distance. She might have a very real need of it. It was much better protection than the pepper spray.

That strange cold wind was blowing in from the north again. It seemed as though she were the only one in the world at this moment in time. She stood beside her rental car, the trunk open and a gun held carefully in front of her, considering that five years ago she never would have guessed that she would be in this place, at this time, doing what she was doing. But then she hadn't known that a man who owned a gallery in Soho, who sometimes showed her work, would be mugged and shot before her very eyes, triggering a mass of unconscious images she had suppressed for more years than she cared to count.

As soon as Vincent Grase spread the word about her upcoming purchase of the old house on the Poteet land, there would be some consternation. But who would be the most concerned? And what would they do in order to protect themselves?

Mignon put the pistol in her purse and put the purse beside the driver's seat. She closed the trunk and drove back to the bed and breakfast in Natchitoches.

In her room, she dropped her purse on the table beside the door, and caught a movement out of the corner of her eye. Turning her head in that direction, a blur of motion disappeared under the bed with a smooth, repetitive noise that she had to strain to hear.

Mignon assumed it was a mouse or a rat. She had seen mice before, and rats were nothing but big mice with longer tails. *So much for the owner's cleaning methods*, she thought with a groan.

With one knee on the ground by the bed, Mignon stooped to look underneath. One hand lifted the white, lacy bedskirt up and out of the way so she could get a better view. It was the skirt that saved her life.

A great cottonmouth was curled up under the bed.

She focused on the shape under the bed for a split second before it moved directly at her. It was faster than she would have imagined anything could be. It was in that split second that she realized it was a snake, it was striking at her, and her gun was in her purse on the other side of the room.

Mignon couldn't help the scream that issued forth. She yanked herself back, even while knowing that there was nothing between her and the snake. The snake, its body as big as a baseball bat and as long as she was tall, its white lips and gums illustrating its name, hurled itself relentlessly toward her. Jaws opened impossibly wide, revealing huge fangs which slammed shut with a loud clap as it missed her and snagged the lace bedskirt Mignon had dropped as she yanked herself backward, a low hiss of air escaping through her mouth.

She threw herself back and thrust a chair full of pillows on top of the snake. Then she ran for the door, slipping out and slamming it behind her.

Mignon stood shaking in the garden, her chest heaving up and down, her limbs trembling with the onslaught of adrenaline that flowed so freely from the chilling experience. Her room was located outside the main building, like a guest house, but surrounded by lush fall flowers and evergreen foliage. The cottonmouth was a water snake, however, and lived in watery areas like swamps and lakes. It wouldn't be attracted to this garden, much less the country-decorated splendor of her room, and its poison was deadly, especially if it had struck at her neck or throat.

Five minutes later, she watched the owner of the bed and breakfast peer into the window of the room. "My lands," she muttered. "Sure enough. That's a cottonmouth all right, curled up right next to your bed."

The word "Duh" almost slipped out of Mignon's mouth, but she clamped it down and asked instead, "Can you call animal control or something?"

The much older woman nodded distractedly. Her name was Patti Lewis, and she was apologetic and crestfallen at the thought of such a thing happening at her place of business. "I'm sure those folks will come over and take care of that fella. I don't know what he's doing in your room, though. You didn't bring him with you?" It was a half-hearted question at best.

"No, dear," responded Mignon with sarcasm she couldn't suppress. "I didn't."

Mrs. Lewis went back through the garden to the main building to call the proper authorities while Mignon looked around her. It would be easy enough to walk back here with a snake in a bag, jimmy the door or the window, leave the snake, and vanish without anyone seeing anything. But Mrs. Lewis had a full house of guests, and many of them had wandered through the garden while she and Mignon stood there talking about their uninvited guest.

When the older woman returned, Mignon asked, "You might want to ask if your other guests saw anything unusual this morning."

Mrs. Lewis's face twisted unhappily. She had visions in her mind of being sued by the nice young lady who was staying for an unlimited time in her refurbished carriage house. But she wasn't stupid. "You mean you think someone put that snake in your room? On purpose?" *God forbid*, the older woman thought. *Talk about a lawsuit to end all lawsuits.*

Mignon shrugged, happy to be outside while the snake was inside and a shut door stood between the two of them. She wondered how she was going to be able to sleep in that room again without dreaming about snakes. "It's hard to say exactly what people are capable of, don't you think?"

Chapter Ten

Mary, Mary, quite contrary,
How does your garden grow?
With silver bells, and cockleshells,
And pretty maids all in a row.

MARY, MARY, QUITE CONTRARY

IT HAD BEEN A busy week for Mignon. As soon as she had closed the deal with Miner Poteet, she had wasted little time calling various construction contractors in the Natchitoches area. Men who were willing to drive a few miles out of their way to work for some extra money. Men who weren't allied to the St. Michels one way or another, like many of those who lived in La Valle.

As it turned out, the house wasn't as dilapidated as Miner Poteet had worried about. Twenty-five years of neglect hadn't broken its back. One set of workmen immediately set about jacking up the house in the middle where it was drooping. Despite its appearance, it wasn't as difficult a task as Mignon imagined it to be. They were done in two days and the house began to look like a decrepit old farmhouse instead of one about to collapse on itself.

One of the contractors had said to her, "The wood beams are in good shape for such an old bear. But I think you'll have to have all the floors ripped out, some of them are like Swiss cheese."

Money provided a way for men to work on that as well. Another two days of work and a new plywood floor graced about half of the bottom of the farmhouse. In addition, all of the trash inside had been hauled away, leaving only the major appliances that could be used again, such as the pot-bellied stove someone had tried to drag off once, and the stove in the tiny kitchen.

She laughed aloud at her own quirks. Electricity would be the largest problem, and a master electrician had told her the wiring system was relatively simple. Of course, she couldn't use the outhouse, so a chemical toilet was brought in for the time being, and any water she used would have to be carted in by car. The road had been leveled for the workmen right off the bat, finally allowing Mignon to drive right up to the house itself.

Which left the problem of the cistern out back. She wasn't sure what she could do with that. Technically, using rainwater in this day and age wasn't like it had been a hundred years ago. It wasn't healthy to use it for anything except to water the yard. The cistern would have to be filled in so it wouldn't present a danger to anyone walking near it. After a half hour of walking back and forth, Mignon found the cement cap in the backyard under some debris and marked it with bright yellow surveyor's tape, warning the workmen who were filling in the outhouse pit, and those who might take a break outside, not to walk across that particular area.

It was good to spend her money on this place, Mignon thought, feeling inordinately pleased with herself. It was like bringing a grand old lady back into her own, except that this house could never be considered a grand old lady. Rather a mischievous, dirty child who had allowed the mud to dry on her face.

She could envision a bathhouse out back rather than an outhouse. Perhaps a small building with a septic tank nearby and its own water system. A well might have to be dug, or the water tank replaced by one that wasn't rusting into little pieces even as she thought about it. All in all, the old farmhouse might make a decent getaway for her.

Mignon stood on the porch and studied the oil painting on her portable easel. She dipped her round-headed brush into some yellow ocher and lightly dabbed on one side. The painting was coming along just fine. In the bright light of noon on a pleasant September day, her mind was clear and she almost didn't have to think about how her fingers guided the brushes along the canvas, creating light and shape out of nothingness.

Behind her the house was silent. Two men working on the floor had gone to lunch. Another one who was filling in the outhouse pit had walked off into the woods toward the national forest, saying he'd be back in an hour. *Looking for a place to come jacking for deer one night*, Mignon thought. *He's checking out the area for spoor.* He wouldn't be the first in this area. She had found a deer stand perched on a tall oak tree about five hundred yards into the forest to the east, in a little clearing someone had made in order to better see deer and shoot them.

Then John Henry drove up in his official vehicle, disrupting her calm train of thought. He parked next to her rental and looked around as he let the engine idle. In addition to the leveled road, a small parking area had been cleared and the brush obscuring the front yard had been removed. A surveyor's flags marked the length and breadth of the property to all sides. The house had been returned to a level state, which hadn't improved its overall condition in his opinion. Mignon Thibeaux had been busy this week.

Mignon looked at him once and returned to studying the painting in front of her. John Henry was naturally curious. She had made more money off her paintings in a single year than he would see in ten years of work. *It must be something special*, he reckoned. *To be able to do something like that.*

John Henry was required to possess a certain perspicacity in his work. Mignon was at least as smart as he was, if not more. Furthermore, she was hiding something he would very much like to know. However, buying a house near La Valle, the very house she was born in, wasn't a method for getting revenge on the St. Michels. Living near them wouldn't particularly annoy them. No, he knew she had another motive. She had said she didn't want to rake up the coals, but she was doing just that, simply by her continued presence.

Conversely, there were the St. Michels. Eleanor wouldn't have invited the woman to dinner if she hadn't desired to do just that. The matriarch of the St. Michels had her own motives, and John Henry wondered how Mignon fit into the larger scheme.

In the meantime, Mignon had attained a cult status around La Valle, a woman who had been born poor and succeeded. There were those around this area who were proud to have her back here, and implied in many conversations that she and her father had received a raw deal from the St. Michels.

But did Mignon think that?

John Henry turned off the Bronco and got out, placing his Stetson on his head.

Mignon watched him out of the corner of her eye. She put her brush down in a cup filled with turpentine, casting a last critical eye over the painting. Her muse had fled, leaving an empty well of creativity. Nothing more would be accomplished on this work today. She flipped a cover over the painting.

John Henry approached the patio. "Morning, Mignon," he called.

Mignon began to clean her brushes with turpentine and cheesecloth. After a few moments she turned toward him. "Come to threaten me again, John Henry? It doesn't go over as well in the daylight. Maybe you should come back at night." *When I'm at the bed and breakfast, sugar, in another parish. Out of gun range.*

He stood at the base of the wooden steps leading up to the porch, waiting for her sarcasm to fade, an enigmatic expression gracing his fine features. He studied her carefully. She was dressed in worn jeans and an old T-shirt that read "Ancient Oriental Proverb" on the top and had some Chinese characters on the bottom. John Henry almost shook himself. It would have been nice if she didn't look as good in old baggy clothing as she did in that figure-hugging black sheath that showed every inch of her flesh to its best advantage. But the truth was that it really didn't matter what she was wearing.

"I wasn't threatening you," he said, not able to remove his eyes from the curved slopes that tantalized him underneath her loose T-shirt and jeans. He put a booted foot on the bottom step and rested his hands on top of his knee.

"Come on, John Henry," she said. "A graveyard at one in the morning? What's that about? Some strange Louisianan welcome wagon that we Yankees don't know about? What's next, a cross burning on my front lawn? Right after I got the damned thing cleared off, too? But hey, I forgot, I'm not doing anything to threaten the Ku Klux Klan. Yet, anyway."

"Technically, you're not a Yankee, Mignon. And on reflection, maybe I shouldn't have picked that graveyard." John Henry sighed. "I was sure that you had pulled a fast one on Eleanor St. Michel."

"And you're not now," Mignon asked carefully.

"Your hands were like ice, you were shaking like a leaf, and damned if I know what happened to the table. My foot was on yours. All I can think is that two of the other people at the table did it. Two people who were sitting together." He shrugged. "I've seen some strange things in my life, but that one, well, I've never seen something like that."

Mignon sighed, as well. "It's never happened to me before.

Leya said I was sensitive. Maybe it's just because I was a little nervous being in the boogey man's house." She *had* pulled a fast one, though. A fast bit of chicanery combined with quick thinking. And that unnameable sense of something else that had been there.

Words died away, leaving only the sound of leaves moving softly around them. John Henry finally said, "I don't get it."

Mignon saw that he was staring at her chest. She resisted the impulse to glance down at her breasts and then understood that he was referring to her shirt. She took it in her hands and turned it to the side, so that the vaguely Asian words became obvious. Although the words resembled unreadable Chinese characters viewed from the front, turned on their side they were simply a Chinese-style font that read in English, "Fuck this shit." She shrugged apologetically. "My friend gave it to me. For when things are a little crazy."

He smiled. It transformed his face in a way that left Mignon a little in awe. He asked, "Can I look at your painting?"

Mignon took a step backward with a little look of surprise on her face. "Why? You like art?"

John Henry took that to be a challenge. "Let's see. When my daughter was younger, she used to draw horses that were mostly lines and she called it art. I like a little of this and that. St. Germaine isn't the height of cosmopolitan culture, however." He wasn't about to admit that he had gone to Barnes & Noble to buy a copy of her book to see what she was capable of doing. He found the watercolors almost as entrancing as he found her. There was a lot to be said about her character in those works that transfixed his eyes as he had turned each page. There was a wealth of color and detail that he didn't know a watercolor painting could possess. Perhaps he couldn't say exactly why he had liked her work, but he wouldn't mind having one on his wall where he could look at it every day. Not any more than he would mind having her in his bed where he could wake up to her every morning. "Other than what I see sometimes in Natchitoches, I don't know much about art in general."

She took another step backward and mutely invited him onto the porch. With her right hand she uncovered the work. John Henry stepped up to look at it. Immediately, he thought it didn't look like the works in her book. It was a scene of the forest just past the curve of the driveway, a primeval forest with the primordial growth springing forth, threatening to obscure all in its path. The colors were jewellike but darker, and the piece conveyed a savage lack of enlightenment and luminance. Unlike her watercolors, this one relied on vague shapes to impart its message of blackened forest, a stunted forest that refused to grow. He found himself staring at it and losing himself in the shapes that covered the canvas. It said volumes more than Mignon ever could about pain and torment. He couldn't even begin to describe what he felt when he looked at the canvas; the only thing that popped into his mind sounded lame and anemic, but he uttered it anyway. "Impressionistic, right?"

"Right," she confirmed, flipping the cover back. "You know more than you let on."

"Not really. Not about art."

Tilting her head, Mignon studied his face and he looked back at her. She asked, "What do you know about snakes?"

John Henry's expression didn't waver. He knew about the cottonmouth in her room on Sunday. "I know not to step on 'em."

"Do you know sometimes they crawl into the damnedest places?"

"Like your room?" he asked, but it wasn't really a question. Mignon nodded. "Just like my room."

"Natchitoches police chief told me about that yesterday. He didn't know I was interested in . . . your well-being."

There was a certain heat between them. Mignon suddenly

became uncomfortable and stepped backward, breaking the spell. "Does he now?"

"Naw, just telling me about something peculiar that happened to a famous artist who happens to be staying in Natchitoches. She came about this close"—he spread his index finger and his thumb about an inch apart—"from being snake bit."

She lowered her head. "Actually, it was a little closer than that."

"Had me a deputy who got nailed by one of those year before last," said John Henry. "Turned his hand black. Man ended up taking disability because his hand will never be the same. Every year we get several people bit around here. Every few years someone dies. Usually a child or an older person. But they die all the same."

Mignon wasn't sure what exactly to say to that. That snake had come so close to her head that she had felt the breeze caused by the rush of his strike. The animal control officer had said that he hadn't seen such a monster for years, and didn't have a clue how it had wandered into Mignon's room.

She had a clue.

"It seems to me like you're biding your time here," John Henry said.

"Biding my time in lieu of what?"

"That's the part I'm not sure of. Either you're just a little gal curious about where she's from, or you know something you're not letting on." He adjusted the Stetson on his head so his sherry brown eyes could better see hers. "Wish I could figure out what."

"I think you can figure it out, if you're as honest and true-blue as you seem to want me to believe." Mignon wiped her hands on the sides of her jeans, removing the remainder of the paint from her fingers and palms. "Maybe you should be thinking about Luc St. Michel and Garlande Thibeaux instead of worrying about this 'little old Yankee.' "

John Henry crossed his arms over his chest, glancing around him. He knew very well that he wasn't a Boy Scout, not with the thoughts that lately had obscured his mind. He had been thinking about Luc St. Michel and Garlande Thibeaux a lot. He had searched the state database for a criminal record for both individuals and found nothing. There were no warrants for either person. There were no records for the State of Louisiana. He'd requested a Social Security work history and received it that very morning. Neither individual had a work history since 1975. Finally, neither Luc or Garlande had a Louisiana driver's license, which didn't mean that they didn't have a driver's license from another state or even in another country. But both people had effectively vanished in a world where records were increasingly easier to access. "You'll give me a call if you have a problem with snakes?"

"I think I can take care of snakes, if I happen to run into one." She paused. "It's the bigger critters I have to worry about."

John Henry left without further ado, carefully turning his Bronco around in her little parking area, and returning up the dirt road.

As he drove he thought about what she had suggested. There was an inherent challenge in her words that he couldn't resist, so he returned to his headquarters just outside of La Valle. Nothing much was going on in the sheriff's department. There was a man in the lockup on a DUI, and another awaiting transportation to Shreveport, where he was wanted on a manslaughter charge. Three deputies were patrolling the parish, and two were working in a large open area in the back. None of the deputies had been in St. Germaine Parish as long as he had, and three of them weren't even from the area originally. No one was familiar with the old scandal except the receptionist, who overheard him asking about Luc and Garlande.

Ruby Wingo had been a fixture of the St. Germaine Parish

Sheriff's Department for more years than anyone could recall. She knew where all the bodies were buried. She knew all of its dirty secrets. She was also the ugliest woman John Henry had ever seen in his life.

She stood five-foot-nothing in her bare feet, but she wore five-inch heels to the office every day. In her fifties now, she dyed her hair jet black and wore more makeup than Tammy Faye Bakker. There was a wart the size of a pencil eraser on her cheek that had a huge hair growing out of it, and she was a chubby little woman with a chip on her shoulder the size of Texas. No one crossed her. No one said boo to her. Her husband of about thirty years, or it might have been forty, was Percival Wingo. She had married very young and her grandchildren were about to enter high school. In any case, Percival was strongly protective of his much beloved wife and came into the station periodically to make sure all the other employees were treating her right, which only added to her menacing reputation.

John Henry thought it was all amusing because Ruby Wingo was one of the best receptionists he'd ever seen. She could handle just about anyone who came into the station with one hand tied behind her back. She could have arrested a gang of burly bikers single-handedly if she had been so inclined. As a matter of fact, he was a little afraid of her himself.

"That woman sure is stirring up a mess of yellow jackets, ain't she?" she said to him.

"Beg pardon?"

Ruby balanced herself carefully on her spiked black heels. Her pursed lips were covered with sparkly fuchsia lipstick, and she stared at the sheriff with one hand on her plump hip. "I've never heard so many people talk about Luc St. Michel and Garlande Thibeaux since 1975. And it was kind of a secret then."

John Henry smiled. "Let me buy you a cup of coffee, Ruby."

"Why John Henry, what would Percival say?"

A vision of the six-foot-six, three-hundred-pound Percival Wingo popped into John Henry's head. Percival was a big, mean man who had not one whit of humor about him. "Well, we won't tell him, will we?"

Ruby giggled with one hand over her mouth, and John Henry cringed.

After Ruby had spilled all the beans she could, John Henry wasn't much more informed than he had been before. Ruby's was just a slightly watered-down version of what he'd heard already. Luc had run off with his mistress, Garlande. Garlande was Mignon's mother. Mignon's father had been forced out of the parish by the then sheriff, Ruelle Fanchon. *Which explains why she isn't enamored of the present sheriff.*

Ruff Thibeaux had taken his daughter over to Texas and ended up dying there. Mignon Thibeaux had disappeared into the system. Suddenly she was back, and not only that, but she was relatively famous as an artist. However, since she used her first name only and watercolors weren't the first thing people rose to speak about in La Valle, her success had been virtually unheard of until she returned. And she happened to be the spitting image of her mother. The only addition to the story was that Luc had been seeing Garlande for years, and it was even rumored that Mignon was Luc's child.

"But that just ain't so," added Ruby. "I knew her mama pretty well. For a few years she was right happy with Ruff. Until he started drinking more and more. Then she done hooked up with Luc and off they went to only God knows where."

Mignon had hinted that all wasn't right with those scenarios. John Henry sat at his desk in his office, staring at the wall. She was looking for her mother, and she had thought that her mother might have come back to this place. But Garlande never had.

Neither had Luc St. Michel. That wasn't surprising considering the gargoyle he had for a wife. Eleanor would give Ruby *and* Percival a run for their money. But money was involved. The St. Michels were multimillionaires. Geraud dabbled in some small business ventures, a chain of stores that competed with Pier I, offering a line of foreign knickknacks, candles, and metal ware. The rest of the St. Michels simply lived a social life, like the dinner last Saturday with Eleanor and Leya mucking around in the world of psychics. That certainly hadn't been the first séance he'd been to out there. But it had been the most interesting.

Why wouldn't Luc St. Michel want any of his money?

There wasn't an obvious answer to that. He started a search for John and Jane Does from 1975, cold cases in which the bodies hadn't been identified. He was going to start with Louisiana and then follow up with Texas, since the Texas state border was less than twenty miles away.

Finally, he was going to have to start asking questions of people he didn't want to ask questions of: Eleanor St. Michel, Jourdain Gastineau, Gabriel Laurier, and Ruelle Fanchon. All of them had been involved.

But the one thing that bothered him most was the snake in Mignon's room. Someone had gone to a great deal of trouble to catch a cottonmouth and put it in her room. On the off chance that it would bite her? On the off chance that it would kill her? Not hardly. But certainly to scare her off. She wasn't the type to be scared off, and consequently whoever had been responsible for the snake was going to become more agitated the longer she stayed.

John Henry shook his head. No, he didn't like any of this at all. *Not one damned bit.*

Chapter Eleven

Here comes a candle to light you to bed,
Here comes a chopper to chop off your head.

ORANGES AND LEMONS

"SAY, MIZ THIBEAUX," ONE of the workmen called out to Mignon about an hour before they finished for the day. "Miz" was the southern equivalent of Ma'am, Mignon had rediscovered, rather than the equivalent of Ms. She found the idiom antiquated, but sort of charming all the same. "Miz Thibeaux?" came the workman's voice again.

"Just a second," Mignon called back, covering the canvas on the easel in front of her again. Despite the interruption by the sheriff, she had managed to find some more creative energy from somewhere deep inside of her. In fact, she had been pleased to focus on her painting again.

The darkness inside the house always surprised her, regardless of the uncovered windows and the door propped open by a rock. She knew white walls and bright colored furnishings would cure that ailment soon enough.

The workman who had called her over was named Horace Seay, pronounced "Say." He was an older man in his early fifties and the same one who had been inspecting her section of woods for possible illegal deer-hunting excursions. He had finished with the outhouse's pit and had come inside to help tear out the old wooden floor, gruffly instructing the two younger workmen with short, concise phrases that sounded odd to Mignon's ears. She had realized that he was truly Cajun, a man who originally came from the southern part of Louisiana, and spoke with more than a hint of colorful Acadian French in his accent.

When she went into the master bedroom, she saw that he was bending over the floor in one corner, looking down intently at something he had found.

The floor was nothing but tongue and grooved planks fitted together, like most hardwood flooring. The men had been tearing out the pieces almost recklessly, because most of it was warped, rotted, or generally useless. But Horace had found a piece of the flooring that lifted out easily because someone had once rigged it that way. When she examined the piece of wood more carefully, she saw that someone had sanded away one side of the tongue; when it was fit into the floor, it appeared as solid as any of the rest of the flooring. However, it could be pulled up easily with the edge of a fingernail or a knife, in order to retrieve one's secret possessions.

Horace motioned at Mignon to look into the hole, and together they stared at an old metal box that had been slipped into the floor sideways and wedged between a piling and a support. The bare earth was dark in the deep shadows underneath the box and to the sides of the pilings. Since the piling was on the side of the house, it wasn't among those that had needed rebuilding or bracing when the house had been jacked up. Consequently, if Horace hadn't seen the box when he was tearing up the old flooring, it might never have been found again.

He glanced at her with compassionate brown eyes because he knew the story about her mother and he knew that she and her parents had once lived in this desolate, broken-down place. Horace didn't know if the rusted metal box belonged to anyone she had known, but he wasn't going to look in it. He was a superstitious man, and his own wife said the *fifolet*, a glowing ball of fire that signaled the coming of terrible things, had been seen in the bayou on three consecutive nights. "Let the young woman take that burden," his wife told him. "*Le Bonne Dieu* will watch over her and her trials."

Mignon reached carefully into the hole, mindful that the other two workmen had stepped up to the doorway and were quietly watching both of them. It took a moment to dislodge the box from its place. When she had the box in both hands, she set it down on the floor beside them. Finally, she said, "I think you've worked enough today. Why don't you guys go home?"

Horace wanted to see what was inside the box, but he didn't want to bring evil spirits down on his head. As for his two companions, if they were dumb enough to want to see what was in the box, then let them hang a noose around their own heads. He barked at the other two men, "I'm leaving. You want a ride with me, no? Else you walk back to Natchitoches."

He walked out of the room without looking back. The other two men parted for him to pass, then looked at each other curiously. One asked the other, "What crawled up his butt?"

The other said, "I don't know, but I ain't walking back to Natchitoches, no."

Mignon waited until she heard Horace's truck start up with a roar and a clunk. He ground his gears backing up, and almost a minute later she couldn't hear his engine anymore. She peered down into the hole again and found there was nothing else there but a spiderweb.

With a sigh she turned to the box. The moment it had come into the light she had known who it belonged to, because of the lock on the chest. It was a little padlock, not even an inch long, silver in color, mostly obscured by rust, and had a little embossed knot running across its body. Garlande had worn that lock sometimes on a chain around her neck. She had joked to her only child on more than one occasion, "It's the lock to my heart, *ma chère*."

Now it guarded the box that had been left under the bedroom floor. Mignon picked up the box and fingered the tiny padlock. It had two little wheels on the bottom with letters on them. It was a tiny combination lock. Mignon didn't want to break it, so she started on the combinations in order. There were only six letters on each petite wheel. She began with *A* on one side, rolled the other wheel to the *A* on the opposite side with the tip of her index finger, and the lock fell open soundlessly.

It dropped off the box and onto the floor. After a moment, the rusted lid yielded to Mignon's prying fingers and it came open with a creak. No one had opened the box for many years.

Mignon sat down heavily on the floor, holding the box in her arms. Had she known something would be waiting in this house for her? Had she been called here to find some mysterious object that would point to where her mother was now? It would be easy to say this was so, but there had been another reason behind buying the old house, one that was more practical in nature. It was true Mignon couldn't have foretold that Miner Poteet would be willing to sell this parcel of land, but once the idea had come to her, she knew that it could be worked into her overall plan. It would be like shoving a needle under someone's fingernails—the same someone who had searched her room and had put a snake inside to greet her return.

Not only was the child of Garlande Thibeaux back, but she resembled her mother in the most eerie way imaginable. Not only that, but she seemed as though she wanted to stay and perhaps ask questions that other people wouldn't want asked, and would *never, ever* want answered.

She looked inside the rusted box and found a diary. It was a cheap one with pink flowers on it, something that obviously came from some five-and-dime store back in the seventies. The diary was fastened with a lock, but the key was still attached, not that it would have stopped Mignon from ripping it open and reading the words that waited for her within.

Inadvertently she tilted the box to one side and a necklace came sliding down, making a small clicking noise on the lower side of the metal container. Mignon dipped a finger in to move the diary slightly out of the way. The necklace glittered in the dim light of the room. It was as shiny as the day it had been put into the box. *No dross, that,* she thought. *This is nothing my father could have afforded.*

The same finger slid under the edge of the necklace and lifted it out into the light. It was a gold medallion with a picture of a saint on it. She looked closer and saw that it was an image of St. Luke, the patron saint of artists and doctors, which Mignon knew because of her own calling in life. Her adopted father had given her a medallion like this once, to wear around her neck for luck.

Deftly her fingers turned the medallion over so that its back was visible in the beam of light coming in through the dirty bedroom window. Engraved on the back were the initials *L. St. M.* It had been a gift to a lover who had nothing and couldn't take the risk of wearing it openly. Had it been a special trinket that represented something to him? Or was it simply a little piece of nothing that a millionaire could easily afford and wouldn't think of twice after pressing it into the hand of his mistress?

Mignon put the necklace back into the box. It had been a gift from Garlande's lover, so valued by her mother that it had been carefully hidden away from her husband, along with a diary that might reveal some of her most guarded thoughts.

Mignon knew that her mother would have no more left these precious things behind than she would have left her own daughter. The wind outside began to howl like a man in agony. She hugged the diary to her chest, and the words popped out of nothingness: "Old King Cole was a merry old soul, and a merry old soul was he, he called for his pipe, and he called for his bowl, and he called for his fiddlers three." She wiped away an errant tear coursing down her cheek.

When she returned to her bed and breakfast just after 6 P.M. she found two telephone messages waiting for her. One was from Eleanor St. Michel inviting her to another dinner at the mansion the following night. The other was from Nehemiah.

She picked up the phone and dialed his number. "It's me," she said.

"Mignon," he said with relief. "I was about to call in the Marines. You should have called days ago. I've been scared half to death. I can't help thinking about what you're doing every waking moment." He paused. "On the other hand, I must admit a certain eagerness to see what happens next. It's very contradictory."

"Tomorrow," she said. "It's on for tomorrow. Time for another little push."

"If only there was another way," he said. "It's not my part, you understand. That I can handle. But you. That's entirely something else. You've put yourself right smack in the middle of the danger zone. I can't help but worry about you."

"So you're ready then," she persisted.

There was a brief silence. Finally, Nehemiah sighed. "Extremely," he said. "And I expect you are, as well."

Mignon was exactly that. She had agitated the murderer before, gambling that her assumptions about who was responsible for the disappearances of her mother and Luc St. Michel were correct. She fully intended to give that person another vigorous shaking.

———

AFTER LEAVING MIGNON, John Henry went to see Jourdain Gastineau in his fancy La Valle office. On his way there, John Henry wondered how a man like Jourdain got to be on the short list for one of the highest judicial positions in the state of Louisiana. John Henry knew Jourdain had been born and raised in La Valle, and had married locally. Although he had been educated at Harvard, he had returned to the same township to begin a lucrative practice, catering to the plantation set. His clients were the richest members of north-central Louisiana, and he had serviced state politicians, spending a considerable amount of time in Baton Rouge and New Orleans. Despite the fact that he had never been a judge before, he would most likely be one for the rest of his life.

The office itself was sophisticated and pleasing to the eye. Expensive cypress wood lined the walls and was stained to a warm, amber hue. Graceful scenes of Louisiana history adorned the walls. The furniture was expensive and of the same shade as the cypress wood paneling. Even the receptionist, an attractive young brunette with large brown eyes and a beguiling, well-endowed figure, embellished the office. Her smile was wide enough to swallow him whole, but she couldn't hold a candle to Mignon Thibeaux's lustrous radiance. This sudden urge to compare the two women was unfamiliar to him, and it made him uneasy.

"Sheriff," gushed the receptionist. "Mr. Gastineau said to send you right in." She waved a manicured hand at the door behind her desk. She wasn't a local girl, either, but someone imported from New Orleans or Baton Rouge. John Henry had heard about Jourdain's preference for young beautiful women to man his offices, a fact that had led to much speculation in town as to what their other duties might be.

Jourdain greeted him amicably enough, but with a curious light in his eyes. He rose from his desk and came around to face him. "What can I do for you, John Henry?" he asked, offering his hand to the other man.

They shook hands and then sat down. Jourdain's office was similar in most respects to the reception area, but featured Jourdain's own wall of fame, including diplomas, certificates of appreciation, and various civic awards. John Henry had never been inside this office before. He had never needed to, because the two men usually met at various functions related to the daily regimen of politicking. They had never sat across from each other in the courtroom because it wasn't the kind of law that Jourdain Gastineau practiced. In any case, it was different now, and John Henry was seeing everything in a new light.

Because I am walking a fine line, he thought. He was angry with Mignon for pricking the bubble that kept all of the doubt locked away. Now, it was starting to spill out and he was looking at every man and woman in his parish as if he or she were a possible murderer or conspirator in the disappearances of Luc and Garlande. He had been true to what being a lawman should mean before, but now something had tainted the parish, a place he had come to regard as his home.

"I have some questions," he said.

Jourdain laughed. "Sounds too all-important for today. They're about to announce the nomination for Supreme Court justice. I just got a call from the governor, and he was mighty pleased with himself. And the rest you'll hear on the news like everyone else."

Which made this all the more difficult. *Who in the name of God wants to piss off a Supreme Court justice?* John Henry sighed. He had to be very careful here. "About Luc St. Michel."

Jourdain's face betrayed his obvious irritation. "I knew that woman was going to cause trouble. What is it? What can she possibly be dragging out of the past now?"

"Luc St. Michel disappeared in September of 1975," began John Henry, and Jourdain interrupted him.

"He didn't disappear, he left. He left with his mistress. Hell, it wasn't a secret."

"I want to know how control of the St. Michel estate came to Eleanor," John Henry said as bluntly as he could. *So much for walking the line. I've picked a side and I won't be crossing back.*

Jourdain leaned back in his tall leather chair and examined his manicured nails. He thought for a moment. "I know what this is about. The question isn't how she came into control, but why Luc didn't take his money with him."

John Henry didn't say anything.

There was a long silence. Finally Jourdain said, "Luc St. Michel was a selfish son of a bitch and he left without taking care of a damned thing. I made up a power of attorney for Eleanor so that she would have something to control him with. She was in urgent need. She didn't have access to the St. Michel trust and they would have been in trouble if I hadn't done something. John Henry, she didn't have anything except the house over her head, and that wasn't even hers. She had to have money to keep the house running and the various accounts active."

"Did she know that you forged his signature?"

There was a pause as Jourdain considered the legalities of the situation. "No, Eleanor thought Luc had signed it in lieu of what he had done to her. She wasn't thinking properly about the whole situation. He had done the unthinkable and then left her and their children without a penny to their name. Although Geraud would have come into his own some years later, Eleanor was in a dire state of affairs at that time. And Luc had a multitude of accounts, some in Switzerland. Twenty-five years ago he was a millionaire. That is tanta-mount to being a billionaire today."

"And no one has ever stopped to ask why? No one ever asked, what the hell happened? Don't you know what that means, Jourdain?" John Henry twisted his face as he asked the question. He didn't wait for an answer. "No one has seen or heard from Luc St. Michel or Garlande Thibeaux since they allegedly left. Not anyone. They might as well have fallen off the face of the planet."

Jourdain's mouth fell open and then snapped shut. His mind was busy calculating possibilities. "Surely you don't think that Eleanor . . . did something to Luc and his mistress?"

John Henry stared at the other man as if he could divine the contents of his soul. Finally he said, "I don't know what to think, Jourdain. I know that you did something illegal, and I know that there's no evidence of a homicide. But someone seems to be damned sure that Luc St. Michel is dead. Why are they asking for him at séances? Why do they think he's haunting them? Because they know he's dead and buried and they know exactly who did the burying. And I have to ask why Eleanor had the judge and the old sheriff run the Thibeauxs out of town like some kind of trash they didn't want to look at anymore."

Sitting forward in his chair, John Henry locked his eyes with Jourdain's. He wanted to know this man's secrets. He wanted to see him squirm with discomfort. Because he knew that if Gabriel Laurier and Ruelle Fanchon were involved, then Jourdain Gastineau had probably been the man pushing them from behind. With all that dirty business, it was clear how Jourdain had garnered the nomination to the Supreme Court. It wasn't a surprise to John Henry. He had played in the same pool that dictated he sometimes let go influential men who had drunk too much or were going a tad fast on a dark night. He had politicked for campaign money from the same families with which Jourdain did regular business. He discovered it wasn't sitting well now.

"It's because of Eugenie's nightmares, that's all," said Jourdain. "She's unbalanced and Eleanor thinks that she's half possessed by her father's ghost. Luc could be anywhere. There's no proof that he's dead. I've tried to talk Eleanor out of these activities with her psychics, but you know how she is. She doesn't want to listen to anyone but her own counsel. She thinks that having that girl, the artist, in her house, will help appease them in some insane manner."

"Jourdain, there isn't any evidence of a crime." said John Henry. "I've told you. I've known you for ten years and you've known me. I've never thought that you were capable of doing something wrong like that. But I understand why you did it. Forging a signature twenty-five years ago doesn't mean crap to me now, and I've no reason to bring it up in the future. But understand this, if you have knowledge of a murder, then you become a conspirator after the fact, and there's no statute of limitations on that. And there isn't much that will protect you. Not even a nomination to the highest court in the state."

"You haven't even read me my rights, John Henry," Jourdain said icily.

"I don't have to because I don't have one shred of evidence that anyone is dead, much less murdered." John Henry stood up and looked steadily down at the older man. "Let's just call it a friendly chat between two acquaintances, and a hearty congratulations on your new job." He paused. "Maybe even a last 'favor' to you."

He left without another word.

Jourdain sat in his chair and steepled his fingers together as he stared at the door.

Chapter Twelve

There was a crooked man, and he went a crooked mile,
He found a crooked sixpence against a crooked stile;
He bought a crooked cat, which caught a crooked mouse,
And they all lived together in a little crooked house.

THERE WAS A CROOKED MAN

DARKNESS HAD DESCENDED UPON St. Germaine Parish and a
man climbed out of a rented car, looking at the levee that ran
parallel to the road. It was an earthen structure built in the
1930s by a stream of men who worked in Roosevelt's Civilian
Conservation Corps under the supervision of the Army Corps
of Engineers. For the unnamed tributary to the Cane River,
the main sluice gates were approximately eight feet wide and
eight feet tall in a moderately-sized dam about a mile north of
the St. Michel mansion.

The man, dressed in a gray suit, looked up at the night sky
where storm clouds concealed the stars. A sprinkle of rain had
begun and he smiled to himself. Mother Nature was on their
side this particular evening. He went to the trunk of the car
and retrieved a set of bolt cutters, fully five feet long, and
whistled as he mounted the levee. He made his way to the
sluice gates and intently observed the simple mechanism that
operated the gates. A large steel wheel raised and lowered the
gates, used most often by those who needed water from the
canal to water their crops.

However, the farmers all had a key to the padlock that secured a chain that prevented petty vandalism to the gate. The man whistled a bit from the theme to *Mission: Impossible*. The average vandal didn't have a handy set of bolt snippers. He broke the lock and used the manually operated wheel to raise the levee gates. Water spilled into the causeway and he smiled. It was a remarkably easy process; the farmers kept the mechanism well oiled to prevent rusting. When he was done, he used the large bolt cutters to break the handle on the wheel so that the the gates could not be shut anytime soon.

When he was finished, the man brushed dirt from his hands, retrieved the bolt cutters, paused to wipe any incriminating prints from the sluice gate wheel, and returned to his car. He was smiling broadly, happy that he hadn't even broken into a sweat. With one last look at his handiwork, he drove off to implement the second part of his plan—to sabotage an electrical transformer that fed power to most of the dwellings in the area, including the St. Michel mansion.

GERAUD WATCHED THE valet assist Mignon from her rental car and wondered why she simply didn't buy a car. After all, it had become common knowledge that she had purchased that godforsaken spit of land where she and her parents had lived when she was a child. Since it had been sitting empty and forgotten in the thick woods near the edge of the Kistachie National Forest, she was most likely paying a small fortune for men to rebuild every part of it. A rental car was impractical at best, if she was intent on staying. Then he brightened. Maybe she wasn't planning to stay, but merely wanted to touch something from her past, just as any human being might do in order to understand his or her heritage.

A long leg became visible for a moment as Mignon stepped from the car. The slit in her dress parted, exposing an expanse of creamy thigh, curving calf, and a nicely turned ankle. Geraud held his breath. He'd been thirteen when Garlande became his father's mistress, and fifteen when his father had decided to leave LaValle with the same woman. Thirteen had been man enough to appreciate his father's perception of Garlande's attractiveness. In his mind's eye, she was the most beautiful woman he had ever laid eyes on, and one he had dreamt of in his teenage bed for years afterwards. There was that long red hair, which seemed to glow with an inner red-hot fire, and the pale green eyes that glimmered with sensual knowledge. Her lips had been full and appealing and beckoned to a man in a wicked manner. There was that lush figure that any hot-blooded male could hold on to, and one that his own wife would have called Rubenesque in a condescending way.

Luc had taken Geraud along a few times when he stopped at the house down the narrow dirt road, leaving the teenager to fend for himself while his father spent time with Garlande. As far as Geraud knew, this had been a ploy to throw off Eleanor. Why would a man take his adolescent son along while he went to see his mistress?

Sometimes the little girl, her hair the exact shade as her mother's, had come out on the porch and stared at the big, luxurious sedan. Sometimes Geraud had wandered through the thick woods until he heard his father calling for him to return. His father had explained to him that wealthy men sometimes married for reasons other than love, that having a mistress wasn't necessarily a bad thing, but it was something to be kept discreet.

Geraud could hear his father's voice in his head just as plainly as if he were speaking to him this very moment. "Geraud, my son. Your mother would not disapprove unless I were to flaunt this woman in her face. That would be rude, not only to your mother, but to our family name. Although I care for your mother, I also care for this woman, and both should be treated with respect."

Geraud hadn't quite understood. He had asked, "What about her husband, Papa?"

Luc had laughed. "I don't think he'll be coming after me with a shotgun, if that's what you mean, Geraud. One simply has to handle these affairs with a sort of dignity. Respect your wife and your mistress. That's the way we do things. *Comprends?*"

That wasn't the way Luc had done it and Geraud bitterly remembered it. His father hadn't been the one driving an invisible wedge into the wholeness that was their family, splintered though it actually was. It had been that woman. His mistress, Garlande Thibeaux. It was her fault that his father did not love his wife and had not respected her. *Her fault and none other.*

The man at the gate had called a minute earlier to let Geraud know that Mignon's car was on its way up the drive. Eleanor had instructed Geraud to escort the young woman inside. And he had made a silent vow to find out a little something about her motives for being here.

At least there hadn't been any more incidents of ghosts walking the halls of the mansion or the grounds. Even Eugenie seemed to be sleeping better this week, as if their mother's ploys with the Thibeaux girl were truly working. Geraud had to be thankful for those small mercies. Perhaps all of this could be wrapped up quickly and then these ridiculous "hauntings" would no longer be fodder for the pulp press.

He focused on Mignon as she passed her keys to the valet. She could be a model with her looks, although she was a bit short. Perhaps an actress, with a figure that men would admire and women would envy. She was young, attractive, and successful in a way that few backwoods Louisianians could ever achieve. *So what does she want around here?* he asked himself.

Geraud stepped forward, with an eye on her breasts. Mignon was dressed in another sheath. Sheer white material over the shoulders became more opaque as it hugged every bit of her shape, hinting at the marble-hued flesh underneath. It was a longer dress that draped elegantly to her ankles and cleverly concealed the slits that reached nearly to mid-thigh on each side. Elegant white pumps on her feet completed her ensemble. He wasn't a judge of designer wear, but he knew that this hadn't come off a rack at any store between Los Angeles and New York City.

"Geraud," greeted Mignon. "You look handsome." And he did. He wore a black designer suit that offset his pale hair and blue eyes. The shirt itself was the exact midnight blue shade of his eyes, and a silk tie that cost ten times more than what he would tip at a good restaurant graced his neck. Geraud St. Michel appeared every inch the successful businessman and wealthy, old-monied Louisianian. And Mignon knew he was.

His stores did reasonably well, purchasing import items from China, Taiwan, the Philippines, and the Asian continent, then selling them at a tremendous markup to Americans who enjoyed ethnic decor. However, there had been a slump in sales of late, one that concerned Geraud very much.

But Geraud had been spending some time at home lately. He had a home in New Orleans where his wife preferred to live, and there was another family house in Baton Rouge, where little time had been spent by any St. Michel in the last ten years. But the eldest and only son seemed to want to keep close to home these days. All the while, Mignon knew from business reports that Geraud's company was in the throes of some twisted type of growing pains. Although its earnings were good, it also needed a fresh influx of money and it needed its CEO to maintain his respectable name.

Geraud offered his arm to Mignon and broke her reverie. He commented, "And you look rather beautiful yourself. I look at you and I see your mother."

"Oh?" Mignon wasn't sure where he wanted to lead her. He had the most anticipatory look on his face, the appearance of a shark circling his prey.

"I knew about your mother and my father, of course." Geraud led her into the mansion, deliberately keeping their entrance to a slow stroll. "Years before they had the audacity to do what they did. I know what he sees in her. She was one hot piece of—"

"And your point is?" Mignon interrupted. She wasn't sure if she wanted to hear Geraud's crude take on what Luc had found so attractive about her mother. Geraud wasn't a nice man. She knew about the teenage mistress he kept in an apartment in New Orleans, a young woman who seemed to spend an inordinate amount of time in the emergency room when he was in town. His only redeeming quality seemed to be that he cared so much about his sister that he'd moved back to St. Germaine Parish in order to spend more time with her, although it was far more likely that he was protecting his own best interests.

"She was a mercenary little bitch," he said amicably. "Just like you."

Mignon smiled. They paused to look at a painting in the long hall. It was an early-twentieth-century George Grosz. Grosz was a German-American artist who became well known for his anti–World War I political views. Later he turned to oils and produced some fine expressionistic pieces that tended to be less controversial. Mignon thought the piece they were looking at dated from the forties; it depicted a scene at a beach with a small house in the background as the shoreline twisted away. Its colors were as brilliant as the day it was completed, and it elicited a solitary emotion that plucked the heartstrings. She had noticed the painting before but hadn't had the opportunity to study it.

She didn't say anything in response to Geraud's comment.

"So what do you want?" he asked after a long moment of silence. She could hear other voices floating down the hallway. They seemed so far away. The translation was clear: *How much do you want?*

"From you?" she finally asked. "I'm not as rich as the St. Michels, but I'm rich enough. I became a millionaire two years ago. My financial advisor tells me we doubled that last year. I don't need money."

"Then what is it? A twisted desire to see the family that your mother ruined? A little appetite for revenge? I'm curious to see what exactly you're up to. That little piece of property in the backwoods doesn't have a lot of appeal, I think. I'm not sure if you are capable of sentiment. Your mother wasn't. Otherwise she would have been happy to remain simply my father's mistress."

Mignon stared at the brush strokes that George Grosz had used over fifty years before. He was a man who had tried to use his artwork to express his unhappiness about World War I Germany, a country that suffered tremendously at the whim of its leaders. He wasn't the most well known painter, but his work was pleasing to the eye and a good investment. She turned to Geraud, "Are you trying to make me angry?"

Geraud crossed his arms over his chest. "No, I just want you to know the effect your mother had on us. You've seen Eugenie, who still dreams of her father at night, so much so that she feels compelled to seek him out. My mother became a cold woman, abandoned by her beloved husband, never to be the same person again, because of the whispers, because of the innuendo."

"And you?" Mignon tilted her head at him. She thought

that Eleanor had been a cold woman long before her husband had vanished. "What effect did it have on you?"

"It taught me a lesson about life."

There was no need to ask what the lesson had been. She had learned the lesson, as well. But Geraud was too self-centered to see that his family's lives weren't the only ones that had been impacted. There had also been the lives of a little girl and her father, who were forced to flee for safety's sake. "And our lives? Weren't they affected as well?" She had to ask the question, just to see if there was any compassion in this man.

"What did you lose? A woman who didn't care about you," he answered carelessly.

"Geraud," came Eleanor's voice from the front parlor. "I insist that you stop haranguing Miss Thibeaux and bring her in to visit with the other guests."

They turned to look at Eleanor as she stood in the doorway. She was dressed in a charcoal-black suit, immaculate from the top of her styled head to the tips of her polished shoes. Her face gave away nothing, but remained coldly serene, the ice queen in her palace of frozen wastelands. *How much did she hear?* Mignon silently asked herself. And then, *What does it matter?*

Mignon went into the parlor, followed closely by Geraud. She did not let him touch her arm again. Inside was almost the same group of people who had been invited the previous Saturday evening. Eleanor liked to entertain her close friends. Jourdain and his wife, Alexandrine, were present, appearing nonchalant as they chatted with Eugenie and her friend, David Something-or-Other. Mignon was surprised the Gastineaus had come, since the announcement for the Supreme Court position had been made the day before.

Gabriel Laurier winked lasciviously at Mignon from the corner, where he was helping himself to some of Geraud's brandy. Geraud's wife, Leya, was staring out the window at the storm clouds gathering into an angry front. Finally, there was a short, fat, black woman dressed in a flowing gown of vivid purple, and beside her a young black man dressed in a conservative dark blue suit. They were talking quietly with Eleanor as Mignon passed through the door.

"Mignon, my dear," said Eleanor. "Here is someone I would like you to meet."

Mignon stepped up and looked at the black woman. She was in her forties with creamy brown skin, doe's eyes, and long black hair gathered into a careful plait down her back. Every finger on her hands was decorated with various gold rings, and more gold glittered at her neck and her ears. She was a striking woman, not someone who could be ignored in any situation, much less at a dinner party.

"This is Madam Terentia Jones," Eleanor announced proudly. "She has had much success with the revivification of spirits from the next world."

Which is very interesting, thought Mignon. Eleanor was widely known to enjoy the company of seers and spiritualists from around the country who came to "enlighten" her. *What does one say to that?* "An amazing accomplishment, I'm sure."

"Let me touch your hand," boomed the woman. She had a throaty voice, attractive and deep, but at the same time feminine and compelling. Mignon presented her hand automatically. Soft fingers enclosed hers and pressed for a moment. Then brown eyes searched her own. "A woman of mystery."

A smile flittered across Mignon's face. Anyone who had been in LaValle for more than a few minutes and had an open ear for gossip would have heard about her and her eccentricities. Terentia Jones went on. "A woman with depths as unfathomable as the ocean."

Her young male companion kept pulling at his collar and tie and Mignon's eyes turned to him. He was obviously uncomfortable here. Too many rich people. Too many white people. Too much authority. He was young and handsome, but annoyed by playing male courtesan to Terentia. Mignon knew that he was something more than that. She shifted her attention seamlessly back to the spiritualist.

"I think a tarot reading would be most informative with this one," said Terentia, the rhythm of her voice almost lulling. "I sense a quandary within her soul, an aura of enigma. A most compelling young woman."

"Thank you," murmured Mignon.

Leya turned away from the window. "Did my mother-in-law tell you about our experiences last Saturday, Miss Jones? It was the most amazing psychic occurrence I've ever witnessed."

Terentia released Mignon's hand reluctantly and turned away to speak with Leya and Eleanor. Mignon rested her hands against her abdomen comfortably, but itched to rub them together, exhibiting a bit of the nervousness she felt. As she glanced up she saw that Jourdain and Geraud were both watching her.

What are they expecting? Mignon asked herself. *I have to be careful.*

"I'm Faust," said the young black man, holding out a large hand. Mignon smiled and shook it, all the while staring at his rich, individual features, searching for the things that motivated him.

"Faust. An interesting name. Did you sell your soul to the devil?"

He grinned. Teeth of the purest white spread his face apart. There was a low chuckle. "Haven't we all, Miss Thibeaux?"

"You know me," she said.

Faust shrugged, showing the spread of muscles under his jacket. "People talk. It's the most amazing thing if a guy happens to listen." He wasn't from the South, any more than

Terentia Jones was. Both of their voices lacked the Louisiana accent she found so pleasing to her ears. If anything, they sounded like her—someone who could speak on the radio or broadcast the news, neutral and without home.

A flash of lightning illuminated the room. It was followed by a crack of thunder and several people jumped. The electricity flickered, and Eleanor announced that they should begin dinner before the lights left them completely.

Mignon wondered where John Henry was this evening. She had a sudden image of him soaked to the skin in his uniform, his muscles delineated by the wet cloth, and shivered involuntarily. *What is getting into me? I never let anyone affect me like this.*

"Cold, Miss Thibeaux?" asked Jourdain, looking at her with cool brown eyes. He was every inch the poised attorney who had been appointed to the Supreme Court. His eyes were assessing and penetrating.

"The storm, Mr. Gastineau," answered Mignon calmly. She stretched out her arm. "See, I have goose bumps."

"Can we expect another intriguing performance tonight?" he asked.

"I didn't expect the first one," she said.

Jourdain laughed. "Well, one never knows what to expect at Eleanor's galas. A séance here. A psychic there. Ghosts from the past. Skeletons from the closet."

"Yes, but from whose closet?"

Jourdain was silent for a moment. Then he shrugged carelessly. "I would imagine that everyone has something to hide."

The group wandered into the large dining room and found their places. Throughout dinner the lights continued to flicker in tune with the pouring rain and strikes of lightning. Not long after they were finished, the electricity went out for good, and the housekeeper lit dozens of candles.

In the quivering candlelight Mignon could see that Eleanor

and Leya were pleased with themselves. They thought it would be a grand night for another discernment. And who better to assist them than a distinguished spiritualist from New York City?

Mignon was amused. After the dinner dishes had been cleared from the table, people began to slip away to drink or smoke. She took a candelabra and began to walk the halls, looking at the many paintings.

There was a library in the west end of the mansion where Mignon had discovered a Carlos Carrà piece from the early 1900s. It was a wonderful oil on canvas, a futurist piece depicting the four horsemen of the apocalypse. As Mignon examined it she realized that she didn't know much specifically about Carrà, only that he was Italian and considered a futurist artist who was ahead of his time at the peak of his career. She held the candelabra up to examine the piece closer and found his delineation and use of color fascinating. She could understand why Eleanor would be attracted to the painting. It was simply striking.

Outside the house the storm was working itself up to an impressive display. Rain pelted the roof with unquenchable frenzy, drowning out any other sounds from the interior of the house. Mignon was lost in the abstract painting with its vibrant primary colors when there was a sudden sound behind her.

The words seemed to originate from nowhere at all, deep and throaty emissions, sounding like something out of Mignon's deepest nightmares. "There was a little man, and he had a little gun, and his bullets were made of lead, lead, lead; he went to the brook, and saw a little duck, and shot it through the head, head, head."

Mignon was frozen in place. It was as if her mother were whispering the words to her, as if she had come from some unfathomable place to remind her only child of a nursery rhyme recited so many years before—and perhaps to remind her that once there had been a woman called Garlande Thibeaux, who had taught her nursery rhymes with an easy smile and a loving touch. Mignon slowly turned her head and her figure followed, allowing the candelabra to cast weird, twisting shadows and malicious black shapes in the gloom.

A nightmarish face made of the purest white stared at her. Mignon swallowed the scream that threatened to escape from her throat. The frail woman standing before her was like a wraith floating in the candle's tremulous light. Mignon abruptly realized who it was, but her heart thundered in her chest all the same.

"It is you, isn't it?" said Eugenie.

Chapter Thirteen

Hark! Hark! The dogs do bark,
The beggars are coming to town;
Some in rags, some in tags,
And some in velvet gowns.

HARK! HARK!

MIGNON ALMOST SAID, "MY God, you scared the crap out of me." But Eugenie's face began to fade away as she stepped back into the shadows of the library like some ghoulish figment of Mignon's imagination. She bit off the exclamation with a soft question. "I'm who?"

"You're her. I see the resemblance. I see what you look like. Only . . . only your hair is short, instead of long." Eugenie had retreated to the other side of the library, visible only as a shape in pale blue silk.

Mignon's eyes strained in the darkness. She took a step forward, raising the candelabra in order to see better, but Eugenie said quickly, "Don't. Don't come any closer. I'm . . . I'm not sure about all of this . . ."

"I'm Mignon," she said softly, her voice as unthreatening as she could make it. "I know I resemble my mother, but I'm just her daughter. I'm your mother's guest for dinner tonight. *Remember,* Eugenie?"

There was silence from the other side of the library. Eugenie was gathering the few wits she still possessed and forming them into some kind of cohesive sense of reality. Finally she said, "I remember, Mignon. I came looking for you. They're about to start the discernment." Her voice was low and scattered. She spoke slowly, as if lost in deep thought. "The thunder and lightning . . . bother me. The darkness in the mansion disturbs me. And your face in the candlelight. It . . . reminded me of someone. Someone I knew a long time ago. . . . I used to play with a little girl with hair the same color. That red, red hair . . ."

"It reminded you of Garlande," Mignon suggested. The idea shocked her. Thoughts ran fast and furious through her mind as she went through possibilities. Eugenie had remembered that they had played together. Where had they played together? Certainly Luc wouldn't have brought Garlande to the St. Michel mansion, but on the other hand, he might have brought Eugenie to the old farmhouse in the woods. *Before they had disappeared . . .*

"Yes, Garlande. You look just like she did. I didn't see it at first. It's been so long since I've seen her."

Mignon took another step forward. Eugenie had knocked the brains right out of her head by reciting that nursery rhyme in the darkness like an incantation from beyond the grave. It had been one of dozens her mother had taught her. "The nursery rhyme, Eugenie. Where did you learn it?"

"The nursery rhyme?" repeated Eugenie dumbly. "The nursery rhyme."

"There was a little man, and he had a little gun . . ." Mignon's voice trailed away as she took one more step closer to Eugenie. Now she could see her face, a confused face, perhaps a little flummoxed from too many liqueurs before dinner, and perhaps a little panicky from the roar of thunder and the crack of lightning. Confusion changed to apprehension as Mignon repeated the rhyme. "And his bullets were made of lead, lead, lead . . ."

"He went to the brook, and saw a little duck, and shot it through the head, head, head," finished Eugenie reluctantly. "I remember the rhyme. There were many rhymes."

"Where did you learn it?" Mignon's voice was more insistent. She wanted to reach out and shake the older woman by her trim shoulders. *Shake her right out of that stupor.*

"There was a woman," cried out Eugenie. "And she used to teach me the rhymes, so I could repeat them. She was in a house in the woods and there was a little girl there with the same color hair. Oh, that pretty color of hair, like the leaves in fall, bright and alive. Sometimes the little girl taught me the rhymes. It . . . it was you."

"Yes," answered Mignon, lowering the candelabra. "You came with your father sometimes. And sometimes we would learn the rhymes from my mother together. And sometimes I would teach them to you." Suddenly it was clear to Mignon as well. There was a startling vision in her mind of a big, new car parked in front of the little house in the woods, and a young, coltish girl with hair the palest shade of blonde. She was five years older than Mignon but it had never seemed that way when they had played together outside on the grass. They had played together like . . . sisters, as if Eugenie were the sibling Mignon had always wanted.

"And sometimes my papa would leave me outside in the dark trees all alone, because I couldn't get him away from . . . *that red-headed whore!*" With that she gave Mignon a quick, unexpected shove and slipped away into the blackness of the hallway.

Mignon struggled to keep standing and not drop the candelabra. She fell heavily on her posterior anyway, and grunted in a most unladylike manner as hot wax was slung across her arm, causing a flash of instantaneous, burning pain. But somehow the candles and their holder remained upright in her hands. "*Merde,*" she swore awkwardly.

There was another voice in the darkness, a rich, redolent voice, tinged with amusement. "Perhaps you should leave this place."

Try as she might, Mignon couldn't hide the fact that she jumped at the unexpected addition of another person in the library. An old, dark mansion. A storm thundering rain and lightning outside. Hints about ghosts. A séance planned. Although it all seemed like a scene straight out of a gothic novel, it was more than enough to give Mignon permanent goose bumps along her arms and shoulders. She remained on the floor and looked around for the owner of the voice, who had apparently overheard her conversation with Eugenie.

There was a flicker of light from a cigarette lighter and Mignon saw Terentia Jones with a long cigarillo in her hand. She lit it, inhaled until the tip glowed red, then the lighter went out abruptly, liberating the shadows again.

"You could help me up," Mignon suggested sarcastically, her hands on her knees. She had to appear the utter fool, sitting on a bare wood floor on her ass while this woman stood in a corner and watched with thinly veiled amusement.

"What, and spoil your big scene with the St. Michel girl? Woman, you've got to be joking. That lady is nuttier than all the fruitcakes at the post office at Christmastime." Mignon couldn't see the short woman's face, but she had a sudden whiff of the cigarillo smoke as it was exhaled.

"That a professional opinion?" Mignon asked as she carefully climbed to her knees and rubbed her buttocks with one hand.

"As professional as I'm going to give, dear." There was a moment of silence before Terentia spoke again. "I don't know if this is going to work, Miggy."

Mignon had managed to wobble to her feet, one hand still on her flank, half an eye on the other woman. "Terri," she said. "Anyone could be listening."

Terentia Jones, an art gallery owner from New York City and one of Mignon's closest friends, laughed. "The only one who matters is Eleanor, my dear, and she believes, oh lord, how she believes. She swears up and down on an old woman in the area who gives her 'readings' and protective charms. It wouldn't matter if God Himself proclaimed that I wasn't a spiritualist."

Glancing behind her, Mignon said quickly, "Yes, but we don't want to trumpet it to the rest of the house."

Terri took another drag of the cigarillo. "My mama used to be so upset that I wouldn't follow in her footsteps. Seventh daughter of a seventh daughter and all of that. I figured out pretty early in life that pretending to be psychic was just another big con job and knew there had to be something better."

"And the art world is about as pure as the driven snow."

"Look, if you think you can get something out of her by doing this, then I'm glad to help. My son is glad to help," Terri said, meaning her only child, Faust, who had taken a brief break from Princeton to give a hand. "My mama thought it was wonderful that I wanted to use some of the old connections to set this up with Eleanor St. Michel until I told her it would be my one and only gig as the infamous Madame Terentia." She drew the words out in a theatrical manner. "But this place is bad news, sugar. I don't think anyone is going to give anything up. I think Nehemiah will tell you the same thing. So if you don't want something bad to happen to you, it'd be best if you leave." Terri laughed as she said it. It sounded like the cryptic warning that a so-called psychic was supposed to give to the mysterious woman who might be in peril. It was downplayed by the laugh, but Mignon knew that her old friend meant the words and that hidden beneath the humor was a mute plea.

The candelabra remained by her feet as Mignon straightened out her flowing dress. She flicked the cooled wax off her

arm and smoothed out the long, white skirt. At last she turned
to her old friend, who continued to stand in the corner of the
library, leaning against a stack of books and smoking. Only
the red glow of the cigarillo and a vague shape could be seen
in the Cimmerian blackness.

"If I had a dime for each time someone told me that
lately . . ." Mignon almost laughed at herself. "Well, I'd have
a handful of dimes, anyway."

There was a chuckle from the darkness. The red tip of the
cigarillo wobbled visibly. Then Terri said, "I don't know if
we're biting off more than we can chew here. Be careful, Migs.
Be more careful than you've ever been in all of your life."
There was a long pause and only the sound of faint thunder
and wind from outside. "They say that girl Eugenie hasn't
been back to Louisiana in over two decades, that the spirits
started haunting this place because she is the only St. Michel
who's . . . sensitive enough to pick them up." She paused
again. "It gives a person something to think about. By the way,
I think Madame Eleanor has changed her mind about the discernment. The storm has knocked out the electricity and the
phones, too. Of course, they have cell phones, but there's
something else."

"What? What now?"

"The river has washed out the road about a quarter mile
from the mansion. None of us are going anywhere tonight."
There was a little snort of laughter. "Wonder how *that* happened."

That river was an offshoot of the Cane River, once a tributary into the Red River. This particular offshoot wasn't just
a tiny tributary, because it had once been used for small barges
to export produce from the St. Michel plantation. Nehemiah,
Mignon, and Terri had hoped for an opportunity to flood out
the bridge and strand them at the house for a night, to give
Mignon time to search for evidence that her mother had been

murdered. Apparently Nehemiah had taken the opportunity. Mignon could only hope that the river didn't flood out homes down the river.

As it turned out, there were more than enough rooms for Eleanor's guests. Mignon was put into a blue room on the second floor of the west wing, along with several of the others. Down the hall were Terri and Faust. Jourdain and his wife were on Mignon's other side. Across the hall was Gabriel, who had given her another salacious glance as she entered her room. Mignon hoped he would not come wandering in the middle of the night and silently vowed to wedge a chair under her doorknob.

It was well after midnight before the guests had been escorted to their rooms. Most of them had hoped that the river would recede, allowing them to leave, but when it became obvious that they were stuck, they all seemed to take the forced restriction with good humor.

Eleanor had laughed and said, "Excuse me, but I have to see that some of the servants get rooms, as well. We'll see you all in the morning over a nice breakfast, and hope the sun is shining down on our heads instead of that mess outside."

Mignon sat in the window seat watching the lightning and rain outside. Although the water was rapidly dissipating, the road was still flooded and not passable. The storm was moving to the east like an enraged god. The rain must have dumped a few inches of liquid upon western-central Louisiana. Each lightning strike revealed tree branches broken by the wind and excessive rain. The ground had soaked up as much water as it could, and the remainder was running off in the direction of the tributary of the Cane. Mignon wasn't disturbed by Mother Nature's wrath because this plantation house had existed for two hundred years, and would most likely stand for another two hundred, horrid thunderstorms aside.

Mignon was tempted to go to Eugenie's room and shake

out any information the woman had about Garlande. Instead, she decided to wander through the halls looking at paintings and seeking any knowledge that she could ferret out. Something in this cavernous house would tell her what she wanted to know, and she would find it. Another chance like this wouldn't come along in a million years and Mignon couldn't afford to waste it sleeping.

There was a light tap on her door, and it opened quietly. A maid said, "Ma'am, I brought some extra towels."

Mignon turned around and smiled. The maid shut the door carefully behind her and put the towels on the bed. Then she said, "Mignon, don't you look like a hottie."

Kate Trent had her grandfather's good looks, the same blue eyes and clear-cut features. Mignon stood up and gave the younger woman a quick hug. "I can't say how grateful I am that you're helping. Doing all the intensive labor when—"

"They're not going after me with a knife or a gun or whatever," Kate interrupted her. "Besides, a few more weeks and I'm off to Europe to study art with the masters. You've more than helped me out." She shrugged, just a twenty-year-old young woman who had come to love her grandfather's adopted daughter as if she were her own flesh and blood, but there was also the excitement of trying to fool people into revealing something they hadn't let go of in over two decades. "But just to remind you, the security measures are strongest around the paintings. It's just as well we're not here to steal them. There's none in the offices at all, and I think he's got a safe under the desk." She looked around. "I could do more of the searching. I'm here sixty hours a week."

"No!" Mignon almost yelled it, then took a breath. "I can't let you take that risk. It has to be me. You promised me, Kate."

Kate nodded. "I've kept the promise. God knows, if that woman caught me snooping she'd have me thrown into the dungeon." She glanced over her shoulder again. "I've got to go. Good luck, Mignon."

After Kate slipped out the door, Mignon waited for people to find rooms, go to bed, organized by Eleanor in whatever way she wanted. Then she would go and look for what she knew must be here.

When she could hear no other noises except the endless cry of the wind and the sporadic splatter of the remainders of the rainstorm, she left her room, still dressed in her evening apparel. Mignon didn't care to be cat-footing around a dark mansion in a stark white dress, but didn't have a lot of choice in the matter. She took a small penlight from her designer purse, a bag no bigger than the palm of her hand. In this venue, a candelabra would only get in the way and alert anyone still awake that she was prowling uninvited through the house.

Mignon's first stop was the home office that Geraud kept at the mansion. She looked through his desk and glared at the computer that she couldn't explore because of the power outage. Perhaps there would be another opportunity before dawn, if the power were repaired. The desk revealed various business records, all aboveboard. There *was* a fireproof safe under the desk, however, and the combination lock seemed simple enough. She didn't expect to find anything of significance because she knew that the St. Michels kept several large safety deposit boxes in various banks around the area.

The combination turned out to be Luc's birthday, 3-16-35. Mignon had tried several other birthdays first, as well as some telephone numbers, before trying Luc's. She found papers showing that Geraud had commissioned a private detective to find his father in 1982, to no avail. The only other thing of interest was the power of attorney supposedly contracted by Luc the day he disappeared. It had Jourdain Gastineau's notary signature on it and was witnessed by Sheriff Ruelle Fanchon, and none other than His Honor, Gabriel Laurier. The power of attorney shifted all command of the St. Michel monies over to Eleanor St. Michel, with Jourdain as the backup.

Mignon read the report from the private detective with utmost interest. The investigator, who was out of Atlanta, Georgia, had been of the opinion that Luc St. Michel would reappear when he felt like it, and expressed himself thus. He could not find a trail of any sort, and only suggested that certain bank accounts be flagged for future activities.

All the information that the St. Michels had had at the time indicated that Luc simply didn't want the encumbrance of a family and had fled to an unknown tropical paradise outside of Eleanor St. Michel's aegis. Furthermore, he was known to have international accounts from which he could live comfortably.

But Mignon could look at it more objectively. How had these men known to cover up for Luc? Because they wanted to protect Eleanor. Because she could pay them for protection. Because they had to, in order to keep the gravy train running on schedule. They had to cover up or lose out. So they must have known that Luc was dead.

She put the papers back into the safe and fingered the small box of jewelry there. Nothing but his wife's diamonds and a few semiprecious baubles. Certainly nothing of interest to Mignon. Then she carefully shut the safe and wiped off the evidence of her fingerprints. Perhaps she could explain her presence in his office, but certainly not her fingerprints on his safe. In any case, she used the long skirt of her dress to cover her hand as she rustled through various items.

Mignon was searching along the backs of various photographs and paintings in the room when she heard voices in the hallway; they seemed to be headed directly for her. She flicked off the penlight and glanced around for a place to hide. It wasn't a big office and there was no closet. There wasn't even an armoire which she could crawl into. The voices came closer.

"Damn it," she muttered.

Geraud and Jourdain came into the office.

"I can't control who my mother invites into the house," Geraud said.

"Good God, it was bad enough when she only had psychics in here. At least they were entertaining."

Geraud chuckled. "That one blonde was more than entertaining. She thought she could up the ante by crawling into bed with me. Talk about a contortionist."

There was silence from Jourdain.

Under the desk, Mignon had pulled her dress up so that it wouldn't be exposed beneath the bottom edge of the front of the desk. She thanked God that the lights were out, because in the bright office light she would have been seen in an instant. As it was, the light from the candles Geraud and Jourdain had brought was bright enough to make her wince. She also thanked God that Geraud's desk was large, wooden, and paneled all the way around the front. Of course, if Geraud wanted to get into his safe—the same one she was crouching on top of—then she couldn't have picked a worse place.

Then Jourdain asked, "You slept with one of the psychics?"

"I didn't sleep, if you know what I mean."

"I don't want to know what you mean," said Jourdain. "You're as bad as your father."

"Which brings us back to the subject at hand." Geraud's voice was uncomfortably close. "I know Mignon is suspicious about her mother's disappearance, but what can she find out?"

"No more than anyone else, I suppose," said Jourdain. "She's already got John Henry sniffing around. He came to my office to ask about your father and his mistress. About powers of attorney. About who might have seen them last." He paused. "And all because of that girl. God, she looks just like her mother."

"I wouldn't mind a piece of that, because she looks like she'd be twice as good as her mama," speculated Geraud crudely. "Hell, man. I'd like to know what she's up to. But all John Henry can do is ask uncomfortable questions. And Mignon can't hurt us."

"She can rile up Eugenie."

There was silence from Geraud as he considered that. "She could also rile up the press and my mother," he said slowly. "I think something should be done."

The candlelight began to move as the two men went back toward the door. Mignon resisted the sigh of relief that wanted to escape from her throat.

"I just want to lock the door since she's in the house," Geraud finished. The door shut and the lock clicked. "You know, my chauffeur told me he saw you over at Natchitoches with Ruelle Fanchon a week or so ago. Funny how bad pennies keep turning up."

There was a terse silence. Then Jourdain said, "Maybe your boy shouldn't carry tales."

Geraud paused. "Maybe he shouldn't."

Mignon listened as the two pairs of feet walked down the hall. Jourdain said, "We have to protect your mother."

The last thing she heard was Geraud's reply. "My mother?" he said in disbelief, his voice muffled by the walls. "What about my company?"

She carefully edged out from underneath the desk, lamenting silently that the designer dress she was wearing wasn't up to this kind of treatment. Then Mignon stared at the door. "Well, crap," she muttered. "How am I going to get out of here, so I can worry about what Geraud and the lawyer are going to throw at me next?"

A letter opener sprung the lock in about ten shaky minutes. Mignon quickly discovered that she couldn't relock the door, so there was little point of lingering in the vicinity for Geraud or someone else to discover her presence and conclude that she had been rifling through his possessions.

Then Mignon paused for a moment. Something had changed. There was a dead silence around her and she caught a scent of something, something that called to her. It seemed like the smell of perfume lingered in the air, the scent of a woman who had been dead long ago. Mignon's eyes widened and the hair rose up on the back of her neck. She felt as though someone was watching her. Someone who couldn't be seen or touched, but who was interested in her all the same. Mignon moved her head about slowly, discovering she was alone, and the dead silence was interrupted by the sound of the wind, still strong and persistent outside. Abruptly, the odd feeling vanished.

Mignon slowly walked down the hallway. She had other things to be concerned about, such as why Jourdain had returned to see the old sheriff of St. Germaine Parish and whether it had anything to do with her.

Chapter Fourteen

> Three wise men of Gotham
> Went to sea in a bowl:
> And if the bowl had been stronger,
> My song had been longer.

THREE WISE MEN OF GOTHAM

IN THE DARKNESS OF the grand hallway Mignon felt a shiver run down her spine, alerting every inch of her body, signaling every one of her senses that something was amiss. She looked around her in the stygian gloom. Only vague shapes were visible. A table there. A lamp over here. The slight glint of gilt on the frame of a painting. Black shapes that coalesced out of nothing at all as she inched her way quietly through the passage.

Shivering again, Mignon wrapped her arms around her body. Suddenly it seemed so chilly in the hallway, and the bit of sheer cloth that she called an evening gown wasn't much for concealment, much less warmth. She was alone in the darkness, she reassured herself. No one else was there. It was only that eerie feeling again that something without form, without eyes or shape, floated about her, near her, watching her, perhaps following her.

Something brushed along her bare arm and goose bumps broke out in a rash, spilling across her flesh like a delicate fall of water over a ridge of sheer rocks. Mignon spun around to face whatever had touched her skin. It was the same as it had been outside Geraud's office. It whirled around her and pressed against her body, shifting away almost mischievously, taunting her with a touch that was ethereal and unexplainable.

After a moment it was gone. Mignon clutched her shoulders and let out the breath she had been holding. She had never counted on the eerie feelings of misgiving that surrounded her, enveloped her when she came to this place, as if someone, some*thing*, was trying to warn her.

Mignon had never believed the stories. She knew that Eleanor believed them, and if Eleanor wasn't responsible for Garlande and Luc's disappearance, then she most certainly knew who was. It was only a matter of persistence and trickery. Now she had doubt.

She stopped at the end of the hallway, at the base of the great staircase, and touched one mahogany rail, feeling its smooth surface, shined to a soft gloss by generations of slaves and servants alike. Through the windows that framed the huge front doorway she could see the wind still moving treetops in the distance, their forms barely perceptible in the darkness.

A shape dressed in white roamed through the base of the trees and Mignon's head snapped around. She hurried to the door and opened it, peering out into the night shadows. With her mouth open wide enough to trap a bear, Mignon watched the trim figure clad in only a long, pale garment disappear into the forest.

Who in the name of God was that? Mignon glanced over her shoulder at the staircase. If someone came down the stairs, they might wonder why Mignon was still up, and furthermore why she was wandering around downstairs in the dark, fully dressed.

It has to be Eugenie, because she's a little strange, she thought. *Kate isn't supposed to play ghost tonight, not while*

I'm trying to search for some kind of evidence. Then she berated herself for the briefest of moments, realizing that no one else was up to go after whoever was out there. She would have to do it.

She narrowed her eyes and searched through the darkness to locate the white figure. The moon was waxing, more than half full, and peeked out of the clouds from the north. It shed a meager amount of bitter yellow light on the disarrayed landscape.

The wind was still howling and there was a sting of debris as it was flung across Mignon's face. She frantically scanned the panorama in front of the mansion. *How could one slender woman in a lily-white nightgown have disappeared so quickly? It has to be Eugenie.*

Behind her she could hear the front doors of the mansion banging shut in time with the wind. In front of her the formerly immaculate yard was littered with leaves and bits of branches. Mignon sank to her ankles in mud, almost losing her shoes, while she searched for Eugenie's white-clad form in the darkness. Terri's words repeated in her mind. *The river has washed out the road about a quarter mile from the mansion.*

And Eugenie could easily get swept away and drowned. No one would ever know until her body was found.

Except me, concluded Mignon unhappily. *And it would be my fault. My fault.* There wasn't any time to waste.

Mignon pulled up her dress and ran toward the front gates. The intricate wrought iron creation hung limply on its hinges; the wind had bombarded it severely. The security system had gone down along with the electricity. No one would have seen Eugenie run away into the night.

Slipping sideways through the gate's opening, Mignon followed the road as best she could.

Staggering through the mud was like something out of a

dream, in which one was running and running and getting
absolutely nowhere at all. It pulled her into the earth and
balked at letting her go. Mignon struggled to stay on the road.

The tributary had crested less than a hundred yards down
the road from the St. Michel mansion. In the moonlight, Mignon could see some smaller trees and brush being swept down
river. It was a churning black mass of water.

Eugenie was nowhere in sight. Neither was anyone else.

"Eugenie!" Mignon screamed over the roar of the wind.
"Eugenie! Where are you?!" She twisted around looking. Eugenie could have left the road. She could have headed away
from the river. She could be anywhere north or south of the
mansion, in the chilling wind.

Mignon shivered and repeated her call. Her voice died away
and through the rumble of roiling water and wind she thought
she heard some faint noise. *An animal?*

Picking her way along the edge of the water, Mignon
avoided logs and debris, almost slipping into the blackness of
the river herself several times, sliding down a muddy bank.
The waters lapped violently at the channel it was quickly ex-
panding to fulfill its needs. She continued to follow the noise.

As she moved awkwardly through the shrubbery, the brush
and trees became heavy and thick, almost impossible to break
through, and the noise became a kind of humming, like someone singing a familiar song. Mignon shivered as she realized
that it was the same tune she had heard in the old house that
first night. A lingering song that hinted at memories buried
deep in her subconscious.

She stopped at a ridge that overlooked the surging waters
beneath her, a bubbling, writhing flood of mud and debris,
and searched for something, anything. Mgnoni already knew
the answer. Eugenie wasn't out here. Neither was Kate. It was
only her and something that was leading her. She looked
across the heaving, angry water and suddenly realized she

stood only a quarter of a mile from the old farmhouse, not ten feet from where an old footbridge used to be. Mignon had played in the canal once here, under the supervision of her mother's watchful eyes, and she knew that Luc had once used this path to visit his mistress in the woods.

But the bridge was gone. Time had rotted it away and Mignon could go no farther. As the wind buffeted her body, slinging wet material against her face, for a moment she thought she saw that same white-clad figure moving in the forest beyond the canal. She stood stock-still and searched eagerly, trying to find that shape again, but it was gone.

Then someone gave her a shove into the turbulent, opaque waters, deliberately planting a palm in the small of her back, and Mignon fell into a river of murk and flotsam.

The water chilled her body far worse than the wind and rain had done, and her breath seemed to freeze up in her chest. She struggled to keep her head up and tried to look back to see who had pushed her into the canal, but the darkness and the roiling waters obscured her vision. After a moment she was far away from that spot, whirling through a force that sought to pound at every bit of her body, grasping her with untenable fingers, pulling her in every direction.

Another moment passed when her head was forced under and she took in a mouthful of murky water. She bobbed back up and spit the water out, trying to gather oxygen into her rapidly deprived lungs. Her hands and legs struggled to find something to grasp, and just when she thought her straining muscles couldn't take anymore, she felt a large branch within reach.

Mignon grasped the branch with frozen fingers and began to pull herself up. The water pushed at her frantically, as if determined not to let her go, clutching at her limbs and pulling her away from the branch. There was a sickening crack as the branch began to break with the additional weight, and she was afloat again.

The gasp of distress tore through her lungs and she thought she was going to drown. Suddenly, she felt fingers curled about hers in a bone-crushing grasp. Someone had her hand in a firm grip and kept her motionless as the branch pulled away and disappeared into the seething water. The raging current tumbled over her body and tried to thrust her out into the center of the coursing canal once more, but the hand held firm.

They weren't moving. Mignon felt a shiver of fear run down her back. She was in the most precarious position she could imagine. Whoever was holding her could simply let go, and she wouldn't have a chance in the chilled waters pulling at her with little icy currents, trying to grab her away from the shore. She slowly turned her head and saw . . .

"John Henry!" Mignon shrieked. "You trying to threaten me again, or is this better than the bayou?"

John Henry was trying to get a better grip on Mignon's hand, as well as avoid sinking into the muck where he stood. He had called the air and rescue patrols after one of the local farmers reported that the sluice gates had been sabotaged, and they had given him a lift over the river in their boat. Two of his deputies were working the east side of the river, and he was working the west. Half the homes along this tributary had had to be evacuated due to the rising water, but it seemed as though it was under control. Once the sluice gates had been closed the river quickly began to recede. It was purely coincidental that he had seen Mignon's figure falling into the canal, and only by the grace of God that he had grabbed her hand just as she would have been swept away.

John Henry threw Mignon an exasperated look of disgust. Then he gave her a yank she would feel for a week and pulled her out of the water as if she weighed next to nothing. The next thing Mignon knew, John Henry had her by the waist, his large hands warming her flesh, grasping her firmly. "Can you walk?" he asked.

"I can walk, but my shoulder's probably dislocated," she complained, rubbing the joint of her upper arm.

John Henry took off his windbreaker and pulled it around her chilled body. "Would you rather I threw you back in?" he snapped. Then he brightened. "It would make a hell of a fish story."

Mignon studied his rain-soaked features for a long moment and decided he was angry, tired, and irritated enough to be half serious. She scrambled up the bank and back into the safety of the tree line. She was exhausted. Her cold body was beginning to feel as though it was warm, signaling the start of hypothermia. She needed to get inside, just as he did.

Then the wind stopped and the night became clear. After a moment a nightingale began to sing.

"Well, isn't that just hunky-dory?" she asked no one in particular. But John Henry chuckled behind her all the same.

When they returned to the St. Michel mansion, Mignon caught the distinct aroma of Cuban cigars in the air. An involuntary shiver ran through her body, but she didn't say anything.

The household had been roused. Blankets and brandy were provided for Mignon and John Henry.

"I don't think this is recommended for hypothermia." Mignon's teeth chattered as she spoke.

John Henry shrugged. They were on a couch in the entertainment room at the back of the house. The decor was much more conventional and contemporary. There they wouldn't drip all over hundred-thousand-dollar rugs and on wood floors that had been hewn from cypress a century before.

Mignon shivered and pulled the blanket around her form more closely. She was still in her wet, dirty, torn evening dress.

Her hair was a muddy, sodden mess, and she was sure she didn't have a bit of makeup left on her face. She'd lost her mini-mag someplace, probably at the bottom of the canal, and she thought that she'd swallowed about a gallon of muddy water. Eleanor had wanted her to go upstairs with Eugenie or a maid and soak in a hot tub, but Mignon had refused, hating the thought of spending even another minute alone in this house.

Instead she sat and shivered on a comfortable couch with a large snifter of brandy in her hand. People wandered in and out to check on them. Geraud had been in once. So had everyone else in the household, just to peer at the two of them as they sat surrounded by candles. She had looked at them all carefully, even while she was shuddering, trying to see who else showed signs of being damp. Three had wet hair—Geraud, Jourdain, and Eugenie's date, David—but Eleanor had mentioned that the three had been outside with the groundskeeper trying to repair the generator. No one else had wet hair or clothing, and she realized that whoever had pushed her had had more than ample time to come back, remove a rain slicker, and change. If Mignon had cared to look, she was willing to bet that there was a damp coat in the mudroom. A coat that could have been used by anyone, perhaps even boots. Had they seen her leave the mansion and followed, seeing an opportunity? Shoved her into the canal hoping she'd drown in the night?

"So, John Henry," Mignon said, relieved that the chattering of her teeth was starting to go away. "You swim across that river?"

John Henry managed to laugh. "I wouldn't be here if I had, *chère*."

Mignon's head snapped up. It was a shock to hear him use the endearment, and for a moment he reminded her of her father.

His knee nudged hers on the edge of the couch. Even under fabric, his flesh was hot next to hers and she ached to move closer, to draw in the heat from his body to warm her cool flesh. "What the hell were you doing outside?" he asked.

Reality came back to Mignon. There was more than met the eye in this place. More than she could ever find out in a hundred years, much less a few weeks. Every single thing had a nuance. Every person had a secret. Even John Henry probably had a few in his Dudley Do-Right career. Maybe a perp who got handcuffed a little too tight, or a handout from some guy on the road who didn't want another speeding ticket. Perhaps he looked the other way when a buddy went drinking too hard and did a little driving. In fact, maybe he was even on the St. Michels' payroll, the kind of payroll that no one reported to Uncle Sam. But if that was the case, why would he go to Jourdain and ask "uncomfortable questions?" At least that wasn't one of John Henry's secrets.

Even Mignon had a parcel of her own secrets that she didn't dare hint at, much less give away. Such as trying to fool Eleanor St. Michel into thinking she was possessed by her mother's ghost and scare her into giving up some of her own secrets. "I thought I saw someone out there," she said.

"Uh-huh," he murmured. "In the darkness, in the rain? Someone like who?"

Mignon wasn't sure if she really wanted to tell John Henry that she thought she'd seen her mother's ghost. And telling him that someone had pushed her into the canal would be worse. Either it was someone he might be protecting, or he'd want to start a huge investigation which would keep Eleanor from inviting her back to the house, thus ruining her plans. He had simply assumed she was outside trying to create trouble and had fallen into the swollen canal.

John Henry's eyes glittered. "Did you see a ghost, then?

Perhaps it was some kind of scam, like . . . things crawling over your feet and being buried alive?"

"I didn't say those things. I think it was just your imagination. That séance stuff is complete crap." Mignon's mouth tightened. *Moral outrage, that's the way to go,* she decided, but she felt a twinge of guilt at fooling this man. *Offense is the best defense.* "I think you people yank someone in like me just to play silly little games. First someone breaks into my room, then there's you and our little trip to the cemetery, and there's someone wandering the night like some kind of Fruit Loop. Then there's that damned séance and that snake in my room, waiting to send me to art-heaven. I've never been around such a bizarre group of people in my whole life, and this includes some of the weirdest flakes in Soho and the Village. On one hand you're accusing me of being some sort of super con artist. On the other you're pulling me out of the river and looking at me like . . ."

"Like what . . ." His voice was almost a whisper.

"Like you want to kiss me," she finished, her voice trailing away.

John Henry turned his head to look at her, and his eyes were focused on her lips. He took a deep breath, as if something was paining him. One hand put the snifter of brandy on the table by his side. The other reached for her face, cradling it tenderly. Then his head came closer to hers and she had all the time in the world to say no or back away, but she didn't.

He tasted of brandy and a male aroma she found dark and stimulating. It was a slow, sweet kiss that shook her to the roots of her hair and to the depths of her soul. Without thinking about it, one of her hands came up and twisted around the back of his head, pulling him closer to her. The kiss changed into something different, something more feverish, something almost insatiable. Their lips moved against each other's, and his other hand caressed her face, trying to soak up her very essence.

Abruptly voices could be heard coming down the hallway, and Mignon managed to pull away. She and John Henry stared at each other. She could feel her heart thundering in her chest and could see that she had had a similar effect on him. "Jesus Christ," he whispered.

Mignon didn't say anything. She couldn't say anything. She was sure that it would come out as a long moan that would betray everything her body was experiencing.

In the doorway stood Terri. She had changed from the glittering purple gown to a silver one. The golden rings twinkled on her fingers, and the earrings were still in place. Her hair was still in its careful plait, and flowed over one of her generous shoulders. A bit of gold glittering at the end bound it together.

Terri's arms were crossed over her bosom as she regarded the pair of them with a practiced eye. Behind her, Faust peered around the edge of the door with a sly grin on his face. Mignon had the grace to blush, knowing her friend had accurately guessed what had just occurred.

"Mrs. St. Michel has changed her mind," Terri announced. "She thinks that the presence of so much psychic energy in the area would be too good to pass up. And she would like you to stay, Sheriff Roque. I'm assuming that's who this handsome dark man is, of course."

John Henry rose up from the couch, the blanket still wrapped around his shoulders. "I don't know you."

"She's Madam Terentia Jones," said Mignon. "She's a spiritualist, John Henry. Maybe you can ferret out some crime she's committed since it doesn't seem like you're going anywhere either, with the roads like this."

His face went through a series of expressions, most notably one of irritation. He was attracted to a woman he thought was up to something. It irked the hell out of him and made him want to shake her like a dog would shake a rat. Then he wanted to kiss her again and not stop there, but not with this other woman watching, a devious, patronizing look on her face.

Mignon turned to Terri. "He doesn't believe. But then again, neither do I."

Chapter Fifteen

Little Tommy Tittlemouse
Lived in a little house;
He caught fishes
In other men's ditches.

LITTLE TOMMY TITTLEMOUSE

JOHN HENRY CALLED THE sheriff's department with Geraud's cellular phone. His own had succumbed to water damage. His men told him that the rain had stopped, and the National Oceanic and Atmospheric Administration had reported that there hadn't been enough rain to flood the area to begin with. Furthermore, no more rain was expected for the remainder of the week. The problem was that the tributary to the Cane River was going to be up at flood stage almost all night and none of the search and rescue teams would be able to pick him up for hours. Since neither he nor the St. Michels and their guests were in any kind of danger, they were stuck there until further notice.

His deputy said that the sluice gates on the levee to the tributary had been forced open and the heavy locks had been cut; it appeared as though kids had vandalized them. John Henry had thought that perhaps someone had tried to flood the St. Michel grounds, hoping to kill people in the process, and that was the reason he had rushed over to the house. Too many odd things were happening. Mignon's return. Reports of hauntings. The snake in Mignon's room. She had also let slip that someone had broken into her room, which he hadn't known about. Then she had ended up almost drowning in the canal. He'd seen her fall, and he could've sworn he saw someone push her. And hadn't she cleverly avoided telling how she'd ended up there? Someone was up to no good, and it was not something John Henry cared to miss.

Furthermore, Mignon was up in the middle of the night, fully dressed. It didn't take a genius to realize that if Mignon suspected her mother had been murdered, then the one with the most obvious motive was Eleanor St. Michel. If that were the case, perhaps evidence of a crime still existed. Consequently, how did one get an opportunity to look for evidence? One manufactured a situation in which guests were forced to spend a night at the mansion.

The groundskeeper finally managed to get a generator running, but it provided only marginal lighting for the house. John Henry silently ruminated over the information Mignon had told him in her angry rush. He wanted to know who had broken into Mignon's bed and breakfast room the same day she had arrived in town. He wanted to know why she was here, and he wanted to know why she was keeping secrets from him. While John Henry was on the phone, he had also asked for a records check of one Terentia Jones, alleged spiritualist from New York City.

Geraud had loaned John Henry some clothing that was a bit tight, but wearable all the same, and Mignon was wearing something that looked like it had been taken out of Eugenie's wardrobe. The khaki pants and creamy silk shirt didn't suit her dramatic coloring the way it would have Eugenie, any more than the jeans and polo shirt from Geraud suited him. But the clothing was dry and it was better than what they had had on before.

Mignon was not happy about this discernment, and voiced

her disapproval at length. "It's after three A.M. and no one has had much sleep."

No sleep for me, dammit, she thought. *But I can't tell them that, especially not Mr. Nosy-Good-Kisser-John-Henry-Man. Not to mention I'm not sure if Terri is completely ready for this evening's show.* She added, "This isn't going to accomplish anything."

Eleanor glided into the room as though on wings, dressed in a velvet robe. She seemed comfortable and at ease. "On the contrary, Mignon," she said. "I think it will clear things up. And we can't afford to wait."

Madam Terentia finished covering the large windows with heavy drapes, closing out any negligible light from the half moon. "I agree. This place has an unearthly stink to it. Otherworldly creatures have been in this place, touching their spectral hands upon all that dwell within. I could smell it all evening and protected myself with a charm. But the smell still lingers like the devil's hands are wrapped around all of our hearts, waiting for the right moment to squeeze." She paused. "And worse, it is the smell of fine cigars which no one has been smoking."

Faust was standing in a corner, tall and dark, waiting for some kind of instruction. Geraud was present, as well as Leya and Jourdain. Eugenie was not there, which Eleanor chalked up to fatigue. Finally, John Henry rounded up the group, totaling eight.

"Eight," murmured Leya, inadvertently echoing Mignon's thoughts. "Eight is a bad number for a discernment. It's bad luck."

Terentia waved her hand at Faust. "Faust will not participate, so it will be seven only. We shall have no more malignancy than is already present in this place."

Geraud said, "Faust can participate instead of me. I'll go have a drink. Happily."

Jourdain said, "I thought you'd be interested in this, Geraud. Very interested, considering what happened last time."

"Yes," boomed Terentia. "We must include Mignon Thibeaux. She seems to be a focus here. A very important figure in our discernment. Her energy is crucial to our success. We must use her to find out why the evil spirits have come to this place, and find out how to appease them."

"Money, perhaps," suggested John Henry. He pulled up a chair and sat down, resting his elbows on its arms, and steepled his fingers together in front of his chest, staring at the group of people before him.

"A disbeliever, as she has said," proclaimed Terentia. "It is good to have skepticism with us. It keeps us focused. You will help us, Sheriff Roque. We shall sit."

"Maybe I'll stay instead," grumbled Geraud.

The lights in the room flickered. The generator hadn't been used for a while and it was not a consistent supply of power. Everyone glanced around. Geraud said, "It's the damn generator. Nothing more. Let's get this over with, Mother. I for one would like to go to bed and get at least a few hours of sleep."

Everyone sat except Faust. He still wore his white dress shirt with his suit pants and didn't appear to be rumpled at all. When he winked at Mignon, she bit the inside of her mouth to stop laughing. She found herself next to John Henry again and pulled her arm away from his before she realized what she had done. She saw out of the corner of her eye that his eyes narrowed at her.

Faust left, closing the door behind him after turning off the lights in the room. Before the door shut, the only light came from the hallway and then the room was pitch black. Not even a sliver of moonlight made its way through the curtains.

There was silence for a long moment. Finally John Henry said, "So whose cigar smoke was it?"

Geraud snickered. "My mother believes that my father has come back to haunt us. Surely you've read the articles in the tabloids."

"I thought your father was gone," John Henry said. "Away from here. Living somewhere else."

"He is gone. But now she believes that he's dead. That he's died somewhere and that he's come back to torment us all." He paused. "As if he hadn't tormented us enough while he was alive."

John Henry digested this. He wasn't willing to share the results of his investigation with people who might very well be responsible for Garlande's and Luc's deaths, even if it couldn't be proven that either of them were, in fact, deceased. Beside him he could feel Mignon squirming in her chair.

"What makes you think he's dead, other than the smell of cigars in the house?" he asked.

"Not any cigars," Eleanor answered thoughtfully. "Cuban cigars. The best money can buy. He bought those from a man in Florida with his own contacts in Cuba who had links to the best tobacco plantations there. These are very rare cigars and their aroma is very distinct. It fills the house sometimes. But no one smokes here. I haven't allowed it in years."

A vision of Kate Trent in her neat little maid's uniform lighting up a fat stogie purchased from an exclusive dealer in New York City popped into Mignon's head and almost made her smile. Nehemiah's granddaughter had walked the hallways at night, not too often, to leave the lingering aroma. An old article about the St. Michels had provided the information about the cigars, and they weren't above using it in this manner. *Well, it sure isn't Terri's cigarillos*, she thought.

Eleanor went on. "This all began when Eugenie returned to St. Michel. She's very sensitive."

John Henry felt like a jackass talking in the dark about a man who might very well be alive. This lack of evidence stung his professional instincts. Just because Luc had vanished didn't necessarily mean he was dead. John Henry had worked a dozen missing person cases in which the families were positive that their husbands or fathers had been kidnapped or killed, only to discover they had set up housekeeping in Miami with their large-boobed secretaries. "What exactly began? And why haven't you told me about this before?"

"What can law enforcement do about a haunting?" Leya asked simply.

Eleanor went on as though she hadn't been interrupted. "Eugenie has visions of both of them in her dreams. Luc, my husband, and Mignon's mother, Garlande. It is, after all, only appropriate that Mignon be here. An act of fate has brought her to us at this time. She can help soothe the spirits that beset us. Perhaps it is time for the St. Michels and the Thibeauxs to forgive each other for past sins.

Mignon squirmed in her seat. John Henry would have given his right arm to see the expression on her face, but there were many things going through his analytical mind. "Have you . . . heard from him since he vanished?"

"There was the power of attorney, but not a word otherwise. He wanted to sever all family connections, that's for sure," answered Geraud, his voice cold. There would be no forgiveness from him. If his mother wanted to play these games, then play them she would, and he wasn't one to stop her. Besides all of that, he had his own plans for Mignon Thibeaux.

This is all a little too coincidental, thought John Henry. Eugenie St. Michel returns to LaValle, and then things started to happen. Mignon Thibeaux showed up professing utter innocence. And no one knew what really happened to Luc St. Michel or Garlande Thibeaux. They could be living in Bermuda with their feet up on a plush ottoman and glasses of Chardonnay in their hands. "And you think that tonight Mignon here is going to go into one of her little trances, like before."

"I don't have trances," insisted Mignon.

"You did last Saturday."

"So you say."

"Hush!" said Terentia. "There must be no disagreement here. We must agree that we are here to seek out whatever is harming this house and these people! Can we agree? Can we focus on that?"

Silence ensued. Finally John Henry said, "I think I can agree if we can do something to prevent some kind of hoax here."

"Are you suggesting that Madam Jones is some kind of chicanery artist?" Terentia demanded, speaking of herself in the imposing third person. "I have performed discernments with the richest people in this country and all over Europe."

Eleanor's voice cut in. "I think the sheriff is only trying to protect all of us, Madam, and there is no need to take offense. What is the suggestion, John Henry?"

"We can tie Mignon to her chair," Terentia replied quickly.

Geraud chuckled.

"Yes," agreed John Henry.

"We can also turn on the lights," suggested Geraud.

"There must be total darkness," said Leya. "The spirits will not come in light when called. Light repels those souls in limbo. Dark beckons them. Only when the room is devoid of the warm light from God's grace will they seek out those who call to them. It's the way it must be done."

"This is true," agreed Terentia. "Darkness calls to evil ones in a way that cannot be ignored."

"Then tie her to the chair," repeated John Henry stubbornly.

"Gee, thanks, John Henry. This is the best way I can think of to end one of the most memorable evenings I've ever had," said Mignon.

Suddenly the lights came on; Terentia was standing beside the switch at the wall. Everyone blinked and gazed at her. She said, "The sheriff must tie her to the chair. Perhaps the one he was sitting in, with the arms."

John Henry gave her a long look and stood up. He pulled out his chair and checked it, looking underneath it for hidden objects. He rattled the arms and frowned because one side was loose.

Eleanor objected, "John Henry, that's a Chippendale and it does not respond well to harsh treatment. Rest assured it has been in this house for longer than your grandfather has been alive, and consequently must be considered free of conspiracy."

He shrugged, and motioned for Mignon to take his place. She glared at him. "This isn't my idea of fun, but for the sake of argument I'll go along with it."

"Good," he muttered. "Something to tie her with." He looked around.

Geraud smiled brightly. "You could always use your handcuffs."

"I'd have to explain that to the taxpayers," joked John Henry. He saw the curtain ties lying on the table between the two adjacent windows. "Ah, there we go. Velvet and satin in order not to chafe her arms, but secure enough to please me."

Mignon sat down and aligned her arms with the arms of the chair. She looked steadily at John Henry as he bound each arm to the chair, tying a double knot in each.

"And her feet?" murmured Eleanor.

Jourdain had been oddly quiet the entire time, taking in everything and missing nothing. He said, "It should be as it was before. Our feet on each other's."

Terentia went to the door and summoned Faust, who was waiting outside. "My bag, please."

The young man handed her a dark valise, not unlike a doctor's bag. She closed the door as he withdrew. At the table John Henry yanked at Mignon's binding and looked thoughtfully at her feet. "We could simply move her away from the table."

"There is another way," Terentia said. "There will be just the two of us, facing each other. My feet on top of hers. That will suspend suspicion."

"Unless you're in on it with her," responded John Henry dryly.

Terentia tilted her head at the sheriff. "I believe that there is no one you trust. This says volumes about the manner in which you were raised."

"Madam, are you a psychic or a psychologist? It comes with the territory. How about Eleanor instead? Her husband; Mignon's mother. Eleanor doesn't take kindly to fakers in her house. She won't allow Mignon to pull a fast one." John Henry turned Mignon around to face another chair beside the table. Then he turned that chair toward Mignon. "Eleanor, if you don't mind?"

Eleanor rose and took her place. She carefully put her feet over Mignon's. They faced each other with carefully neutral expressions. If anything, Mignon seemed slightly irritated and almost bored.

Terentia was pleased enough. From the black valise she took out a little handbell with phosphorescent tape on it. "This will glow in the dark, showing us its position at all times." She put it on the table next to the two chairs. "Here is a token of Luc St. Michel's," she said as she took out a man's fob watch. "Mrs. St. Michel told me that he wore it frequently. It was given to him on his wedding day by his father." She attached a bit of tape to it, while Mignon wondered why no one attached importance to the fact that if the fob was so prized, why hadn't he taken it with him? "So we can see if the spirit reacts to its physical energy."

She looked at Mignon carefully. "Do you have a token from your mother?"

Mignon thought of the metal box with the diary and the golden medallion. The diary held expressions of love from her mother to the man who had stolen her heart away. She had believed in Luc St. Michel as if he had been her fairy godfather. She had written about her naïve trust in this rich, handsome man, fifteen years older than she was, who had a wife he would almost certainly never divorce, as well as children. It was the first thing of her mother's that Mignon ever had in her possession. "No, I don't have a token," she lied.

Finally, Terentia removed an egg from the bag. She also pulled out a small glass bowl and placed it on the table. She held up the egg for a moment. "Mrs. St. Michel removed this egg from her own refrigerator, not an hour before." She put it next to the handbell, balancing it carefully against the table so that it wouldn't roll off. Then she opened the bag so everyone could see that there was nothing else there—not a substitute egg or any other item that could be used for trickery.

"And that symbolizes what?" asked Jourdain.

"The egg is purity itself, Mr. Gastineau. It will show us the extent of evil present in this household. We must believe this because the egg cannot be tampered with beforehand. The egg is whole, undefiled, and a vessel for those who taint this place and these people." Terentia waved gold-encrusted fingers over the egg. "It is a blessed thing, the egg of the chicken, and it comes from the home in which spirits are reputed to roam. It will tell us what we need to know."

"That's one hell of an egg," said Geraud.

"Sit," said Terentia. "We shall sit and wait for those who will come."

John Henry turned off the lights and took the seat that Eleanor had vacated. After a brief rustling there was a hush in the room.

"We must believe that our answers will be found," intoned Terentia solemnly. "One does not have to believe in the other world, but merely that possibilities exist. Relax your bodies and believe in our Lord, Christ in heaven. All answers stem from Him. He will guide our experiences here."

Someone said, "Amen," but Mignon couldn't tell who it had been.

Terenita ignored it and proceeded with her delivery. "Concentrate on that which plagues this house. Concentrate." Her voice was lulling and seductive in the dark void where they sat. "We must believe in that which taints this world."

Another long silence ensued. Someone was breathing more heavily than the others. Minutes passed and people shifted restlessly in their chairs, listening to their own breathing and to the hollow sound of the wind outside. In the blackness, the tape glowed on the little handbell and the watch fob.

There was a soft moaning sound. It started out low and grew louder like an animal in pain. As it filled the room, all the subtle movements ceased suddenly. Terentia asked, "Spirits, are you with us?"

The moaning noise continued, varying in tempo and volume. It caused a chill to run down John Henry's spine.

"It's Mignon," whispered Eleanor at last. "It's coming from her."

"Spirit, we long to be informed of your desires. We want to understand your presence." Terentia's voice was level, calm, and determined. "Spirit, speak to us. Communicate with us."

"There is no light here," came another voice. It was a deeper voice, unidentifiable as male or female. An electric voice, full of anxiety and anger. Everybody strained their ears to hear.

"Who was that?" said Geraud.

"Who speaks?" asked Terentia. "What spirit is with us now?"

The watch fob moved suddenly. The phosphorescent tape showed its path along the table. It slid toward Mignon and Eleanor.

"Did you see that?" said Eleanor incredulously, a tremble in her voice. "There's no one by the watch. Did you see?"

"Silence," ordered Terentia. "If this is Luc St. Michel, give us a sign."

Slowly the watch fob began to coil up, then it lifted into the air, floating, floating.

Someone gasped.

The watch fob dropped to the table just as slowly as it had risen.

The bell began to trill as if someone were shaking it.

"Luc St. Michel," intoned Terentia. "You must tell us why you are here. What troubles you?"

The bell tinkled again.

There was a sudden movement in the room, as someone lunged for the bell. It dropped to the table with a loud clunk. That person grunted, and then there was movement across the room as John Henry scrambled for the lights.

There was no one near the bell on the table and the watch fob lay still, as if it had simply been there all along. John Henry cursed loudly as he went back to the table.

Mignon had slumped forward in her chair, her arms still tied to the Chippendale with the curtain ties. Her chin rested on her chest and her eyes were closed. She seemed to be unconscious. Eleanor's feet were still on top of hers.

Eleanor removed her feet and leaned forward to touch Mignon's face. "She's like ice," she whispered. Her midnight blue eyes raised up to meet her son's. "Geraud, what is happening here?"

Terentia brought the small glass bowl close to her and swiftly picked up the forgotten egg. With one hand, she cracked the egg on the side of the bowl and delivered its contents to the glass dish. The egg was full of blood. She made a gasping noise. "Dear Lord above, protect us from evil," she cried.

Jourdain gazed at the bowl filled with blood, his face a mask of horrified dismay. "What does it mean?"

"This family is cursed," murmured Terentia. "There is blood on the family name. It is cursed by evil, and if something is not done, someone will die."

Chapter Sixteen

Hickety pickety, my black hen,
She lays eggs for gentlemen.
Gentlemen come every day
To see what my black hen doth lay.

HICKETY PICKETY

MIGNON WAS PAINTING ON the porch of the small farmhouse, alone. Horace Seay had left a message at her bed and breakfast that the workmen wouldn't be able to come until Wednesday because of "unforeseen difficulties." The truth was that his wife had sworn that she had seen the *fifolet* in the bayou the night the tributary had cut off half the homes near the St. Michel mansion, and it was surely an omen not to be ignored. But Mignon, after sleeping almost twelve hours the day before, was relaxed and unconcerned with the fact that for the first time there would be nobody around.

The storm had passed to the east, leaving the ground moist and debris strewn over the ground from trees, brush, and houses. Mignon had picked her way down the long dirt road to the farmhouse because it was too muddy to drive her rental car down the road. At the house itself there was a little note from Miner Poteet, who had come by Sunday to check on the place. Mignon made a mental note to go and thank him personally.

She had finished her previous work and was busy with another. The start of this more abstract piece was beginning well and she was pleased. Next to her on the old porch was an ancient rocking chair she had rescued from the side of the road.

Mignon put her brush down and stepped back to observe her efforts, nodding. Then she began to hum idly, resuming her work. In her art she could lose herself, working for hours at a time, losing track of time and even location, until her shoulders and arm cramped with overuse. This piece was another oil, instead of her preferred watercolors. She was so into her painting that she didn't realize she was murmuring words to the tune she had been humming. "Bobby Shaftoe's gone to sea, silver buckles on his knee . . ."

The brush returned to the bottle of turpentine. She thought about what she had said. It was another of her mother's rhymes. It was the oddest thing. She couldn't recall when she had ever heard it. It had just popped into her head out of nowhere. She repeated it softly to herself. "Bobby Shaftoe's gone to sea, silver buckles on his knee . . . now what's the rest?"

The trees around the old house were rich and green despite the late month of the year. Some were beginning to turn the rich yellows and reds of fall, but the evergreens reigned supreme and surrounded the house like a collar of vivid green. She stared into the foliage searching for an answer and found something deep inside of her.

"Gone to sea, silver buckles on his knee," she repeated again. Then slowly came, "He'll come back and marry me, pretty Bobby Shaftoe."

The sound of an engine nearby, coming closer, made Mignon realize that someone was driving down her road. Without electricity and no sounds except for those that Mother Nature provided, it was easy to tell when someone was drawing near. She chewed on her lip as she considered the source of her rhyme. Like most of the others it had popped into her mind unwanted, at an odd time. Now it remained like a mystic chant, going through her mind again and again. She supposed each of the rhymes had some kind of meaning. Some were more obvious than others, Some were simply nonsensical. Garlande had liked the sound of them. Her mother had taught her some, her grandmother had taught her others. She had wanted to pass them onto her sole child, preserving one of the few traditions in her family.

Though the engine was coming closer, someone was taking his or her time on the road. It might be days before the mud completely dried. Mignon had decided that the road would have to be re-leveled and filled with gravel. Eventually an asphalt road would be best.

She sat down on the rocking chair and grabbed her purse beside it. She removed the Beretta, took the safety off, chambered a round, and placed it on her lap. Then she covered it with a newspaper, staring at the edge of the woods where the road emerged.

A white Bronco appeared and parked in front of the house. Mignon let her shoulders sag slightly. This was no ordinary henchman. It was her own personal, gun-toting savior, none other than Sheriff John Henry Roque. He'd had his opportunity to get rid of her at the river early on Sunday morning, and he had missed it. Or he had never wanted it to begin with.

There had been other missed opportunities. She was almost positive that John Henry was exactly what he seemed. He was a lawman first and foremost. Second, he wanted answers to his questions, no matter what the cost. Finally, she wasn't falling down at his feet like tumbling dominos. Perhaps her obstinacy was part of the attraction. His history was readily apparent. He wasn't crooked and there wasn't a blemish on his professional record. No one had complained about police brutality relating to him. No one had ever reported him taking a bribe. He'd never been investigated for any kind of police-related misconduct. And she'd heard Jourdain himself complain about John Henry asking questions on her behalf.

John Henry climbed out of the Bronco like a great feline, all lean muscles and bunched energy. In Mignon's mind she could find much to appreciate about his sinewy body. Not only was his face something she would enjoy putting on paper or canvas, but so was his physique. Here was the man who had snatched her hand as she was about to be swept away in a turbulent current. Here was the man who had kissed her like the world was on fire. She couldn't help the secretive smile that momentarily curved her lips.

But there was that nagging question. *Am I sure enough about him to risk my life?*

John Henry propped one foot on the bottom step of the porch much as he had done before and looked solemnly at Mignon, his sherry-brown eyes warm in the light of early afternoon. After a moment he said, "Nice rocking chair."

"Found it. You believe someone threw it out?"

He shrugged. "Hard to believe a lot of things around here."

"You mean about Saturday night? Which part?"

"Let's start with how you came to be outside," he said.

"I thought I saw someone. Someone in the woods, dressed in white." Mignon rocked her chair back and forth slowly, knowing that it sounded amiss, knowing that she sounded like she was admitting she had seen some kind of ghost. "It was a little hard to miss."

"You were still dressed in your evening dress," he stated.

"I'm surprised you could tell. I had trouble going to sleep." Mignon reached up with her left hand to scratch the side of her nose lazily. "I was still up, watching the last bits of lightning outside." *How in the name of God can I tell him that I was up tossing the joint for a notarized confession that doesn't exist?*

"Did you know that the sluice gate had been jimmied open? That someone let the tributary flood out the road so that none of you could leave?" His eyes seemed to penetrate hers.

Mignon couldn't look away, she couldn't even blink. "Why would I know that? It was raining, too. I thought that flooded the road."

He smiled grimly. "It had a little help. Like the transformers that fed electricity to the tributary area had a little help being turned off."

The color of his eyes was like the sweetest kind of blended whiskey; she thought she might fall into those eyes and never come up for air. She didn't say anything.

"Okay, then, what about the séance?" John Henry rocked back and forth on his resting knee. The movement of his large body was hypnotic as she watched the muscles slowly move back and forth.

"You tied me, and then everyone was freaking out about that stupid egg," Mignon said. "You'd think you'd never seen an egg turn out that way."

"You have?"

"Sure, my mother and father kept a few chickens. It was a chore of mine to fetch the eggs." Mignon was surprised with herself. This was a memory that had previously escaped her, like the rhymes had. But now she remembered it as if it had happened yesterday. "There was a chicken coop." She pointed to the south. "Down that way." She turned her head to look. It was gone. Long gone, but it existed in her mind, standing in the shadow of the forest as it had over two decades before. "I haven't thought about it for a long time. My mother would fry up fresh eggs every day on the stove in the kitchen, or sometimes on the potbelly if the electricity was off. Farm eggs aren't like the kind you get from the store. Double yolks. Other stuff. It happens, but they mostly get weeded out by the time they hit the shelves. It's a way of life."

John Henry watched Mignon as she looked off to the south. He could see that her mind was lost in the past. He glanced over to where the chicken coop would have stood, and when he looked back he found her incredible green eyes on him again. She had the most innocent expression on her face. She was thinking about the past, like a little girl lost in oversized hand-me-downs.

He fought the urge to take her into his arms and give comfort in the only way he could. Instead, he took a deep breath. "And the bell ringing?"

"The bell rang?" asked Mignon curiously. "No, it didn't. I was sitting there the whole time. It was right next to me. I think I would have heard it."

"What about the watch fob?"

"Right on the table in the same spot." She paused. "Weren't they?"

"Do you believe in ghosts, Mignon?"

Mignon studied him closely. "I know what I would have said a few weeks ago, John Henry."

"You didn't believe," he said softly. "And now you wonder if something is happening to you." She nodded ever so slowly, and he added, "So do I."

Neither one of them seemed to move, but a moment later Mignon was in his arms, right where she belonged, fitting there as though they'd found the part missing from both of them all of their lives. The Beretta and the newspaper were forgotten, sliding to the porch with a low thud. All she knew was that his lips were intoxicating and that it felt good to think about nothing but the sensation of their bodies rubbing against each other. He carried her into the house, and she directed him to the pantry where she had slept as a child. She had placed a twin bed there, for when the house was finished. The workmen had finished the floors in the tiny room, but it was empty except for the bed, which wasn't nearly big enough for the two of them.

They didn't, however, care much about that.

Later Mignon was propped against John Henry's chest. He rested against the wall behind the bed and slowly stroked her thick red hair back from her face. It had been sweet and satiating, and he was already wondering if they could repeat it. So he satisfied himself by studying the lines of her body. It was a lush body with curves many women would envy, full breasts and a trim waist, full hips that jutted out from her midriff in the manner of a woman who was shaped like a woman. She was stretched out at his side, her upper half resting on top of him, one of her hands playing with the hair on his chest. "What's the gun for?"

"Snakes, John Henry, what else?" she whispered. "I suppose I should go fetch it off the porch because it doesn't do me a lot of good in here."

"Like that?" he asked, amused. "Like Venus rising out of the half shell?"

Her head came up. "And who's to see?"

"I wouldn't look away," he replied with a little rasp in his voice, enjoying the thought of her walking naked out to the porch to retrieve her gun, the gun he had pointedly ignored when he had almost snatched her into his arms. And the vision of her long flanks glowing in the warm afternoon's golden light was tempting beyond belief. "But don't go away. No one will come. Not with the cruiser out there."

"Why? Will they think you're interrogating me?" Mignon laughed huskily. "Is this what you do with all of the new artists in town?"

One of his large hands cupped her face, tilting it so that his brown eyes could stare directly into her green ones. "I don't do this with anyone else."

Mignon shrugged lightly, but she didn't break the contact between them. She lowered her head, and John Henry couldn't see that she was staring at the wall like it would fall before her eyes. "Someone doesn't want me here," she murmured.

"I know, and I can say that it isn't me," he murmured back as he stroked her hair gently. "Why are you here, Mignon? Why have you come back?"

"Why do you want to know?"

"I see the most attractive woman I've ever met. With green eyes the color of the sea, and vivid hair, and the most sensual body, and an apt mind, an incredible mind. She has this wonderful talent, and she has pulled herself out of the ashes unlike anyone I've ever known. I wish I had met you years ago. I see all of that, and I see someone who's playing with fire." John Henry's voice was rough, but tender, like the soft rumble of an old tomcat. "Looking for something that might not be there. I see it, and I feel like I'm helpless to do anything about it."

Mignon sighed reluctantly and raised her head to stare John Henry in the face. "And the St. Michels?"

"The St. Michels are people who would do anything to protect themselves. They would and they have. I've walked a line with them. Maybe I've even walked a fence with them. I've tried to be careful not to fall on either side, but sometimes it can't be helped. Sometimes my only redeeming quality is that I stubbornly crawl back up on that fence. My only fortune concerning them is that they've mellowed in recent years. Eleanor's interests lie in the supernatural and Geraud works in New Orleans, well out of my jurisdiction. But they ask me to come to their house upon occasion, just like some of the other plantation families do. And for politics' sake, I go. Some of these people are good people. Some of them aren't." John Henry stared back at Mignon, hardly even blinking.

"And that satisfies you?" she asked curiously. "Walking this line? Walking the fence? When you know that they've broken the law."

"When I can prove they've done something wrong, I won't walk the fence." His rumbling voice warned her that he didn't like being questioned on this matter. Mignon didn't care.

"So you want to know what makes me tick? What really brings me back?" She sat straight up, and reached over the bed to pull a T-shirt off the floor and over her head. When her mop of red hair reappeared, John Henry was genuinely sorry that the rest of her bare body had disappeared. "Was that what *this* was all about?"

"Hell, no," he exploded and kissed her again. It was a long time before they drifted back to the present. When he released her they were both breathing heavily. He looked at her seriously. "I asked around about Luc and your mother. No one said boo about them except they up and ran off, not until years later. There was speculation about them being dead. But then there was also information that indicated Luc had sent some paperwork from New Orleans, after he left here with your mother. They might not be alive now, but it's not because they were murdered that day." He hadn't found any proof of their deaths, not in the cold case files from Louisiana, Arkansas, or Texas. But what he kept from her was that he hadn't found any proof of their lives either. He knew damned well that they should have left some kind of trace, but there was nothing. It didn't prove that they were dead, but what other answer could there be? And secrets like this tended to stay secret.

"I suppose that would be what you might think." Mignon spoke softly, picking her words carefully. "But you need to consider the source of the information about this 'so-called' paperwork from Luc St. Michel. I'd be willing to bet we're talking about a power of attorney granting control over the St. Michel estates and money to Eleanor." She didn't want to let on that she knew a great deal more than he would have expected her to know, but there was a point where she knew that she had to trust him. She had made love with him, she had trusted him in the most intimate manner possible, and she couldn't deny that. The only thing left was the question of how much information she should impart to him. How much of it was safe? And what would endanger her and her friends?

"That's part of it." His eyes had narrowed, wondering what her source of information was.

"And there was nothing else? Not a Christmas or birthday card to Geraud and Eugenie?" asked Mignon. "Not a post-card?"

There was a long pause. "I've seen men do it before," John Henry said at last. "Hell, I've seen women do it. Cold-blooded individuals who walked away and never looked back."

Mignon stood up and walked over to the door of the little room. She stood there, dressed only in a T-shirt that fell to the tops of her thighs. "Did you know that this was my room as a child?"

"No, how could I know that?"

"Of course not," she said. "My father pulled down the shelves in here so that I would have a little space to myself, or perhaps so that he and my mother would have a space to themselves."

John Henry grunted. "You're feeling sorry for yourself. If that had been so, then they would have simply stuck you in the kitchen by the potbelly stove."

She smiled quickly, and it faded away just as fast. "I didn't think of that. But here was where I slept for years as a child. I was born in this house." She pointed toward the master bed-room. "In that room." Resting one shoulder against the door-jamb, she glanced over her shoulder. "I asked you a question about whether you had dreams that came true or not. I have them. Last year, I was at the peak of my form. I was made. If I wanted, I could never work another day in my life, and I would never lack for anything. All I have to do is live off my investments. I did everything I vowed to do when I was a little girl. Everything, and then last year there was a mugging."

There was a heavy silence before she went on. "A friend was shot while I watched. Mugged by some kid in the street. There was blood. A lot of blood. He lived, my friend. But . . . I started having these dreams."

"What dreams?" he asked as her voice trailed away.

She took a deep breath. "Dreams of death, of blood, of screaming, of my mother dying, and dying violently. I try to help her and I can't do anything because I'm frightened beyond words. Death and pain haunted me, day in and day out." Mignon turned to face John Henry, and he could see the lines of pain etched on her face. "I couldn't sleep. I couldn't paint. Finally, I went to see a psychiatrist in New York City. A good man. The best. And we decided that I was dreaming about my mother's abandonment. If I could simply come to terms with it, then I wouldn't dream about it."

"Go on."

"What better way could there be than to confront my mother personally? So I put some of my money to good use. Instead of taking the Prozac the doc prescribed, I hired a private detective, just like Geraud did in 1982. Only I didn't know that then." She shivered a bit and John Henry sat up in the bed, looking at her carefully. "A good private investigator named Potter, a former feebie. Expensive as hell, but worth his weight in gold."

"He told you something."

"Potter told me everything I needed to know."

Mignon stepped back to the bed and sat on the edge next to John Henry. "Potter looked for the cold, hard facts. He didn't find any." She went on to tell him about the unused Social Security numbers, the missing driving records and work histories—much of which he already knew. But then there was something he hadn't considered. "There's no record of use of a passport since 1975 for Luc St. Michel. My mother was never issued one, not then, and not since then. Luc was driving a 1975 Mercedes Benz, a metallic gray sedan. The most expensive sedan one could buy from Mercedes at the time. It has never turned up. It was never sold to anyone, and never registered in another state under its VIN."

"They could have changed their names, bought new identities," suggested John Henry. There was a natural reluctance to tell her he had found out much of the same information, that he was still looking at cold cases from 1975 and 1976, but he wasn't sure how she would react when he told her. Trust was already the biggest wall between them, and he didn't want to build it even higher. "Eleanor is a vindictive woman. You haven't seen it yet, because you haven't crossed her. You're bringing her something she wants, albeit strange to most folk. But Luc probably had a very good reason to hide from his wife. She would have sued him for every penny he owned and then some. Adultery in 1975 was still seen as a sin, and she would have won."

"You don't understand. My guy obtained a copy of the power of attorney that Luc supposedly signed. It was forged, confirmed by a handwriting expert, and despite that it was notarized by Jourdain." Mignon looked deeply into John Henry's eyes, not willing to admit that she had seen a copy of the document in Geraud's safe. She also didn't want to admit that the private detective had provided dossiers on all of the principals in the area, from Eleanor St. Michel to Sheriff John Henry Roque himself, from their shoe sizes to their grades in grammar school, and photographs when available. "I found things in this house that my mother treasured profoundly. She wouldn't have left me. I know that now. You have to know that they never left this place. They never left Louisiana. They're dead, and they were murdered."

Chapter Seventeen

Lavender's blue, dilly dilly, lavender's green;
When I am king, dilly dilly, you shall be queen.

LAVENDER'S BLUE

THEY WERE DRESSING WHEN Mignon noticed that something seemed wrong with John Henry. She wasn't sure what it was, whether it was the expression on his face or the way he stood by the window after he finished buckling his belt. She tucked her T-shirt into a faded pair of Levi 501s. John Henry ran his fingers briskly through his hair, looking out the dirty kitchen window.

"What's wrong, John Henry?" Mignon asked quietly, and answered it herself. "You can't think that anyone would be that shaken up by my presence here? All I've gotten are warnings. Stupid warnings. If they thought I could accomplish anything here then I probably would be dead, lying in a grave out in the Kisatchie Forest right now." *That was easy to say,* she thought. *But then he doesn't know about the violent shove into the canal.*

John Henry turned to look at Mignon. "Maybe they don't think you're a threat, yet. But all this psychic séance bullshit . . . What if you're right? What if they *were* murdered that very day, by Eleanor or her hired man? Wouldn't she see you as a threat to her, someone who could expose her? Don't you think that you've put yourself in a position of danger?"

"You heard what she said. She feels guilty. She believes that her husband is haunting her because of the wrongs she did me and my father. Perhaps she thinks that by inviting me to the mansion for her little discernments she's keeping the ghosts at bay. Maybe she didn't say that, but that's what she means." Mignon shrugged. "It doesn't make sense if she's the kind of woman you say. But the St. Michels have always been above the law in St. Germaine Parish. You know that. They've got more politicians in their pockets than loose change. Maybe she doesn't see me as a threat and maybe she's developed a conscience after all these years. Being haunted by your dead husband's ghost has to be somewhat . . . cataclysmic."

"I don't see Eleanor St. Michel like that," John Henry muttered. "I see her as someone who would be quite willing to squash anyone who got in her way."

"And you think she's like that, yet not capable of murdering her husband?"

He didn't answer and she started along another avenue of thought. "Then there's the psychic phenomena. She's so into that, she thinks she's got a pipeline there. Maybe that's the reason. I don't understand everything here, but if this is a ticket for me to find out something about my mother, then I'll use it."

"But you're not doing anything. You're not psychic," he said. "Or so you say."

Mignon rolled her eyes, shoving away the sharp knife of guilt that she felt about keeping the rest of the information from this man. "Ever the malcontent, fault-finding fussbudget. I could have a signed affidavit from God and you'd still be, 'I dunno, she's awful suspicious, even though I slept with her.' "

"*I dunno,*" he began and laughed. "Maybe if you came over to my house for a change and slept there."

"Are you inviting me?" she asked. "Because I think you can do better than that."

"I have work to do today and lots of it. But I wouldn't

mind if you came over and let me feed you some of my pat-
ented seafood gumbo. Best in the whole parish." He winked.

Mignon smiled at him. Then she asked, "Was there something else that was bothering you?"

"Yeah, how did you know?"

She shifted restlessly, trying to read his body language,
which was difficult. He kept a stoic face.

John Henry crossed his arms over his chest, staring out the
window as if he were looking for something in particular. Finally he cast an eye back at her, looking at her for a moment
before looking away. "I haven't been . . . honest with you."

"What does that mean?" Mignon suspected she knew what
it meant, but she wasn't sure if she wanted to hear it from his
mouth, the same mouth that had been used so expertly to
enhance their mutual pleasure—not to mention that she knew
she hadn't been completely honest with him, either, and had
little intention of doing so at this point in time.

"There are a couple things. One is that I didn't discount
you completely. I looked into your mother's and Luc's . . . disappearances. I found pretty much the same things your ex-FBI
agent did. Although there are a few more reports due back to
me that will take some time." He turned and glanced at her
again. Mignon was stunned, but he went on. "I couldn't find
anything that indicated they are still alive." She started to say
something, but he interrupted. "But I couldn't find anything
to indicate they're dead, either. There's no proof of anything."

"Of course they're dead," she almost shouted. "People like
Luc don't just disappear. He was a millionaire. He left everything behind. Do you really think he would do that? Do you
really think my mother would have simply abandoned me?"

John Henry would have held her then, but she shifted away,
angry that his disbelief was coloring the conversation so completely. "I don't know that she would have," he muttered.
"But neither do you. You were only five years old."

"I know." She stared at him. "I know it. Because somebody wants me to leave. And why else would they be trying so damned hard?"

John Henry stared at the woman before him and knew that everything she said had already gone through his mind, things he had ruminated over for days. "There is something else," he admitted.

Mignon locked her green eyes on him.

"The old sheriff. He was crooked, like a lot of Louisiana politicians. Once he retired down to Baton Rouge, he managed to get himself into a bit of trouble. Drugs, I've heard. The IRS is still ripping his income tax returns apart. If anyone knows where a body is buried, he would." John Henry sighed.

"So?" Mignon's voice was skeptical. She remembered the old sheriff's cruel face as he told her father to get out of LaValle and never come back. She remembered it in her nightmares because she had felt like a criminal back then, all because she was the daughter of the wrong woman. She also remembered what Geraud had said about his chauffeur. The servant had seen Jourdain with the old sheriff a few weeks earlier. *Why? Because Ruelle Fanchon can use the help of a state Supreme Court justice right now, more than ever, and boy does he have some dirt on His Honor.* "Why would he tell you anything?"

John Henry smiled grimly. "He has motivation now. Drug sentences are harsh, especially for law enforcement. And I don't think he wants to spend a lot of time up to Angola, where he's personally acquainted with half the fellas there. No, I don't think he'd like that much."

"You're going to talk to him."

He nodded. "I'm going to do just that."

"What about his connection to . . . powerful people in the area?"

With a stare that would have shaken another woman, he

looked at her, attempting to follow her train of thought. "You mean, Eleanor St. Michel, maybe? Or Jourdain Gastineau? Eleanor wouldn't help him, and Jourdain's got too much to lose."

She thought, *I wouldn't bet on that,* and knew that she couldn't tell him what she knew without compromising herself and her friends in the bargain.

When Mignon smiled at him, John Henry almost forgot that she had a reason to be angry with him. He smiled back, and as his arms went around her he felt as though she was the thing that had been missing from his life. How could this woman be guilty of anything but wanting to know about her mother? "I need to go. Will you call me at work so I can tell you how to find my place?" John Henry didn't tell her that he had also checked on Madam Terentia Jones and the young man, Faust, last name unknown. Nada. No record on either of them. At least there were no current outstanding warrants. What he needed was their fingerprints and not their *nom de plumes*, or rather their *nom de connes*. He wasn't going to do anything unless a crime was committed, and as yet nothing had revealed itself except a lot of supposition and rumormongering, neither of which was illegal.

"Hey, you can drive me up the road to my car," Mignon suggested, linking her arm in his. "Then I don't need to go tripping through the mud."

Neither one of them saw the figure who watched them from the dark woods. The figure had watched them for the last hour, seeing their shapes in the windows and then nothing for a long time. This person watched and waited patiently for an opportunity.

WHEN MIGNON RETURNED to her room at the bed and breakfast, she found she had another visitor.

He was reading her mother's diary while laying across her bed. A tall man in his early sixties with white hair and blue-gray eyes, he was dressed in blue trousers; his jacket hung over a chair in the corner of the room. He looked up when she unlocked the door, then went back to reading the diary without saying a word.

Mignon gasped and backed out of the room.

"There's no need to do that," the man said.

Mignon glanced around, then she entered the room and closed the door. She stared at her intruder. "What the hell are you doing here?" Her voice was all outrage and indignation.

The man flipped a page in the diary. He pointed with a long index finger. "This is interesting stuff. She was having an affair with Luc St. Michel for years. For a womanizer like he was, that's an eternity. Do you think he really meant to take her away with him?"

Mignon put her purse with the Beretta inside it on the table by the door. She glared at the man. "How dare you read that?"

"Well, you didn't hide it very well, my dear," he commented. "And my God, is this a scene out of *Green Acres* or *Petticoat Junction?*" He waved at the room around them with a finely shaped hand. "This is decorated like a bored hausfrau lost her mind with a sewing needle and a heart motif. I've never seen so much gingham and raffia in my life."

"It's supposed to be rustic," she said, not understanding why she was defending the bed and breakfast owner's taste in decor.

"Rustic," he repeated, considering carefully. "I wouldn't have called it that, no."

Mignon continued to glare at her visitor.

"I like your eyes, but it is an odd color," he said. "Do you suppose anyone's noticed that you wear contacts?"

"Lots of people wear contacts," she replied. "What are you doing here? I thought we agreed that—"

"I wouldn't come unless you needed a little extra support,"

he finished for her. "How about I wouldn't come unless you were about to blow it."

"This isn't about the usual stuff," she said. "You knew that when you agreed to help me, Nehemiah."

"Call me Dad, sweetie."

Mignon finally grinned. "You old fart. Did the B-and-B owner see you come in here?"

"Of course not. Did I tell you your locks here are made of cheesecake?"

"I'm aware of that already. And I didn't call you because I didn't want to listen to you whine about how I'm messing things up." Mignon stepped forward. "Buying the house wasn't part of the plan. Getting into the mansion so quickly wasn't part of the plan. But you have to admit that I needed to find some way to get into the house, and that was a golden opportunity. So was Saturday night, for that matter."

Nehemiah flipped another page in the diary. "It was a golden opportunity," he admitted. "With a little assistance."

Mignon stared at him. "Oh God, Nehemiah, did you have to open the sluice gates while it was raining?"

"More like I pried them apart. You wouldn't believe the size of the locks they put on those things."

"Nehemiah, people's homes were flooded."

"Posh. Land was flooded, my dear, and you got to search the house. No one was hurt. And if you've any guilt about that, you can sell another one of your paintings to pay them off."

She continued to stare at him, although she was seeing an image of herself, almost lost in the riotous water. Her adopted father didn't have the same kind of scruples that she did, except when it came to immediate family. He didn't know about the break-in, or the snake, and she was damned sure not going to let him know about the shove into the water. If he knew about any of that, he'd pull the plug on her so fast her head would spin.

Mignon sat in the chair where his jacket was hung. If people had been hurt by the rising water he would have told her, because she would have found out herself anyway. "And I suppose the electricity was your handiwork, as well. I would have paid out of my own pocket to do a great many things now."

"But darling," protested Nehemiah in his crisp, accentless voice. It was pure California, close to what one might hear on any news station. "That would be no fun at all. After all, one never knows what might happen in a situation like this. The killer could clam up and never admit anything. Is there another invitation on hand?"

"No, but there will be," she said. "You know why, and for God's sake no more messing with sluice gates. The sheriff had an idea that I was down there in my designer dress forcing open the gate with a crowbar in my little hands."

"My dear, you had to have a chance to search the mansion." His voice was serious. "Let's talk about what you're doing now."

Mignon sighed. "I knew you would do this. You want to pick every nuance apart and plan for every type of equation."

Putting his palms face up in the air, Nehemiah asked, "What? A man can't be prepared?"

"What do you think I'm doing wrong?"

"The sheriff, darling," Nehemiah began. "For one thing."

Mignon didn't say anything. She stared at her adopted father and thought about the first time she had ever seen him. At sixteen, Mignon had all but lived on the streets of Los Angeles, having hopscotched through the West in orphanages and foster homes. Prostitution hadn't claimed her yet, but it was knocking on her door. Her foster family didn't care if she lived in, but they cared if the monthly maintenance check arrived. So she spent time drawing pictures on Hollywood Boulevard. She did quick portraits on cheap sketch pads for fifteen dollars a head. The price went up for a pastel drawing. On slow days, sometimes she would reproduce a drawing of the Mona Lisa on the sidewalk, leaving a hat or a jar beside it for donations. The cops thought she was funny and cute and left her alone. The owner of the building she chose to draw in front of didn't care if she marked up the sidewalk with chalk.

One day Nehemiah Trent had walked by while she was reproducing the famous painting. When he stopped and deposited a five-dollar bill in her jar, Mignon had looked up and thanked him. Five dollars made a big difference in her day; it meant she would be inside. Spending the night outside in late November meant that she would be cold, because the winds had been blowing inward from the sea that day. He had asked her, "Can you paint, as well?"

Mignon had admitted that she could do many things in various media. She could draw, paint, sculpt, and carve wood. She had taught herself everything she could while she passed from foster home to foster home. Art had been a way of escaping, and changing media had been necessary sometimes because of material availability. The older man had requested to see her portfolio and she said she didn't have one. Then he asked if she would like a bed for the night, no strings attached. He was an art dealer and was always interested in new young artists, ones with talent such as hers.

Laughing, Mignon had refused. She wasn't stupid. She had thought the older man a lecher, and at best someone who would slip into bed with her at three in the morning to fondle her breasts. She had refused without a thought. But Nehemiah had kept coming back to her corner, viewing each of her pictures as she drew them. Eventually she had learned to trust him, and he had never let her down.

After a lawyer had finalized their legal relationship, Mignon had attended the best art schools in New York and Europe to develop her talent.

"The sheriff is just an amusement, Nehemiah," she lied,

unwilling to admit her attraction to the man. "An afternoon snack. And I get to keep an eye on him. He's very suspicious. It's in his nature."

Nehemiah regarded her with amusement. Sometimes he wished that Mignon was his real daughter. His real daughters wouldn't work with him in his chosen business, but Mignon was the next best thing, as close to family as could be. He loved her like any father would love his daughter, and they were just as close. He could tell she was lying and that was part of the problem. He had never felt so alive as he did now, attempting to expose a murderer by the most devious means possible. But he didn't care to see her rotting in a rustic jail in rural Louisiana because she'd trusted the wrong man. "Well, then, about this farmhouse. Do you think you'll rile someone up too soon, before you're ready?"

"Everything is a risk, Nehemiah," Mignon said, happy to repeat words that he had thrown at her time and again. "Everything. If I'm caught, only I will suffer. No one else. You don't have to worry about that."

"No one is worried that you'll expose us," Nehemiah protested. She knew it was true. "That's silly, darling. But your landlady, who, by the way, is quite talkative, mentioned a problem with a snake." His eyes narrowed. "A poisonous snake in your room. One that had no business being out of a swamp."

Mignon examined her fingernails with great interest. Finally, she said, "What am I supposed to say? Someone tried to scare me, Nehemiah. It means I'm getting close."

"Close to a murderer!" he thundered. "It's all well and good for Kate and Terri, who are well concealed. But you— you've become a great walking target for some mad idiot who's afraid of what you're going to dig up."

"It's already done. The sheriff is investigating. He might even find out what I can't possibly get from them. Like where their bodies are." She uttered the words before she had a chance to think about what she was saying.

Nehemiah closed the diary with a loud thump and pushed himself off the bed. "I don't want you to vanish like your mother, Mignon."

"I have the gun," she murmured. "I have the pepper spray. And I'll get some more ammo when I go to get another mini-mag."

"Another . . . ? Never mind," Nehemiah sighed. "I don't want to know. You must realize that you're in a great deal of danger, my dear. And I can't allow—"

"You have to, Nehemiah," she insisted. "You have to give me a chance to finish. Terri planted the egg full of blood and Eleanor was so horrified, she would have agreed to just about anything. We're so close."

He looked at her seriously. "I know the sheriff is a very handsome man, but you must remember he's one of them." Nehemiah shook a warning finger at his daughter. "And he cannot be completely trusted."

She pointed at the diary. "Did you read it all?"

"I skimmed through it, dear." Nehemiah appeared a little sad as he said it. "All these reminders of your mother and your father. It must be difficult. She wasn't like you, was she? She was, forgive me, a little naïve, but oh, how she loved you." He saw that his words had affected her and moved on to another subject. "You found it in the old house?"

"Under the floorboards in the bedroom," she said. She wasn't offended by what Nehemiah had said about her mother. She knew him much better than she had ever known her mother, and knew very well that he meant no offense. Backhanded compliments were his forte, and he used double-talk and witticisms endlessly. "With the gold necklace in the box."

"Yes, it has the most interesting initials on it."

"You know, I think Luc was going to go away with her," Mignon whispered. "That was probably what precipitated the whole event."

"And their bodies?"

"In the bayou? In the forest, in shallow graves? Well, probably deep graves." She lost herself in morbid thoughts about their resting places.

Nehemiah examined his daughter closely. She could never hide anything from him. She was good at concealing her emotions from other people, but he knew her giveaways, a cheek muscle twitching, fidgeting hands, darting eyes. "This is a little too trying for you," he stated definitively. "This is too much. I think you should leave, and leave now."

"No!" Mignon cried. She grasped Nehemiah's arm and turned him toward her. "No, it's not. It's hard. I'll admit that. We all knew it would be. But we're close. I'm close. I can find out what I want to know. I have to."

"You're going to blow it. You're going to endanger yourself."

"Then I'll be the one taking the consequences. No one else."

"But we're not talking about jail. We're talking about someone doing to you what they did to Luc and your mother."

They both digested that information with biting silence. Then Mignon said, "But the séance, Nehemiah. There was something so very odd about the séance."

"What?"

"I didn't . . . follow the plan. I didn't move the bell and the watch fob. The last thing I remember is the lights going out for the second time, and then there was a bitter cold."

Nehemiah stared at Mignon, his mouth a grim, set line.

"Terri said the bell rang and the fob moved and that I was moaning. But Nehemiah, it wasn't me. So if this is what Eleanor wants, then she might very well be getting it."

Chapter Eighteen

TUESDAY, SEPTEMBER 21

Pussy cat, pussy cat, where have you been?
I've been to London to look at the queen.
Pussy cat, pussy cat, what did you there?
I frightened a little mouse under the chair.

PUSSY CAT

THE WITCH-WOMAN LED ELEANOR into her neat little shack once more and smiled broadly. It had been a fine month for her. She thought maybe she had enough money from the wealthy woman to buy a new set of dentures; the old ones didn't fit so well any more. She had visited three times this month alone, and the woman was often generous with tips. After all, it was she who had told the wealthy woman to invite the young artist to the house to soothe the specter-ridden mansion.

Eleanor was dressed as she always was, elegant and sophisticated, with her hair neatly coiffed. She asked the witch-woman her questions, and the elderly woman used a wooden bowl with bits of mercury in it to divine the answers. When the witch-woman could say no more, Eleanor passed her two hundred-dollar bills and left.

After she drove off, Nehemiah Trent stepped from the tiny back room and put five hundred dollars on the table next to the two hundred already there. He smiled down at the witch-woman and said, "That's exactly what she needed to hear."

The witch-woman nodded, thinking of new dentures that fit snugly into her mouth and eating hot, buttered corn on the cob once more. Her mouth watered at the thought. "It is so. She already knows what she wishes to hear. A cleansing of the house of the spirits, just as your friend has said. I don't t'ink she will be back soon. A pity. She is a good client, no?"

Nehemiah's smile broadened. He reached into his jacket and pulled out another five hundred dollars. He placed the money on top of the other bills. "This should make up for any inconvenience."

"I have other clients." The witch-woman grinned and gave a careless shrug. "And once I knew Garlande Thibeaux. She would like to rest, dat one."

"What do you mean?" he asked curiously.

The witch-woman began to count the money on the little aluminum table before her. She didn't look at Nehemiah again. "I t'ink you know. Best you look out for de young miss. I hear stories about signs of evil a-coming. De blood on de moon last night, de crickets no want to sing at night, de Martinezes' cows giving of sour milk. Signs of badness to come. I t'ink maybe I go to Bossier City and spend a little time on de river boat."

Nehemiah gaped.

"I like de slots, no?"

PERHAPS TWO MILES away, John Henry came out of the sheriff's department rubbing his tired eyes. He had been going through files upon files, hoping to find material to use on Ruelle Fanchon. He had also spent a considerable amount of time looking through cold cases of unidentified bodies discovered within a hundred miles of La Valle. He'd expanded the limits of his search to the eighties and even the nineties, trying to account for bodies which might not have been discovered for years.

Many of the cold cases were just that, as cold as the ice in the Arctic. Sitting unsolved for years, sometimes decades, with no detective following up on them, no clues to pursue, and no leads that hadn't already been followed a dozen times, they had left John Henry with a big, fat zero. Surprisingly, unidentified bodies were not particularly common. At least, bodies that remained unidentified were not particularly common. They averaged one or two a year, and he'd eat his badge if some of those hadn't been solved throughout the years and the files simply were not updated.

Some of the cases could be discounted because of the victims' race. Corpses of black men or women could be dismissed outright. A few were far too young. There were two cases that he would have to look into, but both seemed unlikely. One was a woman who was the right age, but she had short blonde hair and the file specified that the color was natural. The other was a man approximately in his forties who had been found deep in the Kisatchie National Forest five years before, but he appeared to have been dead for only a few years. It hardly fit Mignon's theory that her mother and Luc had been murdered the day they supposedly left La Valle.

But John Henry's eyes were starting to cross from reading chicken scratches on old papers, and he needed a break. He suspected that if Luc and Garlande were truly murdered, then Ruelle Fanchon would know something about it. And his desire to make a deal to save his hide might be the only chance that John Henry and Mignon had to ever uncover the truth.

He drove to the café in LaValle and parked his Bronco in front. It was too early for the lunchtime crowd so it was only himself, Eloise the waitress, and two old men playing chess in a corner booth.

John Henry sat at the counter and ordered the strongest, blackest coffee they had on hand. Eloise hovered over him after she poured the coffee, and he pointedly ignored her. Finally she drifted to the opposite end of the counter and began cleaning up after a customer who had left.

He was halfway through his coffee when Jourdain and Geraud came in. John Henry stared at them in the mirror. The two men nodded at him and went to a booth. John Henry wondered why a man just appointed to the highest court in the state suddenly wanted to hang around in what might arguably be one of the smallest towns in rural Louisiana.

Because, John Henry answered himself silently, curling his hand around the coffee cup, *he's protecting Eleanor. He's always had a thing for Eleanor. Any fool can see that. Even his own wife sees it and barely tolerates it. Which is why he usually spends more of his time in Baton Rouge.* He looked to one side and saw Eloise whispering with the two men playing chess. Their gazes were locked onto Jourdain and Geraud as if Satan and his minion sat within their presence. One of the men made a motion across his chest, crossing himself for protection.

John Henry watched as Geraud realized what the three people on the other side of the café were doing. His face grew crimson with rage and John Henry wondered what would happen if he started having some of the bayous in the area dragged. And he thought that maybe he would start with the one nearest to the old Poteet place, near the farmhouse Mignon had purchased, an act that had caused much ruckus.

Geraud leapt to his feet and stalked out of the restaurant with a bitter curse directed at the two old men and the waitress. Jourdain sat quietly and waited for Eloise to serve him. Once she had done that, John Henry rose to his feet, taking his coffee with him, and went to stand beside the lawyer.

"Shouldn't you be in Baton Rouge making an acceptance speech, Your Honor?" he said.

Jourdain looked up at John Henry and smiled coldly. He took a sip of coffee. "The beginning of January, John Henry. You should know that. The governor likes to wrap up his packages nice and tidy."

John Henry put his coffee down on the table and took a deep breath. "I suppose that gives the press time to ferret out all the skeletons in the closet. Maybe it gives the governor time to have an . . . alternate selection." He stared into Jourdain's guarded eyes. "Time to dig up bodies . . . or maybe even drag a bayou. I guess a fella has to know where to look."

Jourdain's lips curled up into a facsimile of a smile, but there wasn't a bit of warmth there. He said, "Perhaps you should be careful about what you're saying, John Henry. It might be construed as a threat."

John Henry laughed. "Oh, no, sir. No threat there. Not a bit." He turned on his heel, tossed money on the counter, and left without saying another word. All the while Jourdain stared straight ahead into nothingness until his coffee grew quite icy.

MIGNON FOUND HERSELF humming again as she painted on the porch. Everything was almost exactly the same as it had been the day before. She was working progressively on her painting. The sun's early afternoon golden light shone down on her, illuminating dust motes in the air as they floated majestically about her body. And someone was driving down the dirt road again.

She had spent the previous evening with John Henry, suspicious sheriff tendencies and all. They hadn't talked much, but had eaten and made love. His seafood gumbo was, in fact, the best she'd ever tasted, and she had eaten too much. He kept wine at his modest home, and she had enjoyed looking around at his house. Everything was simple and there was a lot of wood. The house was neat and tidy inside and out, and looked like it belonged to a single man. While he wasn't looking, she had casually rifled through his closet and hadn't found a single piece of clothing that belonged to another woman. She hadn't found any files connected to the St. Michels or to herself lying around, either. But then she hadn't expected to, because John Henry was compulsively organized.

Mignon had tried to broach the subject of her mother and Luc, but he had deftly sidetracked her and led her down the path he wanted to travel. When she had woken up that morning, she had slept better than she had in months. No nightmares. No dreams about her mother. No insomnia half the night. It seemed that sleeping with John Henry was good for her, but she knew better. It couldn't last. He wouldn't forgive her for her lies, and she couldn't be one hundred percent sure that he was on the right side.

They had drunk coffee this morning sitting on his patio and made plans for meeting later in the week. Mignon had stopped at a little art shop in Natchitoches and retrieved a recently finished piece of her work from the trunk of her rental car. She had paid extra to have it framed immediately. They had it finished by lunch and she picked it up before coming out to the old house. It was a sunset done in oils, perfect for John Henry. It would brighten the earth tones and browns that dominated his home. She also picked up extra ammunition for her gun and another mini-mag to replace the one that had disappeared into the river.

Studying the work on her easel now, she frowned. When she tried to focus on it, it became an odd, amalgamated pattern of nothingness. Conversely, when she stepped back it seemed to be a dark figure in the depths of the forest. A blackened, menacing figure that threatened the viewer. Mignon frowned harder. It hadn't been her intent to paint such a grim scene.

The workmen hadn't been back to the house, but she had known that they wouldn't be. The road had been leveled again, however. She suspected Miner Poteet had dragged his tractor with the grader blade down the road for her, leveling out the potholes that the heavy storm had caused. Consequently, she had been able to drive right up to the door instead of parking on the road. Miner probably still felt guilty that he hadn't done more when she was a child. Mignon didn't know how to tell him that she never blamed him, that she never felt he was at fault for what had been done to her and her father. Miner had been railroaded by the St. Michels just like a hundred other people. This only gave her another reason to stop by his place later and see if there was anything she could do for him or his granddaughter.

Then the car came around the corner and Mignon saw that it didn't belong to John Henry or Miner Poteet.

It was Geraud St. Michel and Mignon immediately reached for her purse, then cursed under her breath. She had left it in the rental car. There was no way she could rush down to get it without running right into Geraud. He looked at her through the windshield and then got out. He was dressed casually in buff-colored Dockers, a white polo shirt, and brown loafers. Mignon hoped he had come with another invitation from Eleanor and that was all, but he glanced around him carefully, as if sizing up the situation.

Mignon set about cleaning her brushes, but not before she laid the piece of canvas cloth across her painting. She didn't want Geraud looking at her work.

He waited on the edge of the porch, just as John Henry had, but with a different appearance altogether. His silvery-blonde hair seemed all the lighter in the bright afternoon light, and his eyes appeared a deeper blue than when Mignon had seen him in the evening. He seemed to be in the prime of his life, a strong, tall man with not a spare ounce of flesh on him. She knew that he spent a lot of time on the golf course or the tennis courts, working off superfluous energy. She also knew that he was a womanizer like his father had been before him, and that he might try his charms on her. The vision of a photograph of a battered sixteen-year-old girl appeared in her mind. Mignon's detective had gotten her a copy of the photograph from a hospital record in New Orleans.

"Mignon." He greeted her only after thoroughly scanning the area. "You seem to be all alone."

"It's a good time to work right now, with the light so good."

"Ah, yes, your painting," he responded, not moving. "My mother tells me a few of your pieces have sold in the six figures range."

"A few have gone that high." Mignon had been fortunate that some of the most select galleries in New York City had chosen to feature her works early in her art career. But she knew that Geraud didn't give a damn about her art. He was here for a specific reason. Her only question was, *How far is he willing to go?*

His conversation with Jourdain came back to her: *I think something should be done.* But what? The St. Michels weren't habitual murderers, even on the level of thugs. They tended to bully people out of their parish with roundabout threats, such as the one from the old sheriff about "finding" illegal drugs on Miner Poteet's son. People left the area rather than buck the system that was the St. Michels.

But someone had murdered Luc and Garlande. Her unconscious mind reminded her of it on a nightly basis.

Geraud glanced around him again. "No workmen here today?"

"They're around," she lied.

"Huh. I wonder if you'd be interested in the advertising business, Mignon," he said. There was an expression on his face that she couldn't quite identify. She would have said that he was irritated about something, but as far as she knew nothing new had happened and she hadn't been needling him about his father.

Mignon thought about what he said. Nehemiah had suggested that the St. Michels might attempt that route. Bribery was first on the line. She couldn't afford to be sidetracked by this maneuver. "I don't do advertising." Her words were flat.

"My company would be willing to pay a substantial amount for your work to advertise our products. Your pieces would be influential in selling specific lines. In addition, it would make you a household name." Geraud wasn't going to give up easily. The unspoken portion of the offer would be that she would have to leave town and stay out of Louisiana.

"I'm flattered," she responded, trying to keep her tone neutral even though she was offended by his attempt to buy her off. "But I'm quite busy. I have a series to complete." She motioned at the covered painting in front of her. "I have plenty on my plate, and very soon I'm returning to New York City for a gallery showing."

"But you're coming back," he added, taking a step up onto the porch. Mignon tried not to flinch at the subtle change in his tone of voice. She realized that he was angry. He was hiding it fairly well, but underneath his calm facade he was seething with rage. "To this place, I mean. Why else would you be renovating this . . . dump?" Geraud looked around him slowly. "It hasn't changed a bit from when my father used to come here to fuck your mother."

Mignon's lips tightened. She would have swallowed, but it felt like something was choking her. There was a palette knife on the shelf of the easel. It was a thin, flexible thing, not really a knife at all, but it seemed to be all she had. She didn't look at it, but she rested her hand on the shelf just over it.

"So you've come back to drag all of that history into the present." Geraud took another step toward her. He was about five feet away from her. "And you said you weren't interested in all of that. I wonder if you know that the lock on my office was forced the other night, the night the tributary was flooded. Deliberately flooded. A person might think you were attempting to dig something up."

A cold chill ran down Mignon's back. She was more alone than ever. Doubt flooded her. *What was I thinking? That someone would wait until I ran and got my gun before coming to confess to the murder of my mother and threatening to kill me? Fool. Fool. Fool.* There was no one to rescue her. No one would know that Geraud St. Michel had come to do her in.

But there was something else to consider. If it were true, then Geraud must have killed his father and her mother when he was only fifteen years old. It was more than possible, but it seemed so unlikely. He had known about his father's mistress. He had known, and he hadn't cared. What reason did he have for murdering the two of them? "What is there to dig up, Geraud?" she asked carelessly.

A sly expression crossed his fine, angular features. "It's not that easy, Mignon. *Mignon.* What a pretty French name. Just like Garlande. A man wouldn't know you come from redneck white trash around the poorest part of Louisiana. You don't care that my business is suffering because of these malicious stories, and that your presence is causing my sister to have the worst kind of nightmares."

Mignon kept her mouth shut. There was nothing to say to him when he was like this.

Geraud took another step forward. He was now only about four feet away from her. His hands hung at his sides and they contracted into fists every ten seconds like clockwork. "For a long time I hated your mother. Oh God, I hated her. She disrupted our family. She almost destroyed my life. *My life.*"

Her hand closed around the palette knife, and she stepped back, bumping into the porch railing. To get away from him, she would have to turn her back to him and leap over it. In the time that would take, he would be on her. He was taller than she was and outweighed her by eighty pounds, but she ran regularly. If she could get on the ground, she would fly.

She didn't respond. Anything she said would be twisted against her anyway. He took another step forward and looked her up and down. Little worms of blue crawling up and down her body, leaving slimy trails. "I wonder what you'd be like. Would you be like her? My father loved to fuck her. He loved coming here. She had that same fiery hair and that same fiery spirit. Maybe that's what I need."

Mignon spun around and leapt. Her feet were in the air when there was a sudden yank on her hair as Geraud dug his strong fingers into her scalp. She stopped in midair and came back the way she'd come, falling heavily on Geraud as he pulled her back over the railing.

"Where do you think you're going?" he whispered into her ear, holding her tightly against him with one arm wrapped around her waist like a piece of steel. The other viciously jerked at her hair once more and dropped to her breast. He cupped it slightly, rubbing at the nipple with his thumb. "Someone might think you don't like me."

The palette knife was still in her hand. She plunged it backward into his thigh as hard as she could. Although it wasn't sharpened, the edge was very thin and cut effortlessly through his pants and the flesh of his upper leg. With an outraged yell, he let her go. She pushed him away from her and ran to her car, but someone else was waiting for her there.

Chapter Nineteen

Little Miss Muffet
Sat on a tuffet,
Eating some curds and whey.
Along came a spider,
And sat down beside her,
And frightened Miss Muffet away.

LITTLE MISS MUFFET

"THAT LITTLE BITCH TRIED to kill me!" Geraud cried.

Miner Poteet stood between Geraud and Mignon. He had approached silently through the woods, and the cultivated lands in their last growth cycle of the season. His arrival was timely, but Mignon knew that Geraud wouldn't consider the seventy-year-old man much of a threat. However, he was carrying a thick walking stick made out of some heavy wood, which he held ably in one arm, as though he were quite willing to use it.

Mignon had barreled down the porch steps as if she were on fire, and had almost run into the old farmer as he walked around the cars parked in front of the house. She had been so glad to see him that tears poured down her face.

Miner Poteet had taken one look at Mignon—crying, her lip bloody where she had bitten it when she had been yanked backward, her face flushed red, and her T-shirt torn on one shoulder—and stepped in front of her protectively.

Geraud had been busy yanking the palette knife out of his thigh. The blade had gone about an inch deep, and the wound was bleeding freely enough to create a stain the size of a pie plate on his pant leg. He held a blood-covered hand against the wound and limped after Mignon, pausing when he finally realized that Miner Poteet was standing in between him and his prey.

"It looked like you were trying to rape her," said Miner, without even a bit of sympathy. For one thing, Geraud was a whole lot bigger than Mignon. For another thing, she was running away from him. For a third thing, the older man had seen what Geraud had been doing to her before she stabbed him with the funny-looking knife. Miner smacked the cane against his other palm with a loud thump. "I know when a man might be mistaken about an event."

Geraud began to snarl, "I'm not mistaken about—"

Miner interrupted him. "He might have had a little accident which caused him to be cut, just like another man might have been mistaken about what looked like attempted rape." His voice was cool and collected as he suggested a course of action for both of them. "That's what happens ofttimes. A man is simply . . . mistaken."

Mignon had her car door open and her hand on the butt of her Beretta. One false move and Geraud was going to hell where he belonged. She wasn't sure if she could stop the shaking in her hand long enough to plug the bastard, but it wouldn't be for lack of trying.

A variety of emotions flashed across Geraud's face, from anger to surprise to understanding. Mignon could see it plainly. It had taken him a moment to comprehend the combined threat and bargain Miner offered. If he didn't cry assault, she wouldn't cry rape. Miner Poteet didn't know it, but Mignon couldn't afford to cry attempted rape on Geraud, not if she wanted to go back to the mansion to see what else she could find out.

Miner tossed Geraud a red handkerchief he'd pulled out of his pocket. Geraud caught it and pressed it to the wound. Miner said, "Maybe you oughts get to Natchitoches to the clinic. A few stitches will take care of that. A man should be careful when he's . . . walking through the woods and trips on a deadfall."

"I agree," Geraud said after a pause. He limped to his Land Rover, got in, and shot Mignon one last sullen look before driving off.

Mignon wiped the blood away from her mouth with the back of one hand and sat down in the front seat of her car.

Miner watched the road where the Land Rover disappeared into the woods. He said, "Don't suppose I'll see that handkerchief again."

Her knees were shaking so hard they knocked together as she sat there and stared at Miner. "Thank you," she whispered. "I would have killed him. I would have gotten this gun"—she placed the Beretta on her lap—"and I would have shot him dead." She was horrified with herself. Despite all of her planning, all of the scenarios she'd imagined, she had never thought that this might be the conclusion, and it would have been the worst one possible. She would have killed him and then she would have never known who had killed her mother.

"*Mais non*," protested Miner. He shuffled over and patted her awkwardly on her shoulder. "He is not worth the trouble, that one. He is a selfish one. He philanders on his wife, and visits young women in the area. Nothing good has ever come of that one, and shooting him would only bring a touch of evil upon you." He frowned. "You must not come to this place alone, daughter. There are too many who don't want to see you here."

"Daughter?" she repeated. "I wish that could have been. Did I tell you about my adopted father?"

"No." Miner patted her shoulder again. "Tell me about this man."

"He saved my life, too."

Miner moved about restlessly. He opened and closed his mouth several times as if he wanted to say something, but finally he closed it and continued to pat her shoulder. It was a long time before Mignon could stand again, and she put the gun back into her purse as if she were watching herself from afar. It was surreal.

Miner said, "I didn't save your life, Mignon. You would have reached your little gun there, and you would have shot him as dead as I shoot dead the crow who plucks at my corn. I only prevented you from making a mistake." He looked at her gravely. "You do not want the blood on your hands, little Mignon. It's a terrible burden."

Mignon stared at him with large, luminous eyes. "You have that burden?" *What is he trying to tell me? That he killed my mother and Luc St. Michel?*

Clearly Miner could read the thoughts running rampant across her face. He shook his head. "No, *chère*. I did not do that fearsome thing. But there is something else I should tell you."

She waited and he went on. "There was that day the sheriff came and told us what would happen. What would happen to you and your father, and what would happen to me and my kin if I interfered. That day, so long ago, that your mother left with her lover. We found you earlier, hours earlier, my wife and I, as you walked up the little road to our home. Covered with blood and not speaking a word. And in one of your tiny little hands you held this." One hand retrieved something from a large pocket. As he held it out, it glittered in the sun, and Mignon took it without thinking.

In the palm of her hand was a delicate bracelet. It was made of eighteen-carat gold and gleamed as if it had been purchased from some expensive department store that very day. However, anyone could see that this was no mass-produced object, but a finely wrought, exquisite piece of jewelry. Mignon turned over the little pendant that was attached to the gossamer chain. It was an oval engraved with a large *E*. She shivered again. There was still dried blood on the bracelet. Little blackened flakes of blood, preserved by time and by Miner Poteet, floated off as she turned the bracelet in her hand. The clasp was broken as if it had been wrested from its owner's wrist.

"We were afraid, you see," Miner whispered, his old voice hoarse with the pain of remembering. "And soon I will go to God, confessing to Him for my sins, and the one I can never forgive myself for. When we didn't try to help you as we should have."

The bracelet lay in her hand like a tiny golden snake. Mignon wanted to fling it away before it could bite deeply into her flesh, wounding her forever. Her eyes went to Miner's. "Are you saying I was there? I saw it all?"

"You weren't wounded, but you were covered with blood," Miner murmured. "I can see it in my mind. Such a tiny little petite, your white pinafore almost completely red. We thought an animal had got at you. My wife, she bathed you, dressed you in the clothes of one of our daughters, while I called for Ruff. He had been in Natchitoches drinking, as usual. I went to the old store at the crossroads and called five taverns before I found him. He came to pick you up, and found some of his belongings packed and waiting on the porch of the old farmhouse. The judge was waiting there. And the old sheriff visited me, then he go to Ruff, too. . . .

"I put that bracelet away in a box and hid it under the bed for twenty-five years because I was afraid of what it meant. And I knew that something dreadful had happened. Days later

I went to the old house and found that it had been cleaned from the ceilings to the floors. Some of the walls had been painted. It was as if you and your family had never been there." Miner turned away. "I don't know what they did with their bodies, Mignon. I think you won't be able to find them. But at least you know, she's not out there, living somewhere without you. She wouldn't have left you, no."

"I know that. I knew it almost as soon as I saw the old house," she said. "But you don't know who?"

His eyes went involuntarily to the bracelet held in her hand. "You know who, *chère*. You know it better than I."

Her gaze dropped to the bracelet, as well. The *E* etched into the gold seemed as big as life, an elegant shape that denoted the wealth that had purchased it. Like the saint's medal in her mother's rusted keepsake box, this wasn't a piece of dross. The air was humid and still as she whispered the name that they both knew so well. "Eleanor." The sound was like the wings of a small bird escaping through the forest from a vicious predator.

After a while, she muttered, "Let me drive you home, Miner. I'm going back to Natchitoches. I won't stay here alone anymore." She paused. "You wrote that letter to me, didn't you, Miner? It had to be you."

Miner nodded hesitantly. "My granddaughter, she write for me. Her mother saw the article in the Alexandria papers. There wasn't a picture of you, but your last name was mentioned there. She knew and she sent the article to me. I kept it for weeks before I got Mary Catherine to write some words to you. That girl, she said your address was available on the computer . . . the Internet, she calls it." He paused and chewed on his lip. "I didn't know what to say to you, daughter. I felt shame at keeping this secret, at your expense." He passed a hand over his face as if to wipe away an errant tear that leaked from his eye. Then he abruptly changed the subject. "What you do with that?" he gestured to the piece of jewelry in her hand.

"I don't know, but I don't blame you, Miner. You didn't have a choice, any more than I did."

The old man stared at her for a long time. "Perhaps not. But I believe we all make choices we have to live with. Someone comes here at night. Last night, I run them off with the shotgun. They were messing with the property, bringing a truck down to the house. I hear it rumbling off as they leave. They make a bad choice, too. I got plenty of shells for my old Winchester."

Hours later, John Henry was tipping Mignon's chin up to the light inside his house. "How did you get that fat lip?"

"I bit it, John Henry," she answered. It wasn't exactly a lie, but it certainly wasn't the complete truth, either. She had stopped by to tell him that she wanted to see him later in the week, on Wednesday night if he were free. He had noticed immediately that her lip was slightly swollen.

"What happened?"

Mignon couldn't tell him. Not him. There would be too much risk. He was already investigating her claims, walking on "her side of the fence," as he had put it, and pursuing Geraud would be dangerous for him as well as for her. There would be nothing to prevent Geraud from coming after her again. "I tripped and bit my lip. It was stupid. The workmen tore up the floor in the house. Lots to trip over."

John Henry let go of her chin. He had known from the moment they'd met that she was a stubborn woman. Perhaps she would share it with him later. "What about tonight?"

"I'm claimed by someone else," she said softly. "Jealous?"

"Depends on who it is," he answered.

"Well, Eleanor's invited me to her country club." Mignon

smiled at him. He hesitated because it was a brittle smile, and he thought for a moment that it was a clever facade to keep him out.

"You think she murdered your mother years ago, and yet you want to go to dinner with her?" John Henry couldn't quite keep the amazement and awe out of his voice.

"Maybe she'll confess to me."

"Not likely."

"She's showing me off at her country club, her pet artist who just happens to be the daughter of the woman her husband 'supposedly' ran off with." Mignon shrugged lightly. "I'm going to pick her brains. Besides, I won't be alone with her."

John Henry put on his sheriff's face again. "Don't be," he said and kissed her gently.

Then he pulled back and looked at her solemnly. "If you were doing something illegal, Mignon, you know what I would do, don't you?"

Mignon studied him. Her face was as serious as his. A warning was being issued and she suddenly wondered if he knew more than he was letting on. "I know what you would do, John Henry. I know it's the only thing you could do."

"You understand that?"

She kissed him back, and it was a long time before she pulled away to murmur, "I understand, John Henry. I wouldn't expect less of you."

An hour before dinner a limousine picked up Mignon at the bed and breakfast. The driver held the door for her, and when she got in, she came face to face with Jourdain Gastineau. Mignon was momentarily startled. For the briefest of seconds she thought it was Geraud, even though the two men didn't look anything alike.

Settling into the comfortable seat, she eyed him warily. Jourdain was dressed in black as she was. They were both immaculate, sleek, and soignée. She regained her composure immediately and asked about his wife.

"Another function," he explained. "A historical society charitable event."

Mignon nodded and made herself a bit more at ease. Undoubtedly Alexandrine preferred to avoid events where her husband's beloved Eleanor was going to be.

Jourdain stuck his chin out. "John Henry came to chat with me last week."

Mignon didn't reply because no reply was necessary. So Jourdain went on. "He seems to think that something suspicious happened to your mother and to Luc St. Michel."

"May I have a drink?" she asked politely. "Cognac? Brandy?"

Jourdain turned to the little bar inside the back of the limo and poured her a drink. She sipped it and said, "And what does that have to do with me?"

"You said you weren't interested in raking up the past." His eyes were full of ice.

"Sometimes the past has a way of coming back to haunt us," she replied. "In a way we can't do anything about."

Jourdain was silent.

Mignon continued, "I heard on the radio about your nomination, Mr. Gastineau. Or should I be calling you 'Your Honor?' "

"Not yet."

The bracelet on her wrist slid down as she raised the glass to her lips. It glittered in the reflection of the lights from passing vehicles. His eyes caught it and narrowed to slits. "That looks very familiar."

Mignon watched his face. "Oh, do you like it?"

"It's very . . . exquisite, isn't it?"

It was, and the jeweler who had been paid an extra hundred dollars to repair it this afternoon had thought so, as well. He'd held it in his hands like a priceless gem, and said, "This is a Nairne. He's an exclusive jeweler from New Orleans. A man who's been at the top of his form for over three decades. It's even signed here." He pointed out the tiny initials on the back of the pendant and gushed over the masterful yet delicate work. He hadn't been able to do the first-rate job that he swore the quality of the piece required, but it would stay on her wrist provided someone didn't yank it off.

And Mignon needed to wear it that evening; she wanted several people who would be there to see it, people who might have seen it before.

At the country club Mignon admired the old Southern decor. It was as if they had stepped into a plantation from a hundred years before. Willow trees lined the drive, dripping with Spanish moss. Old gaslights in black lanterns were placed strategically at each corner. Inside was leaded crystal and velvet walls, and people mingled happily in groups. Eleanor emerged from a crowd and immediately escorted her around, introducing her as a famous artist from New York. A few people were crass enough to mention her Louisiana roots in a mildly insulting manner, but Mignon handled those with all the ease she had learned in the Big Apple.

By the time they sat down to dinner, Mignon had been introduced to over a hundred people and she knew she could never remember all their names in a hundred years. But she didn't care about most of them. At their table were Eleanor, Eugenie, and her companion David, with his sullen face and uncommunicative manner. Eugenie was off in a world of her own making, and Mignon suspected that she had been heavily medicated this evening. Jourdain sat on one side of Mignon, and a couple from Shreveport sat across from her. She repeated their names twice, but all Mignon could remember was

Mary and Joseph something. They were friends of Eleanor's, and Mary gushed over Mignon so much that Mignon was afraid she'd have to go to the ladies' room to wring the excess moisture out of her dress.

No one mentioned why Geraud and his wife weren't present. Mignon was pleased that his name didn't come up and didn't bring it up herself. She saw Gabriel once in the distance, and was pleased that he didn't come over and ogle her, as was his habit.

The dinner conversation was mundane. Eleanor invited Mignon to the mansion on Saturday night. "It's a full moon, darling," she said. "We should have a most fascinating response."

"I suppose you'll want to tie me up again," Mignon said sarcastically.

Eleanor laughed. "No, nothing like that. Madam Jones has informed me that a supernatural cleansing is the best route to take in order to scour the influence of evil spirits from the house."

Mary from Shreveport was aghast. "Eleanor, surely you don't believe in these psychics? They're all fakes." Mignon's eyebrow went up as she listened earnestly.

Jourdain chuckled, knowing that Eleanor's response would be perennial and relentless.

"My dear, you haven't seen what I've seen." Eleanor's voice was full of pride and authority. "Madam Jones comes with the highest references from acquaintances in New York. She's been a participant in discernments all over the United States and abroad. If a cleansing is what is required then it cannot hurt to follow through with it."

"But I merely meant—"

Mignon interrupted. "I didn't believe either, but there have been some odd things happening at the mansion."

Eugenie added, "If you could see what happens there, you

might believe, too." Her tone was benign and matter-of-fact. "Ghosts walk the house of St. Michel and it shall be cleansed of its darkness."

The couple from Shreveport was not convinced. Joseph said, "Eleanor, I'm sure you'll do whatever is necessary to reclaim your house. No ghost would dare oppose you."

There was a round of laughter.

Mignon lifted her glass of Chardonnay to her lips in a carefully calculated movement. The bracelet slid back as far as it would go on her wrist, glittering in the muted light of the chandelier.

There was a gasp, but she didn't see whose lips it came from. Eugenie got up suddenly and excused herself. David appeared irritated, finished his glass of wine with a restrained gulp, and followed her without a word.

Eleanor gave a slight frown, but no one said anything.

Jourdain watched the bracelet move sinuously as Mignon turned her wrist ever so slightly. It reflected the light and all eyes were on its glinting brightness as it slid delicately down her arm. She couldn't help the tiny smile that curved over her lips.

Chapter Twenty

> There was a man in our town,
> And he was wondrous wise;
> He jumped into a bramble bush
> And scratched out both his eyes.
>
> THERE WAS A MAN IN OUR TOWN

ON WEDNESDAY MIGNON SPENT some of the day with the workmen at the house. Horace Seay was particularly morose, and didn't speak much. He didn't ask about the rusted metal box, and he didn't speak about anything at all, except the occasional monosyllabic grunt directed at his employees. He and the workmen were finishing up removing the wood flooring in the bedroom, and all three men had seen what looked like blackened stains from years past soaked into the sides and bottoms of the boards. Knowing what the stains must be, Horace crossed himself and motioned for the others to continue on with their work.

Even Mignon picked up one of the discarded planks in her hands and examined the sides. She was wondering if tests could be done on the boards, and how she could ask John Henry about them without being as obvious as the sun suddenly falling from the sky. But in the end she put the board back in the pile with the others and returned to her painting on the porch.

The dark image had become more apparent on the canvas and she was disturbed by the way it was coming along.

When the three men left for lunch so did she, and none of them ever saw the figure in the woods who watched them so carefully.

ON WEDNESDAY EVENING Mignon gave her framed painting to John Henry and he hung it in his living room while she watched. He marveled at what she had done, and said, "No one ever gave me something like this." She noticed that he had purchased her book of paintings, but assumed that she wasn't supposed to know, because the book was on his bedroom dresser, mostly hidden under a book by Stephen King.

As they stood in his plain little living room looking at the painting, she said, "If you don't like it, you can take it down and I won't be offended."

John Henry smiled at her. "I do like it. I'm not one to put something on my walls if I don't."

"I should have known that. Some people say they like your work, then turn around and tear you up in a review on the arts page in the *Times*." Mignon's smile was a bit forced. "I don't think you would understand that. I would much rather hear 'I think that sucks,' than have someone lie to me about it. After all, what difference does it make to me? I'm not going back and change it for them."

One large hand brushed a strand of hair off her forehead, gentle strong fingers skimming across soft flesh. "It doesn't sound like a very nice business." The sound of his voice was a rough murmur. He wondered how he could have been so captivated by a woman in such a short time. She didn't back down from an argument. She was committed to herself and to what she believed in. He had never seen anyone like her before, and he doubted he would again.

"It can be. There are some very not nice people there."

"As there are in mine."

A sense of sadness almost overwhelmed Mignon. She knew this brief relationship would come to a close very fast. If John Henry hadn't heard about the "cleansing" ceremony on Saturday, then it was only a matter of time before someone spilled the beans. Eleanor had mentioned what it involved, and even Mignon thought it sounded distinctly fishy. John Henry would find it decidedly so, as it was an elemental part of him to be logically inquisitive.

A note from Eleanor had been hand-delivered by her chauffeur, pleading that Mignon attend the cleansing ceremony because the spirits seemed so manifestly drawn to her, and Mignon was perversely pleased that Eleanor was so certain about the outcome.

As if I would miss that, Mignon had thought to herself after reading the elegant script on creamy parchment with a large monogrammed *E* on top. She had immediately fixated on that *E* because it was the same style of letter used on the bracelet that she was still wearing around her wrist. *Isn't that coincidental?*

"So John Henry, tell me, how long can you do a Luminol test on blood?"

John Henry had been studying his latest acquisition on the wall; his eyes narrowed and he turned to stare at her. "I never know exactly what you're going to say next, do I?"

"I mean how long can blood be lying around before you can't do such a test?"

"*Lying around?* I've seen a case where the test was performed on a room in which a murder occurred—a violent murder, mind you—about five years after the fact." He continued to study her face much the way he had studied the painting. Her heart began to beat a little faster, as if he could read her mind. He continued, "I've heard of longer in some cases. Blood begins to degrade immediately because it's organic. When the chemicals in blood come in contact with other things, such as a wall or a mattress, it causes a reaction. I forget the exact chemical compounds. But the gist of it is that this reaction sticks around for a long, long time, and even if the blood is washed away, the pattern is still visible under a certain kind of light."

Mignon nodded. "So you don't know if a positive result would occur in a place where a murder took place, say, a decade before."

"You're about as subtle as a sledgehammer," he said. "I think you'd do somewhat better if you told me what you're thinking about. Maybe a specific place you have in mind."

"John Henry, I was simply trying to ask you a question about your work. I don't know anything about police work." Mignon smiled innocently. *Except for when I was arrested that one time. And except for everything that Nehemiah has told me about police procedure. But that certainly didn't include a lesson in forensic chemistry. And it's not like I can go up to the police department and ask point-blank.*

"I should grab you and kiss you instead," he complained. "But I have to go back to the office and keep going over some of those damn files. You know, if it's not one thing it's something else. Blood *lying* around." He snorted under his breath.

"Something else happen?" Mignon asked.

"Some newspaper reporters digging around about Ruelle Fanchon," he said.

"He won't be happy in prison, will he?" she asked, turning away to study her painting on the wall.

"He'll be segregated from the regular prison population because he was a sheriff." John Henry analyzed the line of her back. It was a wondrous back, sleek and long, something for a man to run his fingers along underneath the creamy silk shirt she was wearing. "You're not mad because I didn't tell you about him before, are you?"

"Why? He didn't have anything to do with me," she lied. She was glad that the former sheriff was going away. If not for what he had done to her, then for all the other people in St. Germaine Parish that he had terrorized for years. For people like Miner Poteet, whose only crime was compassion toward his neighbors. For people like her father, who had only been married to a straying woman, and for people like herself, who had been five years old and forced into a living hell for something she had no control over. "So what the reporter is trying to say is that the whole department is corrupt and still is? That must aggravate the hell out of you."

There was silence behind her. She could feel his eyes burning into her back. He said, "That's what the reporter is trying to dig up. Proof of collusion, proof of corruption. If they talked to you, they would have your eyewitness testimony, wouldn't they? You were there when the sheriff and the judge told your father that he had to leave or else. That was a little *collusion*, wasn't it?"

"I was there, but I didn't hear everything," she said. "And I have no intention of talking to any reporters." But a cold chill ran through her blood. She knew that Ruelle had met with Jourdain recently because he wanted protection in exchange for keeping his mouth shut. John Henry wasn't going to get anything out of the old sheriff, but she had to admire him for trying.

His hands wrapped around her shoulders, gently squeezing, fingers kneading the flesh under her shirt. His throaty voice whispered in her ear, "No, you wouldn't, would you?"

She suppressed a laugh. "Now why would you say that, John Henry?"

"Just a feeling." He nudged the seashell shape of her ear

with his lips, and murmured, "I'm trying to break away to talk to him this week. As soon as I can."

Mignon ended up spending the night there, and she wasn't completely unhappy about the way things turned out. Quite the contrary.

JOHN HENRY LEFT the house before Mignon woke up, and drove to the old farmhouse. He knew perfectly well why she had been asking questions about old blood and Luminol. She would have been better off not asking, or at least not asking him. There was only one place where old blood could lie around for years, and he knew exactly where that was.

The early morning light shone down strong and bright as John Henry drove the Bronco up to the farmhouse. He stayed in the vehicle for a moment and contemplated the situation. Had a murder taken place here twenty-five years ago that the former sheriff covered up? Wasn't that exactly what Mignon was hinting at? And if it was not Fanchon, who else would've been dirty enough to do that?

John Henry had known Ruelle Fanchon for about two years before the older man had retired from the sheriff's department. He had headed up the committee that had hired John Henry. But John Henry knew when to keep his mouth shut, and he'd been partnered with a man who knew how to walk a fine line between corruption and piety, so he'd survived Fanchon's reign. By that point in time Fanchon had grown cautious. The sheriff's department was a place that people watched with an eagle eye. The world had changed and video cameras were rampant. Too many people were too anxious to report that a sheriff had shaken them down for a bribe when they had been driving through the parish. Too many people didn't feel the fear they had a quarter century before that. So the old sheriff had mellowed, and although John Henry had a strong suspicion that he was crooked, he hadn't witnessed anything personally.

When finally he stepped out of his car, he took his time looking around. Before long he came across the discarded piles of wood planks and he found the stains Mignon had inadvertently told him about. He took out his pocketknife and shaved away some of the once-sodden wood. When he was done, he was fairly certain that there had been a tremendous pool of blood on the flooring piled before him. He went inside and saw that the tainted wood had come from the main bedroom.

John Henry sighed and knew that he was going to have to speak with Ruelle Fanchon much sooner than he had planned. He took some of the wood and put it in plastic evidence bags that he kept in the back of the Bronco. He marked their location in black marker and initialed the bags, wishing that Mignon had simply told him that she thought there was once a pool of blood in the old house. In the back of his mind he admitted that the house had been empty for almost three decades, and men jacked deer through here all the time. A hunter, wary of the law and Miner Poteet, might drag his kill inside to gut it. He was going to have to talk to a criminal forensics guy he knew in Shreveport to find out about the duration of the blood chemical that activated Luminol, but first he was going to have the board tested to see if it was, in fact, stained with human blood. Then he was going to have to drive down to Baton Rouge to speak to a cantankerous old man who had bullied his way around the parish as sheriff for far too long.

Before any of that, he was going to have to convince Mignon to stop renovating the house until he could find out if he needed a criminal forensics unit to go over it.

Mignon took the news with a grain of salt. She was a little miffed that he had gone behind her back, but she accepted it and promised to keep the interior as it was.

LATE THURSDAY AFTERNOON John Henry drove though a middle-class section of Baton Rouge. The houses dated from World War II, situated on avenues lined with dogwood. It was a pleasant neighborhood; people kept their yards trimmed, and jasmine and ivy curled protectively around the verandas. He was surprised at the neighborhood and stopped to ask himself why.

John Henry had always thought of Ruelle Fanchon as a white trash sort of man. While he'd been a deputy he could do his job, count on most of the others to do theirs in a professional manner, and forget that the sheriff was sometimes a shady individual with a shaky past. But he'd always known it in the back of his mind. It had been the cost of doing business in a place near where his ex-wife and daughter lived. He'd been willing to pay it then, but he wasn't so sure about it now. This place didn't fit in with his mental image of Fanchon. It didn't work.

A minute later he parked his car in Ruelle's driveway, got out, and rang the doorbell. John Henry had looked over the paperwork dealing with Fanchon's arrest and concluded that if the man hadn't been a law enforcement official of some standing for decades, he'd be rotting in the local jail awaiting his trial instead of living in the comfort of his middle-class home. Mignon had been correct about him having friends in high places. Fanchon's lawyer was a well-known criminal defense specialist who happened to belong to Jourdain's exclusive club in Baton Rouge.

A young woman barely out of her teens opened the door and John Henry stared at her. She was blonde haired and blue eyed and appeared a little dazed. He knew very well that Ruelle didn't have any children and suspected this young lady was just another in a long line of women who danced through his home. Perhaps, he judged by her dilated pupils and her stuporous demeanor, she was a fan of the former sheriff because of the drugs he could get for her.

Dangerous, John Henry thought. Ruelle had only been out of jail for a month and already a stoned woman was answering his door. Her eyes dipped toward John Henry's badge and she shrugged. "Ruelle's out back," she said, with a heavy Louisianian accent. "On the porch with a beer."

John Henry took that to mean he could go on through, and he did just that. As he let himself onto the enclosed back porch, he took a moment to study the older man. Ruelle was just as tall, just as broad as he was, but with gray hair and faded blue eyes. John Henry thought Ruelle would have suffered in jail, enduring a lack of sleep because of the close proximity of men who would cheerfully thrust a shiv between the old sheriff's ribs in exchange for a carton of Marlboros. He might have thought that the stress of an upcoming trial would have put circles under Ruelle's eyes, but oddly enough, Ruelle looked well rested. In fact, he looked like a strong and vital sixty-year-old man with easily another decade or two in him.

Ruelle grinned broadly at John Henry. Under his congenial facade was the real man, the one who took kickbacks from local businesses, the one who set up speed traps in the most likely spots, the one who let those same offenders off for a gratuity to the local policeman's benevolent fund, and the one who had worked as an enforcer for some of the most powerful families in the area. "Well, well, well," he said in his smooth Louisianian accent. "I never thought I'd see one of my own men come to visit. I'm like a pariah of late. No one wants to take me to the ball no more."

"You look good, Ruelle," said John Henry. His tone was neutral. He had never liked the man; he hadn't been surprised to hear of his arrest, nor was he particularly amazed that the old boy had possibly been involved in a cover-up that involved the richest family in the parish. There had been a multitude of rumors that Luc St. Michel had used Fanchon to "cure" the labor problems at his paper mills—violent confrontations that resulted in broken bones and men who refused to say who had burst their skulls open. But those things had happened well before John Henry's time, and he had never given them credence until much later.

"And you look like you still the sheriff, boy," replied Ruelle amicably. "I never did like that boy who run up against you. He would have shot the first man he arrested, and then where would the parish be?"

John Henry's eyebrows went up. The man who ran against him had been a friend of Ruelle's. He'd even had Ruelle's endorsement, for all the good that did him. Too many people had too many reasons to hate Ruelle Fanchon. "I came to have a talk with you, Ruelle."

"Maybe you tell me some of what's a-going on up there in St. Germaine," suggested Ruelle. "I ain't heard tell of the old place for a year. I don't hear much of late. Don't understand why those people don't call me no more." He shrugged his big shoulders as if he couldn't understand why he was so unpopular lately, and John Henry felt a surge of anger.

Keeping a neutral expression on his face, John Henry gave a quick account of recent happenings in the parish. He told Ruelle about some of the scandals, like when the mayor of LaValle was caught with a transvestite on one of the more isolated highways. Then he mentioned that a hometown girl who had made it good as an artist had returned to LaValle.

"Oh, yeah?" asked Ruelle. "Do I know the gal?"

"Her name is Mignon Thibeaux."

Ruelle stared at John Henry while he took in the information. It was apparent by the furrowing of his brows that he knew exactly why John Henry had come to see him now. "I remember the Thibeauxs," he said. "That gal's mother done run off with one of them St. Michels."

It was easy for John Henry to be silent and wait, but Ruelle was no fool. He'd been caught red-handed with drugs while returning from a fishing trip in the Gulf—the Coast Guard had gotten him fair and square and he wasn't about to wiggle off that hook—but he wasn't about to admit that he was involved in something much more serious, for which the punishment would be much more severe.

"I got some of the old boards out of the Poteet farmhouse," John Henry said. "I took 'em up to the forensics lab in Shreveport. You wouldn't believe how much money they got going into that place these days, Ruelle. They got equipment there I couldn't even begin to tell you the name of, much less how to spell it. They can do things with a drop of blood smaller than the end of my pinkie. Tell you when it was put there. Even who it came from, down to the Social Security number. Can you imagine that?" He hesitated to let this soak into the other man's brain. "I got a team of investigators out to the old place today," he lied boldly. Actually, he wouldn't be able to do that until the board tested positive for human blood, but Ruelle wasn't going to know that. Then John Henry laid it on the line. "I think you know what happened out there. Maybe you want to roll over on someone before they roll over on you."

Ruelle sat motionless in his chair for a moment. Then he took a drink of his beer and finally tipped the can toward John Henry. "You want a brew, John Henry. Leétice, girl, go get this boy a beer!" he boomed toward the door, then turned back to John Henry. "That girl, she ain't good for much else. Cooks pretty good, though. Do you care to eat a bit?"

"I don't want anything." John Henry fought to keep his voice neutral.

Behind the small talk, Ruelle was busy calculating possibilities. Who would roll over on him? Who would break two long decades of silence? Who could do the most damage? At last he said, "You recording this, John Henry?"

John Henry shook his head. "Nothing to record, am I right, Ruelle? Maybe I just came up to ask an old law enforcement man like yourself about a crime committed back when you were the sheriff. If anyone knows about it, you would."

Ruelle wasn't the sort of man to be scared by ambiguous statements. He knew that John Henry was on a fishing trip. "I think my memory's kind of poor for that far back in time. Long time, that. What, twenty, twenty-five years? I don't even recollect what woman I was married to, much less what all them up at the St. Michel place was doing."

"I think your memory might get better, if I was to offer a deal," John Henry said.

Ruelle locked his faded blue eyes on John Henry's, gauging his sincerity. He stared at him for the longest time and then he laughed. He threw his head back and laughed as if it were the funniest thing he'd ever heard in his entire life. After some time he put his beer down and wiped a tear from his eye. "Damn, I ain't laughed so much since Mrs. Regret took up her shotgun and threatened to pepper Tom Siddel for walking on her flower beds."

"Pretty quick this deal is going to go away, and never come back," threatened John Henry. Inside he was deflated. Mignon had been exactly on target. This man had some sort of protection and he wasn't about to turn his back on people who could make things a lot worse for him than John Henry could.

Deep inside Ruelle was the heart of a sadistic criminal, somewhat smarter than most, but a criminal all the same. If he had been caught with his hands in the cookie jar, he would have pulled out a few more serious crimes to which he had been witness and bartered for his own well-being. If he wasn't bartering about Luc's and Garlande's disappearances with John Henry, it was because he had already bartered with someone else. Someone like Eleanor St. Michel.

And that meant something else. If it weren't worth protecting him, then why bother? Something *had* happened twenty-five years ago. And if John Henry couldn't break Ruelle this way, he'd find some other way to do it.

Ruelle finally shrugged. "You can find your way out, John Henry. Come back some time and make me laugh some more. But best you be quick. I aim to up and leave once they acquit me. Think I'll move to a beach somewheres." He smiled knowingly, making it clear to John Henry that he didn't mean an American beach, but a beach in a country that didn't have an extradition treaty with the USA.

"Where are Luc and Garlande?" John Henry demanded.

"John Henry," advised Ruelle. "You should go back to St. Germaine and keep to arresting folks for *speeding*."

Try as he might, John Henry couldn't get anything out of Ruelle Fanchon, just a cold, arrogant smile that spoke volumes about what John Henry didn't know.

MIGNON WORKED AS hard as she could on her latest painting and finally finished it late Friday afternoon, just as Horace Seay and his crew were leaving the old farmhouse. They had kept to the outside, and Horace was happy to be able to tell Mignon that they were done with the siding. They would come back when Mignon had been given the all-clear to start on the wiring inside the house, and when that was done they would finish work on the walls and the floors. Finally, new appliances would be installed, and the house would be completed for the time being. Just as small, just as desolate, just as haunted as ever, but completed.

And Horace wasn't going to spend a minute there after

dark. Not after what had happened the night he'd come out to plug himself a deer. He had ignored his wife's dire warnings, and had gotten out his favorite Remington rifle to satisfy his taste for venison. After all, he'd seen the spoor out here, fresh and plenty. But as he'd waited, he'd heard things in the dark. Either the spooks that his wife spoke of, or men intent on mischief. Men with flashlights and a truck, who didn't know how to come up on the place silently. Old Man Poteet had loudly stamped his feet through the forest and scared the others off, firing his shotgun into the air. The others had fled, and Horace was the only one left. That was when he had heard other things in the darkness, things that he didn't dare to know the origins of.

He said to Mignon as he walked off the porch, "Best you leave, too, mamselle."

Mignon had lost track of time and glanced up to see Horace Seay climbing into his ancient truck. It barely registered in her mind. She noticed that the sun was beginning to dip behind the trees and the light had changed from golden to twilight. She covered her painting and began to clean her brushes. She glanced up again and found Horace waiting inside his truck for her to go to her car. She waved at him to go, and he frowned. She had continued cleaning up when the truck door slammed as he got back out.

Horace mounted the steps and said in a gruff voice, "Mamselle Thibeaux. You best to go, while we drive behind you. The . . . ah . . . road is still bad, and we want to make sure you don't get stuck."

Mignon didn't catch the urgency in his voice as he peered over her shoulder into the woods. The sun was obliterated by the thick line of trees and the shadows encased the house completely. Horace had seen the shadowed figure moving furtively along the edge of the forest yesterday and again today, but he didn't think that the young woman had. He didn't want to leave her alone, fearing that some evil spirit had set its sights on the beautiful miss.

"There's nothing wrong with the road," she said absent-mindedly.

Calloused fingers touched her shoulder and she turned her head, startled. Horace said, "Please." His fingers stayed just long enough to convey the weight of his message before falling away.

Her mouth opened to say something but then stopped. These people didn't have to be concerned about her well-being, but here one was, just like Miner Poteet, someone who cared enough to ask her to leave while the leaving was good. It was sad, but there were so few people in her life who cared simply for the reason that they were compassionate human beings, interested in the health and physical state of others. She nodded and quickly packed up her painting, putting it into the trunk of her car. Horace carried her paints and easel for her and loaded them as she directed.

She said, "Thank you," and Horace nodded at her. She never saw the shape behind her, at the edge of the tree line, waiting for an opportunity.

Chapter Twenty-one

Fe fi fo fum!
I smell the blood of an Englishman;
Be he alive or be he dead,
I'll grind his bones to make my bread.

FE FI FO FUM!

MIGNON SPENT THE FOLLOWING day preparing for the cleansing ceremony. When she was finished running all her errands, it was time to get dressed. She donned a flowing silk outfit with puffed pants that was the exact color of her eyes. She checked herself in the mirror in her room, pleased that everything was in order.

Eleanor had offered to send the limousine again, but Mignon had declined, preferring to be able to leave whenever she wanted.

When Mignon arrived at the mansion, she saw a string of Chinese lanterns hanging from the wrought iron fence and the trees that lined the driveway. A valet took her car and she mounted the steps to the main door. Jourdain Gastineau met her there, smiling as he offered her his arm.

Mignon couldn't help being suspicious as he chattered lightly about this and that like the cat that had just eaten the canary. *Who is the cat and who is the canary?* she wondered.

Eleanor was serving a buffet this evening and most of the guests ate lightly. Geraud avoided Mignon all evening as he limped around the room, discussing his experience with a rambunctious deadfall in the woods up north. Leya whispered in Terentia Jones's ear once or twice before mingling with the crowd, and Faust stood conspicuously to one side, dressed in the same suit he'd worn last time. Eugenie talked quietly with her friend, David, who was drinking cognac as if it would save his life. She threw some odd looks at Mignon once or twice but Mignon chose to ignore them.

The evening seemed to drag on forever, and by the time the group went to the room where the cleansing ritual would be performed, there were many exaggerated sighs of relief. A living room had been transformed into a pale imitation of a chapel. The furniture had been removed. Mats for kneeling were placed in front of a small altar that held the watch fob, the handbell, and a box of twenty-five-year-old cigars. There was also a pile of handkerchiefs, a sparkling new metal box, a length of thick chain, and a padlock. A large wooden cross, replete with glittering lit candles, had been attached to the wall behind the altar.

Terentia instructed that the candles along the walls be lit, and that all should kneel on the mats. Faust began lighting the candles methodically, while everyone took their designated places. The electric lights were dimmed, leaving an onslaught of shadows that flickered in time with the candles. Terentia walked back and forth in front of the altar, rubbing her hands together while the skirts of her long, gold gown trailed behind her.

The people in the room were conspicuously quiet. Even Geraud was subdued, as if he were waiting for something to happen. That odd disembodied air of anticipation had returned, full and constrained at the same time, affecting each individual within the confines of the room.

Terentia began to mutter, "I can feel your pain. The pain is here. The pain of a lost loved one." Her voice was hoarse with need. It was easy to believe that she was sincere.

Eleanor was transfixed on the front mat. She stared up at the stout woman and nodded.

"There is much pain in this room. Many people here have lost people so dear to them. Mothers, fathers, much loved ones. It is hard to concentrate." Terentia continued to rub at her temples with her chubby hands. "The egg has shown us that there is a curse. The blood is unmistakable. The St. Michel family is cursed with an evil spirit."

Mignon was directly behind Eleanor and could hear several people moving restlessly behind her.

Terentia went on. "We must pray together." She dropped to her knees on the bare wooden floor and began to pray loudly to God. The rest of the group went along but not as enthusiastically. They prayed until Mignon's knees began to hurt.

Terentia suddenly leaped up. "The money, sister," she said to Eleanor. "It is time. We have the witnesses and the moon has risen over the trees."

Outside the window the pale shape of the moon had just cleared the edge of the forest and was beginning its ascent into the heavens.

Eleanor snapped her fingers and Faust brought a bag up from the back of the room. Mignon watched, fascinated. Terentia instructed Eleanor to take the bag, and handed her the pile of handkerchiefs from the altar. Opening the bag, Eleanor removed stacks of money held together with paper wrappers. Mignon's eyes widened.

"Twenty thousand dollars for each person in the household. Twenty thousand dollars for each entity. Twenty thousand dollars for each person close enough to be at this ritual," chanted Terentia, inadvertently explaining the amount and why it was so. Mignon counted in her mind. *Some $200,000. Not a bad amount of money to have lying around.* Terentia went on. "Wrap it in the blessed handkerchiefs, Mrs. St. Michel. Blessed with the sweat of priests in Israel, a most holy land, sweated out through working in the name of Jesus Christ, the most holy son of God."

Eleanor carefully wrapped the money in the handkerchiefs.

Terentia produced a large sewing needle. She said, "A sewing needle hewn from the bones of a saint. The thread is from the hair of a nun. Sew the handkerchief shut and let us continue to pray for the removal of the curse from this family."

Mignon heard someone mutter something behind her. She thought it must have been Geraud but she wasn't sure. Out of the corner of her eye she could see Jourdain with his head turned toward her, as if he were watching her every move. Eleanor sewed the handkerchiefs shut with quick, deft movements using large stitches. The money, enclosed in the white cloths, was placed in the metal box, and the heavy chain wrapped around the box so that it could not be pried open. Finally the padlock was snapped shut, all by Eleanor herself, and she pocketed the key with a rapid, graceful gesture.

At last Terentia took the box from Eleanor and brought it to the altar. She sprinkled what she said was holy water on it. The chanting continued while she marched around the room, continuing her appeals to God to remove the curse from the St. Michel family, walking in front of and behind the group, sometimes swinging the box in front of the large wooden cross, and sometimes over the altar.

Mignon could almost believe that her friend was exactly what she purported to be—a spiritualist that guided those from beyond the grave back to aid the living. She nearly smiled. Their plans had hinged on Eleanor being the superstitious woman she was said to be. When they found out where she went to receive guidance, they had bribed the old woman. Now they counted on Eleanor's beliefs to produce the information Mignon wanted to hear.

When Terentia was done swaying and swinging the metal box, she breathed a great sigh of relief and gently placed the box in Eleanor's hands. Her large hands cupped the older woman's face gently. "These spirits talk of reparation, Eleanor St. Michel. You must make amends to those you've wronged. Only if you do this will any cleansing last in this place. You must agree to this. You must make amends." Her voice was low and soothing and Mignon inched forward to hear a little better. "Confess your sins, Eleanor."

Eleanor was lost in the moment with the smell of the candles burning around her and hushed, tranquilizing Terentia's voice. She nodded, almost desperate to admit that she had sinned in some unnamed manner. "I will agree to that. I will make amends."

Terentia released Eleanor's face with a strong nod, and announced, "The curse has been removed. The money should not be touched for three days. It should be placed in a dark place and not interfered with. The evil will go. God has graced this family. God will protect these people. God will smile upon you and your own."

"Where?" asked Eleanor. She was breathless with excitement. The ceremony itself was almost anticlimactic, but the relief that came with knowing that Luc would no longer wander the halls of the mansion was immense, like an ocean of pain flowing out of her body.

"A dark place. A closet. The basement. Blackness must surround the evil and repress it. After three days it should be moved into the light, where evil will be dispelled into its final resting place, where it will be at peace."

"The basement," Eleanor murmured with a relieved sigh. "Come. We will all take it to the basement."

There were groans as knee joints popped and everyone got to their feet. Candles were taken up in the most interesting procession Mignon had ever seen. No one spoke. No one murmured. No one said anything. They followed, watched, and waited. When they had finished, the entire group of people had followed Eleanor into the basement, a dark, moist place that truly appeared to be as old as the house above, where the box was locked in the wine cellar.

When they returned to the main level, John Henry was waiting for them. With a black expression on his handsome face, he said, "Faust Jones. Terentia Jones. Mignon Thibeaux. You are under arrest for fraud."

HOURS LATER MIGNON reached through the bars of her cell like the most practiced of convicts. If she had a hand mirror, she might have been looking down the hallway for activity. Terri lounged on a bunk behind her. Both were still dressed in the same evening apparel they had worn the night before.

The section of the jail that housed women was small, and two other women were in the cell with them. One was drunk and the other was charged with battery against her husband. Both of them had stared at Mignon and Terentia like they were aliens who had just stepped off the mother ship.

"Come from the ball?" the drunk one asked. She had been caught driving in circles on the highway at about midnight, and couldn't quite understand why the sheriff's deputy had felt it was necessary to arrest her and bring her to jail.

"Yes, dear," Terri answered. "Why don't you lie down?"

"Because the room spins when I do that," she slurred. "And I don't want to throw up."

A deputy had locked them in a cell together and left without ceremony.

Mignon turned to her friend and said, "Well, this isn't the way I pictured spending the rest of the evening."

"Me, neither, dear," Terri responded.

She called a lawyer in Dallas who vowed to arrive poste haste, while Mignon had called Nehemiah, who said he'd take care of it if things didn't turn out the way they'd planned.

Mignon already had a good idea that she wouldn't need a lawyer, but she couldn't let John Henry know that.

So they slept the night away on their respective bunks, ate a wretched breakfast that didn't taste like real food, and watched as the drunk and disorderly woman was released on her own belated, sober recognizance. Another hour passed before Mignon began to speculate on the cause of their prolonged incarceration. "They're searching the entire house to make sure nothing else is missing," she said.

"Well, I didn't steal anything," Terri protested. She paused. "Kate took off yesterday. Didn't want to get caught up in the fireworks. Saw her drive off myself. Quit just like that. I can't imagine how a rich white woman like Eleanor keeps good help. You know she wasn't even paying that girl minimum wage, hmm?"

Mignon smiled. "I'll make it up to her when we get back to New York."

Another hour passed and there was a commotion at the front of the jail. John Henry appeared with Terri's lawyer, a friend of the family's who knew all about the family business. He was spouting a bunch of stuff about the sanctity of the Constitution of these United States, and how people were subject to search and seizure only under reasonable suspicion, and just because the sheriff didn't believe in spiritualists didn't entitle him to charge his client with fraud, et cetera.

Terri perked up immediately. She brushed off her golden, flowing gown, which didn't look so hot in the bright fluorescent lights of the jail, and stood up.

John Henry had the deputy open the cell door and motioned at both of them. "I'm dropping the charges," he said. Mignon could see that he was tired, angry, and about two shakes away from blowing his top.

"Why?" asked Mignon.

The lawyer, who was tall, black, and dressed in an immac-

ulate three-piece suit the color of Texas bluebonnets, answered, "There was a decided lack of evidence on the premises
of the St. Michel property. As a matter of fact, there was no
evidence except complaints from Jourdain Gastineau and Geraud St. Michel, who had contacted the sheriff prior to the
event. The money, which was alleged to have been stolen, was
in actuality still locked in the wine cellar, inside the box that
Mrs. St. Michel had locked herself in the presence of some
seven witnesses, including the complainants. Finally, there was
no duplicate box present that might have indicated a switch
was ever intended." He was a handsome man with skin the
color of chestnuts. His face twisted into a grimace of utter
disdain. "Consequently there is no evidence of wrongdoing on
the part of the three accused individuals."

A little muscle in John Henry's cheek twitched as he stood
holding the door to the jail cell.

The other resident of the cell block called, "You go, girl."

"I'm outta here," said Terri. "Davis, you got a car, because
I need a ride out of this one-horse hick town, just as soon as
my fat ass can get in the car. I've never been so humiliated in
my entire life. Have you people heard of wrongful arrest?
Have you people heard of the Constitution? I'm never coming
back to Louisiana if I live to be ten thousand years old." With
her back to John Henry, Terri winked broadly at Mignon,
who had to bite her tongue to keep from laughing out loud.

"My arm, Madam Jones," the lawyer replied, offering a
solid arm to the harried woman. "Let us sign the paperwork
to have Faust released and leave this den of iniquity. This lair
of wrongdoing. This haven of misdeeds and injustice."

Terri muttered under her breath all the way out.

John Henry stood at the door and looked at Mignon carefully. She hadn't moved.

Finally she suggested, "Maybe if you slept with her, too,
she wouldn't mind the harassment, John Henry." She almost

winced when it came out of her mouth because of the intense wave of guilt she felt at lying to him. If it weren't for protecting the others, she might have confessed all of it to him.

"You knew that if you were doing something illegal, then I would arrest you," he said. His voice was neutral, but she could see the sizzle of barely harnessed anger in his eyes. The remark about sleeping with Terentia had cut to the bone. "I told you and I was clear."

"If I was doing something illegal," she said, knowing full well she had skirted legalities. Terri had purposefully not represented herself as a "real" psychic, but as a spiritualist, a guide for those who would explore the paranormal. Technically, Nehemiah was the only one who had committed a crime in vandalizing the sluice gates and the electrical transformers. And Mignon wasn't going to tell John Henry about that anytime soon. "Then, why am I leaving here, without going in front of a judge? Why are you dropping the charges?"

"Because I couldn't find what you had done," he answered, and it was evident from his voice that he believed she was guilty of something, and that it was only a matter of time before he figured out what it was.

"Isn't it possible that you jumped to conclusions?" she asked him. "Couldn't you have looked in that box before you arrested me? Didn't you break the law yourself?"

John Henry couldn't find an answer to that. He wanted to believe that she was guilty of something, of anything, in order to warrant his actions. As it was he was going to have to explain to his constituents that he had made a mistake. OUTSIDER SHERIFF ARRESTS HOMETOWN GIRL WHO MADE GOOD: That was going to sell some newspapers. He wasn't sure if he could make it sound as if he had been vindicated in making a mistake. Geraud and Jourdain had come to him about the so-called cleansing ceremony and he had known immediately that a fraud was about to be perpetrated. The scam wasn't exactly uncommon.

Typically the money to be cleansed was switched before it ever went into a locked box. But that hadn't happened that way. He couldn't find one tiny shred of evidence that justified his arrest of the three people who had just spent the night in his jail. And if he wasn't justified, then he had wrongfully arrested one very special woman, one with whom he might have fallen in love. He said, "I'll have a deputy drive you back to your car."

He started to walk away and then turned back. "Jesus Christ, Mignon, couldn't you have waited before trying this? You've got money, a lot of money. You sure as hell don't need Eleanor's. That isn't going to bring your mother back, and I talked to Fanchon."

"What?" Her voice was suddenly hoarse. Had they jumped the gun? Was it possible that Fanchon had rolled over on Eleanor St. Michel?

"He's a tough old bastard, but I think I can get him to talk on the condition of amnesty for that crime and leniency on the drugs charges," he snarled at her, and the woman across from them jumped back on her bed in alarm. "Couldn't you have waited?"

Mignon didn't know what to say to him. He went on. "I checked Terentia Jones's record. Took me a while without her fingerprints. Didn't you think I might? Fraud in New York State. Small cons, like being a fake psychic. But then I called a cop I know up there. He said Madam T. is out of that business now. She owns an *art gallery*. An art gallery which happens to feature a breakout artist named Mignon. I called them up and asked them. The receptionist was pleased to tell me about this artist. Dammit. This didn't need to happen."

It was another hour before Mignon walked out of the sheriff's department a free woman, albeit the back way because there were ten reporters waiting out front for the famous New York artist to emerge from the slammer. A male deputy named Elvis Brandt escorted her to his patrol car, and Mignon was surprised she got to sit in front. She thought that maybe John

Henry was looking out his office window on the second floor, but it was hard to tell with the sunlight shining on the windows. There seemed to be a large, shadowed figure there, but it moved away before she could tell who it was.

So much for that relationship, she thought. *It never would have worked out anyway. Big town artist, small town sheriff. Who was going to move where? And who was going to make the sacrifice? Among other things. . . .*

Elvis the deputy wanted to discuss what kind of art was a good investment lately.

"Dead artists," Mignon muttered.

"Beg pardon?"

"Well, you buy an artist's pictures while they're alive, and they generally become more valuable when they die," she explained.

"But you don't know when they're gonna die," the deputy complained.

"That would be the trick."

The deputy stopped at the St. Michels' gate. The security guard let them in without hesitation. Mignon knew they were expected. He let her out at the base of the steps leading up to the front door. Her rental car was nowhere in sight.

Elvis said, "If you know of some artist who was about to die, you'd tell me, wouldn't you?"

Mignon turned back to the patrol car and gave the deputy a cold look. She had just spent the night in the county jail and he wanted free advice on investments. *Jerk.* "No." She turned and walked up the stairs. Her purse and keys were presumably inside, since they hadn't come with her to the jail. John Henry had been in too much of a hurry to arrest them all, confident that he had figured out the mystery.

The door opened before she got there and Eleanor was standing there, her eyes cold and her expression foreboding.

Mignon stopped abruptly and wondered if she'd made another mistake.

Chapter Twenty-two

> There was a little man, and he had a little gun,
> And his bullets were made of lead, lead, lead;
> He went to the brook, and saw a little duck,
> And shot it through the head, head, head.
>
> THERE WAS A LITTLE MAN

"I ONLY WANT MY keys and my purse, Eleanor. Nothing else."

Eleanor sighed and a strange look crossed over her fine features. She was dressed in a sophisticated silk suit as if she were going to a garden tea. As usual, her hair and makeup were impeccable, as if nothing could scathe her.

"There were . . . ," Eleanor started and then hesitated. "No incidents last night."

Mignon stood stock-still. Eleanor truly believed the so-called "hauntings" had ended. She went on. "Geraud and Leya have returned to New Orleans. He decided that his actions are regrettable and that he wants no more of this nonsense." *He decided or you did?* Mignon silently asked. *Has the incident at the farmhouse slithered out of the woodwork?*

"Why don't you come in, and I'll have one of the servants bring your car around?" invited Eleanor with a sad little smile. "Wouldn't you like to freshen up?"

"You know what, I really would like that." Mignon smiled and went in. She suddenly realized that John Henry hadn't told Eleanor about her connection to Terentia. *At least*, she thought, *not yet.*

Almost an hour later she and Eleanor were sitting on the patio facing the sun, drinking coffee. It was a rich French blend with all the flavor and aroma that the jail's coffee had sorely lacked. "I hate to sound like an old television commercial, but that's good coffee," Mignon said.

"Mignon," Eleanor began. "I would like to apologize to you."

Mignon put down her cup on the glass-topped table and stared out at the tree line across the vast expanse of green yard. The trees in the distance were beginning their change in color. There was a hint of orange and red among the green.

"When my husband left me, I was heartbroken. Moreover, I was embarrassed that he had done such a thing. With, of all people and I'm sorry for this, your mother. I was mortified that he had run off with a seamstress. We were the plantation owners and Luc had run off with a lowly *couturière*."

Mignon finally looked at Eleanor and saw that her face was crestfallen. The older woman suddenly seemed to be a thousand years old. All of her fears and all of her heartache had been brought back to her a hundredfold. "I know what that sounds like. And I know that I'm not that much of a better person. A bigot, I've been called. A horrid hag of a woman. A woman so cold I could freeze a tom turkey at a hundred yards." She laughed, and it was an ugly laugh.

There was nothing Mignon could say to this. She couldn't laugh with her. She couldn't cry. She could only listen.

"But when I was in my thirties I was vainglorious. I was prideful. I believed that the things I so took for granted were my right, just like a god in my own world. How can you understand the things I am trying to say?" Mignon opened her mouth but Eleanor stopped her. "No, don't answer. Just listen.

"Luc waited for me in the library that day. He told me that he was leaving me for your mother. That they were going away. That he would file for divorce and marry this woman he had discovered that he loved." Eleanor's eyes were bright with tears. She stared at Mignon, seeing Garlande's green eyes and wondrous red hair, and the fine features that made her beautiful and striking all at the same time. But there was more. There was shock in Mignon's face at what Eleanor was saying. "Yes, he loved your mother. And apparently your mother loved him. Not so sorry a thing. But I wasn't an understanding woman. I had found the gold necklace with *her* initials on it in his jacket pocket, which he snatched back from me as if it were a priceless *objet d'art*. I screamed, I yelled, I threw things, and Luc finally left in disgust. When he had gone I found that Eugenie and Geraud had witnessed most of my dishonor. And Eugenie was never the same.

"So Luc left with your mother and I was so angry that I did something unthinkable. I didn't want to ever set my eyes on another Thibeaux in my life. I blamed your mother. It was her fault. It was a Thibeaux's fault, and they would pay." She looked away, at the shape of the trees on the horizon. "But you paid. And your father paid."

Mignon said, "You told the judge and the sheriff to make us leave."

Eleanor took a deep breath. She nodded. "I didn't want to look at you ever again. And you were forced out like common criminals."

Mignon nodded slowly. The bitterness of that day rushed over her in a blinding flow of resentment. Then it was gone and she felt as though a burden had been released.

Eleanor saw her face and was momentarily nonplussed. "I said . . . I don't remember what I told Ruelle and Gabriel exactly. I was so furious that I wanted to scream, and then Eugenie disappeared. We didn't find her for hours. Even Jourdain looked for her endlessly."

Mignon pulled the gold bracelet from her purse. Its little medallion glittered brightly in the flaming light of the sun. She

dropped it on the table in front of Eleanor, who stared at it.
In Mignon's mind, she could only see one way that this brace-
let had ended up in her own tiny, blood-soaked hands—if
Eleanor had murdered her mother. "Whose is this, Eleanor?
Who does this belong to?"

Eleanor reached out with white fingers but she never quite
touched it. It was like a deadly viper just a hair's breadth away
from her bosom. Her eyes stared at the little bracelet with the
E on it and she couldn't force herself to look away. "It looks
familiar," she finally said. Her fingers quivered.

"Think, Eleanor," Mignon insisted, sitting forward in her
chair. "Have you ever seen it before?"

"It's not mine," the older woman muttered. "I would remember it. But I think . . ."

"What? What do you think?"

"When we went to New Orleans that year before Luc left,
we went to Mardi Gras. We were so happy, my family. I
bought things for all of the family. For Luc, for Geraud, and
for Eugenie. I had a jeweler design that for a gift. He was a
famous jeweler, a master craftsman, you see. I gave it to . . .
gave it to . . . my God, I haven't seen it for years . . . since that
year."

"Eugenie . . . ," Mignon's voice faded away in horror as she
realized the implications of what Eleanor said. The bracelet
had belonged to Eugenie. Eugenie had been sent away during
a so-called childhood sickness to a hospital in Baton Rouge
right after Luc disappeared. But Eugenie had been only *ten
years old* at the time. How could that be?

"Where did you get this bracelet?" demanded Eleanor suddenly.

"I found it," Mignon answered, trying to spare Miner Poteet any retribution. How could she or anyone hold a ten-year-
old responsible for a crime? How would she discover the truth
from a thirty-five-year-old woman who was lost in the hell

that was her own mind? The questions raced through her mind. She stood up and stared down at Eleanor. She was so sure that Eleanor had been the one—either Eleanor or one of her cronies. But it had been Eugenie, and that was almost too appalling to believe.

Mignon knew it. She knew it as well as she knew the back of her hand. Eugenie had heard the argument between her parents. She had heard what Luc was going to do. She had been to the old farmhouse in the woods many times, playing with Mignon or by herself, while her father amused himself with his mistress. It was less than a mile away. A ten-year-old girl could have gone there. A ten-year-old girl might have grabbed a kitchen knife and threatened Garlande, who was waiting for Luc to wrap up any last-minute business and join her. Garlande might not have taken the little girl seriously.

A low moan of pain emitted from Mignon's lips.

Eleanor asked, "What's wrong, Mignon?"

Mignon had a sudden splitting headache, as if her mind had comprehended something she didn't want to remember, something that she hadn't dared to remember for twenty-five years. She had been there. She had seen everything. She knew what had happened all along. "Do you know what happened to Luc, Eleanor? To my mother?" she demanded.

Eleanor's eyes were as big as saucers. She stared up at Mignon like a small child. "Of course not. We were never able to track him down. I always presumed that he started another life with your mother somewhere out of my reach. And that sometime in the recent past he'd died. As your mother must have. They must have felt your pain. They must have known what had happened to you and that it was my fault. Why else would they be haunting this place."

"So you don't know . . ."

"Know what?" Eleanor stood up quickly as Mignon reached for the bracelet. She grabbed it and ran out of the house. She got into her car, started it, and left without another word. In the rearview mirror, she could see Eleanor running after her, screaming, "Know what? My God, what is it that you know? Tell me what you know!"

Mignon didn't stop. In fact, she never wanted to see another St. Michel in her life.

Mignon was so lost in her own thoughts, she didn't realize that someone had hidden in the backseat of her car, crouching down in the foot space. As soon as she drove through the gate and rounded the curve of the road, a man popped up and wrapped a wiry forearm around her throat. A gun was placed at her forehead, and there was a whisper in her ear. "I think you know where we're going, don't you?"

He wasn't visible in the rearview mirror, but Mignon knew who it was all the same. She didn't say anything. She simply drove the car. The forearm cut into her throat and she began to choke. "Do as I say, or I'll shoot you right here. It doesn't matter to me."

There was a hint of insanity in his voice, a suggestion that he would do exactly as he said he would. Here was the person who had gone through her room. Here was the person who was responsible for the snake. Here was the person who followed her out into the night and shoved her into the canal hoping she'd drown. Here was the person who wanted her desperately out of the way before she remembered her secret, or before she uncovered something she wasn't supposed to see. And here was the person who had covered up Eugenie's crime to prevent Eleanor from being hurt. "Where is the bracelet?" the person demanded hoarsely.

As the car turned down the dirt road that led to the farmhouse, the light from the late morning sun shifted and the person behind her moved toward the middle of the backseat. The rearview mirror showed the nondescript features of Jourdain Gastineau.

"I have to say," Mignon said carefully, "that you're not acting like a court justice right now."

Jourdain shrugged. "It was nice of you to leave your gun in your car," he said. "How could you know that the police wouldn't search it?"

"They did," answered Mignon. "John Henry already knew about the gun. He's got a thing for me, and I suppose he was willing to let that little offense go by."

"Ah, the lure of a seductive yet mysterious woman." Jourdain laughed suddenly.

"Just like Luc St. Michel fell for," Mignon suggested. She slowed the car down to accommodate the ever-present bumps and holes in the road. *Please let Horace and his workmen be there.* Then she remembered it was Sunday. No one would be at the old house—no one but her and Jourdain.

Then she remembered the little canister of pepper spray in her purse, which was strung over her neck and shoulder. She thought she might be able to reach it in time.

"Just like Luc," he said. "You don't seem very surprised to see me, my dear. Why is that?" He prodded her neck with the gun.

Mignon flinched with the pressure. "Eugenie murdered my mother. And her father. Right in that house." She pulled the car in front of the little farmhouse and stopped. Then she put the gear in "park" and waited. "She was only ten years old. Since Eleanor didn't have a clue, someone else had to have cleaned up after Eugenie. And by the way, I gave the bracelet to Eleanor." She added the lie cheerfully, hoping to prolong the situation. The bracelet was concealed in her hand.

"Clever girl. Bet you thought it was Eleanor all along." He shifted in the seat behind her, apparently not in any particular hurry to kill her. "Eugenie was a budding sociopath or psychopath, I forget what's politically correct these days. She caught your mother alone, slaughtered her with a knife. It looked like about a hundred stab wounds. I'll never understand how a ten-year-old girl could do that. Then she waited for her father, and when he came through the door, she managed to cut his throat. Luc didn't even get stabbed once. It was your mother Eugenie was angry with. However, you must have been around, splattered by the blood. Perhaps frozen in place. Eugenie wouldn't say anything about the murder herself. It was as though she never did it, but I'll wager you recall it."

Her head dropped a little. A rush of memories flowed into her like an inexorable tidal wave that threatened to flood every one of her senses. As though it were happening all over again, her mind replayed the scene she had witnessed and repressed, the reason for her dreams, and the memories that had tried to burst through her mental barriers.

Mignon had come home from school after the bus let her off. She was allowed to walk down the road by herself, and if she was so much as five minutes late, her mother would come looking for her. Whenever she got to walk down the narrow road by herself she felt as big as any grown-up. She ran, she walked, and she hopped all the way down the green corridor. That day she was skipping happily because it was the nicest September day imaginable, and her mother was waiting inside.

Garlande was packing not only her own clothing but Mignon's, as well, and it stopped the little girl in place. Were they going on a trip? she'd asked her mother, and her mother was glowing in the afternoon warmth. Mama said, "Yes, *chère*. A most wonderful trip. And you get to go, and we'll all have a good time. We're going to an island in the Caribbean. Can you say that, darling one?"

Without knocking, Eugenie had walked in, entering the bedroom almost soundlessly, and almost as tall as Garlande, despite her tender age of ten years. Then the screaming began.

Eugenie was shrieking at Mama not to take her beloved papa away. Mama went to hug Eugenie, to comfort the ten-year-old, but when her arms enclosed the skinny figure she suddenly made a choking noise. She fell away from Eugenie onto the bedroom floor, abruptly clutching at an ever-expanding red splotch at her stomach. She threw her hands up to protect herself, but Eugenie was savage with the knife she had found in Mama's kitchen.

Little Mignon threw herself at Eugenie, trying to wrest the bigger girl away from her mother's body. But Eugenie was wild with anger and tossed her away. Mignon's white pinafore was almost instantly covered with blood, and she was left grasping Eugenie's bracelet in one hand as she gazed in utter shock at the scene before her.

Eugenie stared at what she had done as Mignon got up off the bedroom floor and wandered out. Her mind had blurred then, and all she could think of was that Mrs. Poteet often made cookies this time of day and how good they would taste.

"I never saw her kill her father," murmured Mignon, snapping to the present. "The shock was too much. All I remember is that Mrs. Poteet scrubbed my flesh so hard that it burned, when she washed the blood off me. They burned the little white dress, out back in a barrel Miner used for burning trash."

"The judge and the sheriff came to find Luc, to talk some sense into him," said Jourdain. "Instead they found Eugenie, soaked in blood, playing in between their bodies. It was the most horrible thing I've ever seen. And she went off to some kind of lunatic asylum for children the very next day. Her mother, God forgive me, never knew. But you know that, too."

"I know it now," Mignon said.

"I wouldn't have guessed that you were there, except for that bracelet. We searched high and low for that bracelet for days because it was so unique. Eleanor paid a small fortune for that silly little gift. Eugenie wouldn't have parted with it. Finally, we decided it wouldn't matter if someone found it. Because without a witness or proof, what could it matter? And who would ever believe that Eugenie murdered her own father and her father's mistress?"

"Who would believe," she repeated dully. *No one now. I came back to find this. Who would believe, indeed? Not me,* she thought. *Eugenie murdered my mother in an angry fit. But who would believe that she snuck up on her father and cut his throat?* That smacked of sneakiness. It smacked of premeditation, of control and deception. Her eyes focused on Jourdain's in the rearview mirror. "You killed Luc," she stated. *'It was the most horrible thing I've ever seen.' But he hadn't been there. It was only the judge and the sheriff, because he was otherwise occupied. Cleaning up. After he'd gotten rid of the bodies.*

Jourdain was surprised. He had repeated the lie so often over the past two decades that he had almost convinced himself. If he hadn't been there, then how could he have said that he had seen Garlande Thibeaux's body, the "most horrible thing" he'd ever seen. He saw Mignon's perception of his verbal mistake and nodded. "Yes, I killed Luc. He wasn't going to leave Eleanor with anything. He was a selfish man. He wanted your mother and he wanted his money. Not Eleanor, not his children. He didn't even care about his ancestral home. He was taking everything. And by God, he would have done it, too. I found Eugenie with Garlande, leaning over the body, patting your mother's hair. Then Luc came in, and I just picked up the knife. Before I realized what I'd done, he was dead." He stopped for a moment. "It's easy to lie to one's self. I realized exactly what I was doing. I was doing Eleanor a favor."

Jourdain's voice had gone as cold as the chilliest New York

winter Mignon had ever experienced. He was lost in the past himself. "I would do anything for Eleanor," he added softly. "I would have left my wife, but Eleanor was far too good a woman to have me. She mourned the loss of her husband. I still love her. And if you were to disappear, then all of this would go away. Then your friend, John Henry. He needs to disappear, as well. He's been far too inquisitive. Poking into our affairs, threatening to drag the bayous, harassing Ruelle Fanchon to roll over after I promised him that I would take care of him . . ."

Mignon unfastened her seat belt and slowly let it up so that it wouldn't alarm Jourdain. As soon as he took the gun away from her neck she was going to run. She was going to run because it was the only chance she was going to get. *Screw getting all the answers,* she thought. *I have more than enough. Time for fight or flight.*

"Get out," he ordered. There wasn't an opportunity to run because he moved an arm around her neck and opened the door himself. He never let her go as she moved carefully out of the car, shifting his arms around the car's frame to maintain his grip on her.

Instead of going into the house, Jourdain directed her around to the back. She could see that the outhouse pit had been filled in. The outhouse itself lay in a pile of pieces along with most of the flooring from the inside of the house. There was the tree in the back with her initials on it. There was her whole life, in the backyard.

Suddenly Eugenie emerged from the darkness of the forest. She appeared primeval and menacing, far more than she had as a child. Her hair was a silvery-blonde explosion that moved with the slight wind. She was dressed simply in blue trousers and a silk shirt, and her feet were bare, as if she had been running through the woods like a jungle boy. Her skin was whiter than snow on a crow's back, and she held an enormous carving knife in one hand.

Mignon saw her first. If she had been scared before, then the vision of Eugenie St. Michel slowly walking toward them with a knife was downright terrifying. She forgot about the pepper spray in her purse. She forgot about fleeing.

Jourdain saw Eugenie a moment later and almost let Mignon go. His fingers loosened just a bit, then regained their control. "Eugenie," he called. "This doesn't need to involve you."

"But Jourdain," she said. "It does involve me, doesn't it? She came here for me, didn't she?"

She kept walking towards them and Jourdain abruptly jerked Mignon around in front of him like a shield. *He doesn't trust her*, thought Mignon. *Oh my God, I'm going to get killed by one or the other.*

"What the hell are you talking about, Eugenie?" he snarled.

"Garlande," she answered, her voice as light as the air. The knife slashed through the late morning sunshine once and twice. "Garlande," she said directly to Mignon. "I knew it was you. I knew all along. And you came back for me, didn't you? Because I murdered you."

Mignon's mouth opened and closed. She was completely terrified. There was no way to win this game. Damned by the woman in front of her and damned by the man behind her.

Eugenie's breath came and went deeply. She was about fifteen feet away. "Don't worry, Garlande. I won't let you die this time. I tried to save you, after I stabbed you. But it was too late. I won't let it happen to you again. And then you can forgive me."

"I forgive you, Eugenie." The words came suddenly from Mignon's mouth. She wasn't sure where she found the energy to imitate her mother's throaty voice and Southern accent, but the Louisiana drawl came out as if she had lived her entire life here. *"I forgive you."*

"Shut up," muttered Jourdain. "Just shut up."

"But Jourdain doesn't want my forgiveness," Mignon went on breathlessly.

He shoved the pistol into her neck. "I told you to shut up!"

In the second when Jourdain transferred his attention to Mignon, Eugenie launched herself forward, lifting the blade high into the air. Her shoulder arched into the sunlight, ready to thrust downward toward the struggling pair in front of her. The light reflected off the metal, a bright ricochet of luminance, and Jourdain looked back. He gasped and shifted the barrel of the Beretta.

He shot Eugenie St. Michel. Then he pushed Mignon away from him and shot her, too.

Chapter Twenty-three

One flew east, one flew west,
One flew over the cuckoo's nest.

ONE FLEW EAST

THE DARKNESS WAS ALL encompassing when Mignon woke up. She wasn't sure if she had opened her eyes or not until she felt herself blink. But it was utter blackness, as black as the bottom of a deep pit. She moved gingerly and it became apparent that she was lying on some damp, muddy surface. She could feel the grit under her hands and the mud clinging to her fingers. And the smell. *Oh, God, what is that?* It reeked of decay, the way something smelled after it has been dead for a long time.

She moved again and she realized that she had been shot. She had been shot by Jourdain and had lost consciousness. But Mignon didn't feel as though she were dying. There was a dull ache in her side that bloomed into full-fledged pain when she turned her body in any direction, but that was all. She gently pushed her hand against the wound and felt warm liquid billow up in tiny swells between her fingers. She gathered material from her flowing outfit and wadded it up, pressing it firmly against the wound. It was painful but it didn't seem life-threatening. If she could stop the bleeding, then she could probably walk away from this.

But here was the $64,000 dollar question. *Where is this?*

There was no sound. She couldn't feel anything with her free hand. There was only the odor of decay and a sense that there was a void around her. The faint sounds of her movements seemed to echo back at her as if she were in a cave. Her shoulder hurt as though someone had punched her hard.

She suddenly remembered something that might help. Her tiny clutch purse had been strung over a shoulder when she had gotten into her car, and again when she had gotten out. She felt for the gold string that had been draped over her head, and found one end. It had been broken, but somehow remained lying across her body.

Carefully tugging on the end, Mignon pulled the bag to her. Her hand trembled as she opened the purse and found her new mini-mag, right next to the little canister of pepper spray. Her finger pressed at the button and nothing happened.

Dammit. Dammit. Work, damn you. The thoughts rumbled frantically through her mind and Mignon bit back hysterical laughter. The flashlight finally came on and she briefly closed her eyes in thankfulness.

When she opened them again she was staring at the body of Eugenie St. Michel. Her eyes were open and staring back. Mignon took a deep breath and managed to sit up, slowly inching her way toward the other woman. Pressing her index and her middle fingers to Eugenie's neck, she confirmed that she was dead. After all, Jourdain had shot her right in the center of her chest, undoubtedly hitting the heart. She must have died instantly.

Poor Eugenie, Mignon thought. *God have mercy on your soul.* There was pity there. Not only had Mignon discovered that she had some naïveté left, but she also had pity for the irrational, wretched little girl who had murdered Garlande in a psychotic childish rage.

The flashlight made its way around the place where she sat,

awkwardly clutching her side. Mignon made two determinations. The first was that Jourdain had rediscovered the cistern behind the old farmhouse. This was the same cistern that Mignon's father had warned her about, the same one that she had planned to have filled.

And it was going to be her grave.

The second thing she discovered was much worse. It was already someone else's grave.

Mignon let out a shriek of horror when she saw the decomposed face of her mother's corpse. Garlande Thibeaux and Luc St. Michel hadn't gone very far at all. The flashlight fell from her hand and went out when it hit the dirt beside her.

After a moment Mignon retrieved the mini-mag. The cistern hadn't been used for decades, and it certainly wasn't in use in 1975. Ruff had water delivered to the five-hundred-gallon tank beside the house, instead of using the antiquated cistern. Looking at the walls, she could see large cracks radiating up the sides, as well as piles of cement that had fallen to the bottom over the years.

The two bodies were nearly skeletons; only a bit of flesh and clothing remained. Garlande's red hair was vivid under the flashlight's dim beam, and Luc's blonde hair was just as bright as if it had been washed that very day. Two skeletal grins flashed at her silently. There was a twinkle of gold as she saw the saint's medallion still hanging around Luc's neck, and if Mignon had gotten close enough to turn it over she knew she would see her mother's initials on the back. This was the same necklace that Luc had grabbed back from Eleanor, the one he obviously had treasured. They would be together eternally, their figures mingled together in death.

Mignon closed her eyes and turned toward Eugenie, trying to repress a surge of nausea. Jourdain had removed the cement cap and pushed them both in. Mignon must have fallen onto

Eugenie's body. It was the only reason she didn't have a dozen broken bones from the fifteen-foot drop into the bottom of the tank.

Mignon waved the flashlight around and surveyed her situation. Fifteen feet of sheer cement walls with nothing to grip onto. The bottom had once been full of water, which had evaporated slowly, leaving a layer of silt. Once a windlass had towered over the tank to pull the water out with a tin bucket, but the windlass was long gone, and Jourdain must have heaved the cement cap back on top of the hole. Not that it mattered, because there was nothing for her to perch on in order to try to push it off. Even the large cracks in the walls provided no place to hold on to.

Mignon turned off the flashlight to save the batteries. She knew that she was stuck and laughed inanely, the sound echoing back at her ruthlessly. The air was dank in the cistern, dank and chilly. She would die of exposure before she died of thirst.

Life's little ironies were coming back to haunt her. She lay inside a tank devised to hold water, but would have none. She had come back to LaValle seeking answers and had found every one of her questions resolved, but there would be no one to tell. She had faced her mother's murderer, only to have the woman inadvertently save her own life.

Did Miner Poteet hear the gunshots? Wouldn't he come to investigate?

If he had been home. If his hearing aid had been in. If his granddaughter hadn't taken him to church. *If. If. If.*

Mignon began to scream. She screamed until her voice grew hoarse and then she screamed some more.

She turned on the flashlight again and stared at the walls of the cistern, studying the random cracks that crisscrossed the walls. Heat and the shifting earth had caused many, and the age of the cement had caused some more. Mignon thought that if she could collapse one side of the cistern she might be able to crawl or dig her way out. On the other hand, she might be buried alive. Standing up awkwardly and holding her side, she followed the system of cracks up the walls with the tiny flashlight, looking for the ones that were the deepest and the most pervasive.

One ran almost the entire length of one wall and was a foot wide at the bottom. Mignon aimed her foot and kicked it like she would kick a door open. There was a dull thud as her foot made contact. The wall rippled just a bit and cement dust floated down around her, but the movement caused a wave of agony to undulate down her side. She grimaced and aimed another kick at the wall, this time harder. The wall groaned. A chunk the size of a fist bounced off her arm. She looked up and thought that the cap might have shifted a bit. She kicked a third time, her foot landing flat up against the wall, all of her weight behind it, and the wall shuddered. The crack widened and bits of debris rained down.

But she'd caused the bleeding in her side to start again, and a trickle of blood dripped down her flesh. The world shifted around her as if everything was off kilter and she knew she was moments away from fainting. Mignon rested against the wall farthest away from the crack and turned the flashlight off. She would let the bleeding stop and then try again. The wall would be forced to collapse if only she kept at it.

After a while she slipped into unconsciousness, and words were whispered into her ears.

"Three blind mice, see how they run! They all ran after the farmer's wife. She cut off their tails with a carving knife. Did you ever see such a sight in your life, as three blind mice?"

It was her mother's wondrous voice, a heady voice full of life and love. A smile crossed Mignon's lips in the blackness. She had never believed that she would remember as much as she had about her mother. She could smell her mother's distinctive perfume in her nostrils, the smell of lemons and posies, mixed with the unique scent of a grown woman. There was also the scent of bleach and cookie dough, along with other odors, all things she associated with Mama. And if it were possible, a cool hand soothed her forehead, gently reassuring her.

Her eyes opened with snap. Was it possible? Her breath came in frightened gasps and seemed to burn in her chest. She fumbled for the flashlight. The light went on immediately. She half expected to see someone sitting beside her, reaching out to her with ghostly fingers, *touching* her.

But there was no one there. Mignon was alone in the dark pit.

"It was my imagination," she told herself, simply to hear the sound of her own voice.

However, there was a faint, lingering scent of lemon and musk. It tantalized her nostrils and then it was gone. Mignon swung the flashlight around but knew that she was alone. There wasn't even a breeze in this grave. There was nothing here but her and three dead people. And if she started thinking about *that*, she would be screaming again, and it wouldn't be for help.

The flashlight flickered. Mignon looked at it solemnly and turned it off once more.

It was hard to tell how much time had passed. It might have been hours or days. She dozed and she woke. She screamed for help sporadically. She listened for signs that people were above her, perhaps searching for her. She kicked at the side of the wall several times, but she was getting weak and wanted to reserve her strength. Even Geraud St. Michel would have been a welcome face above her in the hole that led to freedom.

There was another period of unconsciousness, in which she wasn't asleep but she wasn't awake either. She knew that she was going to die in this place, alone and undiscovered, with so much to tell. Then that throaty voice whispered to her again, undulating in and out of her conscious mind like a serpentine creature. "Mignon, *chère*, be brave, my darling one. There was an old woman, lived under a hill; and if she's not gone, she lives there still . . ."

Mignon sat up and air ripped through her mouth in a soundless gasp. Someone was in this place with her! Someone was here! And God help her if she didn't know exactly who it was.

She suddenly realized that she was still holding Eugenie's bracelet, the one that Jourdain had searched for high and low, *because it was so unique it could be traced back to Eleanor St. Michel.* The same bracelet that she told Jourdain she'd left with Eleanor. He was a clever man and would have thought to ensure that it was true. Once he found out that it was not, he would be back for it.

The cement cap began to move above her. There was a low grunt of exertion as someone levered it away from the top of the cistern. The piece of cement fell heavily on the ground next to the top of the tank and the walls shook, shedding cement like a snake's skin, some pieces larger than Mignon's head. She realized suddenly that it was on the verge of folding in on itself. Light exploded into the tank and Mignon blinked awkwardly. She didn't know how long she had been down here, but it seemed like forever. There was a dark shape in the opening above her, someone who stared down at her silently.

For a long moment, she thought that it was her mother's ghostly form, coming to rescue her beloved daughter. Then Mignon regained her senses and knew that it was Jourdain. His gray hair, brown eyes, and almost saturnine features gazed down at Mignon broodingly. She sat as still as a corpse and kept her eyes cracked open just a bit.

After another moment Mignon could see that he was still holding her Beretta in one of his hands. "Mignon?" he said.

Mignon didn't budge. If he wanted the bracelet, he would have to climb down in this pit to yank it from her hands. Then she remembered the pepper spray in her purse. If he had to find a way down to her, then she could use the same way up, if only she could disable him for a minute. If he thought she was dead, he might be careless.

"Mignon," Jourdain said again. "I'm going to fire a round into your leg to see if you're faking." The safety on her Beretta clicked loudly. He chambered a round and Mignon almost gasped out for him not to shoot her again. She forced herself to maintain her pose, slumped against the wall. Since she'd obviously moved sometime since he'd dropped her in the cistern, he must have realized that she had been alive for a while. His only question would be, *Is she still alive now?*

Her eyelids drifted shut. She didn't want to see him aiming that pistol at her body, a bullet ready to tear a bloody path into her cringing flesh. Moments passed and he abruptly sighed. A change in the pattern of the light above her told her that he was no longer crouched at the opening to the cistern. Mignon cautiously opened her eyes. Jourdain was gone and the cap was still open. She knew he would be back in seconds. She fumbled for her purse and found the pepper spray, tucking it into her hand after taking the safety off with her thumb, and resumed her position against the wall.

Jourdain let down a rope, wriggling down it like an athlete, one foot expertly hooked within it. He swung to the floor and dust whirled about him, pieces of cement crumbling away as his body contacted the walls.

For a moment Mignon couldn't tell what was happening. She could feel Jourdain standing still, staring at her. Her eyes were barely open and she could only see a blurred shape. "Mignon?" he said.

She knew he stood about five feet away from her, well within range of the pepper spray, but she had to be certain.

There wouldn't be a second chance. Her heart thundered in her chest, pounding like a herd of wild horses roaring across the plains.

He muttered to himself and looked around the floor of the cistern. His eyes caught the glitter of her clutch and he quickly plucked it up in his hands. The gun was tucked under his arm as he tore through the contents of the tiny purse. He snarled as he threw it away, disappointed in his search. Jourdain stood still for another moment and then took a step toward her.

Mignon's right hand clutched the pepper spray. The bracelet was in her left hand. He took another step and she shuddered.

Jourdain knelt at her side and pulled at her left arm. Her entire body shifted, as if he had moved an inert form and it moved helplessly, in tandem with his persistent pulling. Mignon brought her right hand around and sprayed him directly in the face.

He shrieked and began to strike aimlessly at her with the gun as his other hand scratched helplessly at his tortured eyes. The flaying gun connected with her arm and the pepper spray went flying. Mignon would have scrambled for the Beretta, but he wouldn't be under the influence of the spray forever. Any second he would start shooting just to see if he could get lucky while he was temporarily blinded. She clambered for the rope and found it as Jourdain rubbed anxiously at his eyes, keening and groaning as if red-hot pokers had been forced into each.

Mignon yanked herself upward. Without thinking, the bracelet went into her mouth, the ends dangling out like pieces of spaghetti a child hasn't finished. She was weak from blood loss, but she forced herself to put hand over hand and pull herself to the top, propelling her muscles up the short distance that represented the difference between death and the freedom of the world above her. She felt her flesh rip and blood flowing down her side, and prayed that she wouldn't bleed to death before she could find help. One leg hooked over the edge of the cistern's opening and the pain lessened as her body weight shifted to the side of the orifice. She yanked herself up and rolled away from the hole.

Twisting herself around, she pulled the rope up behind her. Once, twice, three times she yanked on the rope, dragging it out of the cistern's opening, praying that she would be swift enough to trap Jourdain in the same pit that would have been her grave.

Jourdain yelled as he grasped the bottom of the rope, yanking it back. Mignon was flung head over heels toward the edge of the cistern, and came about a heartbeat away from being pulled back into the well. Her head hung over the edge and she stared down into the square patch of light where Jourdain stood, covered with dust, only his head visible in the clouds created by debris melting away from the ancient cistern walls. With his hands on the rope, his face twisted as he looked up at her and saw the bracelet dangling from the sides of her mouth. His eyes were bloodshot and tearing badly, but he blinked frantically as he fought not to let her out of his sight. One hand let go of the rope and aimed the Beretta at her.

Mignon shrieked as she scrambled backwards. The resulting gunshot didn't come close to her. She looked around frantically and saw that Jourdain had tied the other end of the rope to her oak tree. She realized that it would be futile to try to untie the dozen knots before he could climb up. If she'd had a knife, she might have been able to saw through it. Instead, Mignon ran.

Her mind sought some clear path to follow that would lead her away from the madness enveloping Jourdain. He was determined and he was armed with her own weapon. She knew that he wouldn't have left the keys in her car, or even have left her car there for the sheriff to find later. Jourdain couldn't risk someone searching the farmhouse or its land until he'd had a chance to fill in the cistern with cement. She didn't waste time heading for his car. The second most obvious choice was Miner Poteet's farmhouse, where he might protect her or at least call the sheriff's department.

But instead, Mignon went into the dark woods. She didn't dare risk endangering her kind, elderly neighbor or his granddaughter. It was full daylight, late in the afternoon, but the forest was like a canopy which kept the sun's light from entering its domain. It was silent, as if the animals knew that a life-and-death struggle was underway. She looked back once and saw Jourdain's head popping out of the cistern's opening, his reddened eyes searching for her. He was furious, and Mignon knew that if he caught her now she would surely be dead long before her body ever went back into the cistern.

Chapter Twenty-four

> The king was in his countinghouse
> Counting out his money;
> The queen was in the parlor
> Eating bread and honey;
> The maid was in the garden
> Hanging out the clothes,
> Along came a blackbird,
> And snipped off her nose.

SING A SONG OF SIXPENCE

JOHN HENRY SAT AT his desk ruminating over what had happened the night before. He'd been up half the night with deputies searching the St. Michel mansion and checking over Eleanor's insurance lists to compare what items might have been stolen.

The only thing missing was a tray of Georgian silver that was later discovered in the kitchen, where a maid had left it while in the process of polishing each piece. Disgusted with himself, John Henry had returned with his deputies to the station to talk with a state attorney about the alleged crimes that had been committed. Then Eleanor St. Michel showed up at three A.M. insisting that her son had changed his mind about the complaint and was withdrawing it.

The state attorney, the same man with whom John Henry had discussed a deal concerning Ruelle Fanchon, had not been pleased. Nightmares of lawsuits against the sheriff's department and the State of Louisiana danced in his head like sugarplums. He even accused John Henry of being prejudiced in both cases. "You've got to be kidding," the attorney had yelled over the phone. "You don't have any proof that the three committed a crime other than lying to Eleanor St. Michel about their connections. And on the other hand, you want to offer a deal concerning a soon-to-be-convicted felon and two murders that no one is sure ever happened. You don't have bodies. You don't have a murder scene. You don't even know if it's human blood at that . . . old shack. Jesus Christ, John Henry, I've never seen you jump the gun like this. Call me when you have something worth talking about."

The metal box sat in the middle of his desk and John Henry glowered at it. The money had been returned to Eleanor. He was angry. Angry at himself. Angry at Mignon. He couldn't understand why she would want to steal it. Sure, $200,000 seemed like a lot of money. But there were three players, maybe more. There were payoffs to be made. There were incidentals. Research. Plane tickets. Rental cars. The private detective. The list went on. The money wouldn't go very far when all of that was added in.

John Henry had grumbled most of the morning and afternoon away, yelling at his secretary, barking at the deputies, and staring at that damn metal box. Then it came to him, and he almost fell over in his chair. And the hell of it was, if he had been in Mignon's shoes he might have tried something similar himself.

He wanted to yell out, "Why didn't she trust me?" but he already knew the answer to the question. John Henry just didn't like it much.

He grabbed the phone and started dialing the number for the bed and breakfast when his secretary stuck her head into

his office. "Miz St. Michel's on line four, Sheriff," she said.
"Says it's urgent."

MIGNON RAN UNTIL her lungs threatened to explode. Glancing
quickly over her shoulder, she could see nothing at all except
deep shadows and trees that seemed to whisper at her. Mignon
came to a tree with a deer stand, crudely constructed by some
hopeful man anxious to eat a bit of venison, even if it was
illegal to poach on national forest lands. She leaned against
the tree, gathering breath into her tortured lungs.

Mignon knew she couldn't run all night. She pressed more
of her clothing against the wound and hoped that it would be
enough, or that perhaps John Henry might come looking for
her.

Shivering, she heard branches crackling as someone approached. Mignon peered around the tree but couldn't see
anyone. Then she heard his voice, calm and natural as if he
were speaking with her at a tea party. "I left to get my car
from Eleanor's. I disposed of yours, by the way. Parked it back
at the bed and breakfast you were staying at. Much better than
the bayou we put Luc's Mercedes in. My aide gave me a ride
over there, and you'd think that girl would have learned not
to ask questions. Of course, I can't kill her, too. But she won't
put two and two together in case someone should ever stumble
across your bodies."

Mignon thought she could hear the smile in his voice. "I
thought you were already dead. You certainly had bled
enough. And here you are, lively as ever." She knew that his
rapacious nature would make him look over every tree and
every bush, searching out her position so that he could take
care of what he thought he had already done. He went on.
"Eleanor didn't have the bracelet. You lied to me, Mignon.
For shame. All I wanted was to make sure that it didn't point

back to her. After all, it is such a rare bracelet. That master doesn't make individual pieces anymore. He hasn't for nearly two decades. So if you didn't give it to her, then I was sure that you must have it. It wasn't in your car, and you didn't have a chance to go back to your room, and I searched the little farmhouse, as well. Not a sign of it. Consequently, it must be with you. On your very person."

Jourdain was saying that he had to finish her off, because there would be a search for Eugenie St. Michel and Mignon Thibeaux eventually. Perhaps the two disappearances would be connected, but certainly not in the same way that Luc St. Michel and Garlande Thibeaux's had been. John Henry might be suspicious, but he was going to be out of the picture before he raised too many questions. Jourdain added, "The other deputies won't look very hard. Besides I have plans to have your little cistern filled in. With cement or such. But it will be your name on the order, and I'll use a man who won't look inside to see what he's filling up. I was going to move their remains. But your elderly neighbor kept coming down to see what the lights were down at the old farmhouse. An interfering old man. Well, now it doesn't matter, because no one else will renovate that decrepit heap of rotting wood."

Jourdain went on. Geraud's business would suffer as well. But all of that didn't matter. Eleanor had to be protected at any cost. It was a shame that Mignon didn't understand that. "And it doesn't even matter about the so-called ghosts, or those damn dreams of Luc I've been having. I'll be in Baton Rouge and I'm sure that I can convince Eleanor to move to her old residence there."

The sun had slid behind the trees and the shadows began to elongate. Mignon couldn't figure out why Jourdain was concentrating on this area until she looked down and found that she had left a trail of blood that led directly to her. It would only be seconds before he found her again. She glanced around and found there was nothing to be used as a weapon. Boards were nailed to the tree that held the deer stand, but they were securely fastened and she knew she wouldn't be able to pry them loose quickly enough.

JOHN HENRY DIDN'T waste any time getting his Bronco out to the St. Michel mansion for the second time in twenty-four hours. Eleanor was waiting on the front veranda for him. He left the engine running and the door open as he bounded out and ran up the stairs. "Tell me again, Eleanor," he demanded.

"Oh, my dear. Eugenie can't be found anywhere. And Jourdain—" Eleanor put an elegant hand to her mouth, dismayed that she had to speak of such distasteful affairs. "He is acting so strangely. He came this morning. He left his car here for hours, and then returned again this afternoon. The gardener said a young woman dropped him off, but he rushed inside and . . . there was blood all over his shirt, John Henry."

John Henry frowned.

"It wasn't . . . his blood," explained Eleanor. "He wanted to know where the bracelet was. He was so insistent. He even shook me by the shoulders. Demanding to know what I'd done with the bracelet that Mignon gave me."

"What bracelet?" John Henry asked.

"Mignon didn't give it to me. She showed it to me. She said she'd found it." Eleanor's eyes were a little unfocused as she stared past John Henry's broad shoulders. "It was Eugenie's bracelet. She lost it when she was a child and Mignon found it someplace. She wanted to know what it meant to me." She hesitated. "I believe she thought it was mine. Because it has an *E* on it."

"And why would Jourdain want it?" John Henry's voice was peremptory and clipped.

"I don't know, John Henry, but Eugenie's gone and . . .

Jourdain got some rope from the groundskeeper before he left, and Mignon has the bracelet that he wants." Eleanor's shoulders seemed to slump. "I thought this was all over."

John Henry cast her a look that said volumes about what he thought about her now, and ran to his Bronco. He pulled out his cell phone and dialed the bed and breakfast in Natchitoches. As he drove out of the St. Michel mansion, not even bothering to fasten his seatbelt, the landlady told him that Mignon's car was in the parking lot and that a man had been driving it. A man in his fifties with gray hair who looked quite fit, except she was sure he'd had a terrible nosebleed because of all the blood on the front of his shirt. He had tried to cover it up with his jacket, obviously ashamed that his shirt had been so badly stained, but she had caught a glimpse of it.

Jourdain Gastineau. John Henry's heart dropped into his stomach. The lawyer was making so many mistakes now. Too many mistakes. *He's lost it completely. Mignon* . . . "What about Mignon?"

"The young lady? I haven't seen hide nor hair of her today," said the landlady.

"That's what I was afraid of," muttered John Henry and hung up.

MIGNON SUDDENLY REMEMBERED that the beautiful golden bracelet was still hanging from her mouth. She took it out and stared at it. It wouldn't be enough. Jourdain had to kill her, too. The bracelet would only be a secondary motive now. She could hear Jourdain stealthily approaching the large tree.

An abrupt image of her father flowed into her thoughts. His large hands guiding her smaller ones, showing her just how to flick a weighted piece of string to aim at an insect. He had shown her a dozen times, and over the years she'd found she still had the trick of it. Mignon flicked the bracelet now, away from her and in the opposite direction from where Jourdain approached. She knew that she couldn't damage him with a bracelet, but she might give herself a moment's head start. The bracelet flew and ricocheted off a tree, thudding against it as if someone had scraped something against the bark.

Jourdain turned and trotted in that direction. "I can hear you, Mignon! I can hear you! And I'm coming to kill you!"

Glancing around the tree, she saw him disappear into a heavily wooded copse and she didn't waste any time. She ran back to the farmhouse, trying to avoid loose branches on the ground and the brush that seemed to reach out with prickling fingers to snag at her skin and her clothing. She had gone perhaps a hundred feet before she heard the roar of her own gun, and a bullet hit a tree a foot away from her, shedding bark and raw wood in a tiny burst.

Mignon couldn't help herself. She glanced back and found that Jourdain had only been fooled for a moment or two. He was after her now and there was nothing in the way but brush and trees. There was no rope to climb and no pepper spray to use. He was going to kill her and he didn't have a bleeding gunshot wound to slow him down. She ran as fast as she could.

Exploding out of the tree line, she emerged in the large backyard of the farmhouse. The sun's light was brighter here and the house cast a long shadow over the cistern. She paused for a moment, her body growing ever weaker. Dancing spots appeared at the corners of her eyes and she could feel herself losing consciousness. She forced her body across the yard, thinking that if she could only cut across the fields to Miner Poteet's place, she'd have a chance. She prayed that he had heard the gunshots and called the police. She would have to risk his life now. She had no other choice.

There was another roar as Jourdain burst out of the woods directly behind her. She looked back once and was horrified.

He was only a few feet behind her, his face a twisted mask of rage. If he could have put his hands around her throat, he would have throttled her until her head separated from her body. That fresh rush of fear provided Mignon with new energy that propelled her feet to move. She ran across the yard and could almost feel his fiery, angry breath at her back, his crazed voice taunting her with mental images of what he planned to do to her, the touch of metal licking at her flesh as he pointed the Beretta at the center of her back.

Mignon leapt over the cistern, not even coming close to the opening. She leapt with the last bit of power that had been dredged from the depths of her soul. She leapt because she knew that if Jourdain pounded across the top of the weakened cistern he might very well finish what she had started at the bottom of the pit. It came to her that this was her very last chance. He was right at her heels and so angry that he might not be watching where he was going.

Mignon leapt like she had never done before. Ten feet past the cistern's edge, she looked back and found that Jourdain had vanished. It was like he had never been. Her knees buckled and she hit the ground hard.

The cloud of dirt whooshed upward as concrete and mud hit the bottom of the cistern. It disgorged violently outward like a bomb had been set off. Mignon covered her face with her arm and tucked her face down, trying to avoid the heavy mass of cloud and cement-ridden debris that wafted up and out.

Eventually it settled. She lifted her head, and she was the only one in the yard, standing in the shadows alone, covered with mud, dirt, and blood. A large hole punctuated the area, a hole twice as wide as the cap had been. Beside the hole lay her Beretta.

Later Mignon would wonder why she'd done it. Jourdain might have survived the fall. He might even have had another gun hidden on his body, ready to shoot her as she stuck her head over the pit. But those cautions didn't go through her mind as she approached the side of the hole and peered down.

There was just enough light spilling into the cistern for her to see the bottom. Jourdain stared up at her in the most malevolent manner possible. There was a single instant when Mignon was sure that her heart stopped. He was alive and waiting for her. Jourdain would clamber up the sides and descend upon her weakened self, choking her body until nothing but bruised flesh remained.

But the moment passed. She saw that he was half buried in the dirt and that there was something horribly wrong with him. His head faced her, but his back was toward her. His brown eyes were open and staring at her, his head and neck turned at a 180-degree angle to the rest of his body. At first glance he had seemed alive and ready to resume his murderous task. But he had broken his neck under the weight of the crumbling cement walls, and he was dead.

Nearby Mignon could see her mother's bony face above the rubble, gazing at Mignon as if trying to tell her something. Long red hair, as bright and striking as the day she died, moved gently around her skeletal countenance, shifting in the breeze.

It took some time for Mignon to staunch her wounds again. She had to wait for the dots to vanish before she found the energy to move around to the front of the house, where Jourdain's car was parked. He'd locked it, but she didn't even hurt herself when she used one of the blood-soaked boards to shatter the driver's side window. She reached inside and pulled out a cellular phone.

At that moment John Henry drove up, his face paler than a ghost's, and she didn't even finish her call before an overwhelming tide of blackness rose over her.

Chapter Twenty-five

Solomon Grundy,
Born on a Monday,
Christened on Tuesday,
Married on Wednesday,
Took ill on Thursday,
Worse on Friday,
Died on Saturday,
Buried on Sunday;
This is the end
Of Solomon Grundy.

SOLOMON GRUNDY

WHEN MIGNON OPENED HER eyes, John Henry was standing over her in the ambulance. He seemed to be a lot more anxious than she was. At first she couldn't quite understand why, but then she happened to glance down at herself and saw that she was soaked with blood. She was also surprised that John Henry had to be persuaded that the wound wasn't fatal, but nonetheless he waited by her side for hours, holding her hand in his own. Jourdain's bullet had ricocheted off a rib, leaving a wound that was more dangerous because of blood loss than anything else.

Later she was admitted into a small hospital outside Natchitoches. John Henry had finally left, and she relaxed, knowing that she had survived and would live to tell the tale. Then she fell into a deep sleep.

That night Mignon dreamed about Jourdain chasing her over the wide field of wild grass that lay behind the farmhouse. He was close on her heels and his pistol was aimed directly at her. He was about to pull the trigger.

Just as Mignon leapt over the chasm, she stared in front of her in disbelief. There was a blackened figure ahead of her, coalescing shadows in the darkness, much like the one that had appeared in her latest painting, arms reaching out to her, long red hair, the color of a tumultuous fire gone awry, flying out behind her shoulders. Her own mother beckoned her to safety. Her lips moved in her beautiful, glowing face, but Mignon could not make out the words. This time she didn't need to look back because she already knew that Jourdain was dead. She reached out to touch her mother but the figure vanished.

Mignon woke up, sweat pouring from her face. *It couldn't have been my mother, whispering to me inside the cistern. It was shock and loss of blood. That isn't possible. But what about what Jourdain had said about being haunted? And what about what had happened at the discernments?*

The doctors wanted to keep her one more day and she didn't feel like arguing. The loss of blood was a major concern and she had already received two transfusions. That afternoon, John Henry came and sat by her bed while they stared warily at each other.

"I brought your rental car to the hospital," John Henry said, his voice calm and neutral, as if he did not trust himself. "I thought that maybe I could drive you to the airport."

Mignon shook her head. "I can drive. See, they even took me off my IV yesterday. But in any case, I'm not going anywhere for a while."

Did his expression change a little? Mignon thought that maybe it did. It became a little more hopeful. "I would have missed you." His voice was hoarse.

"Regret, John Henry?" She kept her tone impersonal, although there was a hint of a tear welling up in one of her eyes.

"Yes, regret." John Henry stared at her. "I think I understand now."

"What do you understand?"

"I know that your eyes were pale green the other day, and now they're brown," he said.

"Contacts," she said.

"And you knew that your mother's eyes were pale green," he went on.

"Yes, I remembered that much about her. Although I didn't appreciate how similar we are because I never had a photograph of her." Mignon smiled sadly.

John Henry nodded. He took her hand and held it the way he had when he thought she might be dying. "You came here to flush out your mother's killer. You had determined that she was dead, and that maybe by playing some kind of game you could cause this person to expose himself." He laughed shortly. "I figured it out. All of it. You should know that. First, if I called Eleanor St. Michel and asked her, she would tell me that Terentia Jones contacted her first. Not the other way around."

Mignon didn't say anything. He was right, but she wouldn't admit it.

He went on. "The ghost walking in the night was someone you planted. I can't explain how they got away, but they left fear behind, and the smell of Cuban cigars, which Luc St. Michel used to smoke at every occasion. At the first séance you used some kind of chemical ice in your purse and disposed of it before I could find it. You knocked the table with your knee. Your shoes had steel toes in them, which explains how you removed your foot without me feeling it move. Special shoes, just like the ones sitting in your hospital locker right now. You made up all the stuff you said. Of course, your mother and Luc St. Michel were buried somewhere. What else could have been done with their bodies? Blackness, you said. Something crawling over your feet. Logical guesses that could easily be interpreted."

John Henry wasn't happy, but he continued to speak, his voice so low that she had to strain to hear. "At the second séance the chair was fixed. The arm could be lifted so that you could remove your hand and ring the bell, then lift the watch fob. I went back and checked all of the Chippendales and found the right one. I suspect that one of your accomplices put the ice on your face that night. And you acted out the rest, saying what you thought would smoke out the unknown murderer." He paused and took a deep breath, about to say something else he didn't like. "You used me. You used Eleanor St. Michel. You used all of us. You knew that I would be suspicious and that I would act on it."

There wasn't a lot to say. Mignon couldn't tell him that what he had surmised had been the plan, that with the assistance of Nehemiah's niece, the room had been prepared for the fraudulent acts. However, something else had interceded, something otherworldly, and she certainly couldn't tell him that. In any case, Mignon liked John Henry, but she had used him. And John Henry wasn't a man who took kindly to being used. "I couldn't trust anyone from this parish, John Henry. I think you can appreciate that. I had to know what happened to her."

He shrugged his powerful shoulders. He could understand it, but it had still hurt in a way that he didn't like at all. "You could have trusted me."

She tightened her lips. "I do trust you. I learned that I could. When I was down in that pit I prayed you would come for me, because I knew that you wouldn't let Jourdain kill me. I knew you'd do the right thing when it came down to it. You wouldn't have covered up my murder. Nor would you have helped pull the trigger."

John Henry didn't say anything.

"John Henry," she said. "I do care . . ."

"Don't," he interrupted savagely. "Don't say that. I understand your reasons. If I had been put in the same position, then maybe I would have done the same thing. Let's leave it at that."

"What are you going to do?" she asked.

"About what? Jourdain tried to kill you. He did kill Eugenie St. Michel with your gun. The evidence is as clear as day. Your hands tested negative for gunshot residue. His test positive. His fingerprints are all over the back of your car and your gun. There's his body, your mother's, Luc's, and Eugenie's. You said he admitted everything. It answers a helluva lot of questions all the way around," John Henry said. "Eleanor wasn't involved, as you said. Neither was Geraud. Gabriel Laurier and Ruelle Fanchon will be questioned as to their parts in the cover-up. There's nothing more that I can do. You might have been up to something, but as far as I can tell there wasn't anything illegal about it, except the vandalism to the sluice gates, and I can't prove you had anything to do with that."

"John Henry . . ."

"It was *never* about scamming the St. Michels for money, was it?" he asked suddenly, and Mignon knew that he wasn't expecting an answer. "You never intended to take the money. It wasn't about that at all. I can't do anything to you, Mignon. I won't do anything to you. But . . . I'll never forget you."

He stood up and a cascade of emotions crossed his face. He bent at the waist and pressed a tender kiss to her cheek. His masculine smell was heady as he leaned close to her. "Goodbye, Mignon Thibeaux," he said, and then he walked away. She saw one of his hands wipe something away from his cheek.

But Mignon wouldn't cry.

The next day she checked herself out of the hospital. A nurse insisted on putting her in a wheelchair and rolling her to the hospital's parking lot. There Mignon got into her car and put her bag in the back. The wound on her side ached from the extra movement, but she ignored it and drove back to the bed and breakfast, where she would start making arrangements for the interment of her mother's body.

Mignon knew that she had to make restitution to several people, including those people whose lands had been flooded when Nehemiah opened the sluice gates. Also, Miner Poteet would receive an anonymous check for a significant figure. Maybe she didn't owe it to him for remaining silent all these years, but he had been there when Geraud St. Michel had attacked her. He wouldn't have to worry about money for the rest of his life.

As she passed through the city, she saw John Henry sitting in his Bronco along the side of the road, but she didn't stop. He sat broodingly in the driver's seat, watching her go past, never slowing down.

Mignon had always known that she would be the focus of someone's anger. All she wanted to know was what had happened to her mother, and she was willing to poke and prod until she found out. Her own status as an artist provided an opportunity, and Eleanor's obsession with the paranormal was the key.

Once inside Eleanor's circle she had several opportunities to search for information, to try to get Eleanor to slip up. She had been so certain that Eleanor was responsible, long before Minor had given her the bracelet with the *E* on it.

Her closest friends had finally confronted her about what she was doing. Mignon had kept most of what she had discovered to herself. Once she found out that her mother was most certainly dead, she became angry. She wanted desperately to know what had happened to Garlande, and although Terri, better known as Madam Terentia Jones, had tried to talk her out of it, Mignon was determined. So they had helped, pleased to return some of Mignon's generosity over the years. They tried to push at Eleanor until something broke.

Early on Kate had donned a long red wig and walked the night as Garlande Thibeaux, careful to tread the grounds only on the nights when the fog was heaviest. But none of them had dared to walk the halls of the mansion that way, and now Mignon suspected that it hadn't been a figment of Eugenie's imagination. Garlande might very well have been haunting the antebellum home. Perhaps she had wanted revenge, or to protect her daughter. And Mignon had to wonder, *Why now?* Why had her mother's ghost started haunting the parish now, of all times? Eugenie St. Michel had stayed away from the mansion for the past two decades. Perhaps her return had been a catalyst, which was only spurred on by Jourdain's return, and finally by Mignon's. The three of them must have forced a circle that prompted some otherworldly events to occur.

They were gone now. Gone like shadows in the dark. Irrevocably and forever.

She would never really know for sure.

A WEEK LATER Mignon was dressed in black as she attended her mother's funeral at the same graveyard where John Henry had taken her weeks before. Days earlier Jourdain Gastineau, Luc St. Michel, and Eugenie St. Michel had been interred in separate private services, their remains cremated. Mignon wasn't invited, nor was she surprised that she wasn't.

Eleanor had taken a trip to the islands, supposedly to stay for the winter. Mignon thought that she might not come back.

She was a proud woman, very much like Mignon herself. She almost pitied the older woman. She hadn't liked being lied to, and Mignon hadn't cared to lie to anyone.

The sheriff's department held back the cameras while a young priest held the services. It was a small ceremony. Bill Martinez the pharmacist was there, as was Mrs. Regret. Horace Seay showed up with his wife, looking appropriately sad. The witch-woman put in an appearance, praying briefly over Garlande's coffin. Vincent Grase hadn't known the Thibeaux family, but he'd felt obligated since he'd helped Mignon purchase the old farmhouse, and Miner himself was there, looking distinctly uncomfortable in a tight black suit that was probably older than Mignon herself. His granddaughter was with him, patting her grandfather's arm as the service finished. Nehemiah held Mignon's arm and whispered in her ear that Terri and Faust thought it was too risky to come. Mignon nodded, and tried to concentrate on what the priest was saying.

When it was all said and done people shuffled past Mignon and Nehemiah, apologizing or expressing their sympathy. Mignon almost cried then, because it seemed like there were so many people who genuinely cared about Garlande.

Nehemiah left her side and Mignon stood alone by the grave. The men who would complete the digging waited patiently in the shade of the church while she stared down at the white casket. Finally she sat down on a nearby stone bench and contemplated the weeping willows and magnolia trees that dripped moss like cobwebs hanging from ancient walls.

Mignon felt a certain amount of relief. It was over. It was well and truly over.

A shadow blocked out the sun. She would have turned to look, but she already knew who it was. She'd seen him earlier, standing by the cemetery's gates, dressed in a black suit that was obviously tailored to fit his strong body. "You mind if I sit down?" asked John Henry. His trademark Stetson was held capably in his hands.

Mignon smiled. She didn't mind at all.

"How's that wound?" he asked, arranging himself on the bench. He laid the hat on a nearby tombstone of a family named Laitsch, dated 1893. "You hurting right now? You've been standing a long time."

"It aches." Mignon didn't look at him. She wasn't exactly speaking of the injury, although it did hurt when she tried to do too much. Then she said, "The man in the wilderness asked of me, 'How many strawberries grew in the sea?' I answered him as I thought good, 'As many as red herrings grow in the wood.' "

"One of your mama's rhymes," John Henry said. "I've never heard that one before."

There didn't seem to be a lot to say. When Mignon glanced up she found Nehemiah looking smug as he leaned against the rental car. She detected a certain gleam in his eye that told her he knew exactly what was going on.

"I see that the workmen are still working on the little farmhouse. They took it up once the crime scene techs were done with it," John Henry said. "I guess I don't need to tell you that it was human blood on all those boards. Enough of it to indicate foul play, but my man over to Shreveport tells me it's too degraded to tell who it belongs to, although it doesn't seem to matter now. Everything is settled." He paused and then added bluntly, "I want a second chance." He hesitated. "I tried to think what I would have done to find my daughter, if she suddenly went missing. I think I would have done almost anything, and I think I understand why you did what you did. Why you *had* to do what you did."

She looked at him then, surprised. His handsome face was serious. Mignon opened her mouth to say something and one of his large hands gently grasped her cheek, cupping the flesh gently. His fingers caressed her skin as if it were the most delicate thing imaginable. Then he lowered his lips to hers and gave her a slow, sweet kiss that she felt all the way to her toes.

When they were done, she looked up and saw that Nehemiah had driven off, leaving her alone with John Henry. "I suppose I have to give you a second chance now, don't I, John Henry?"

He laughed. "What?"

"Or else I'll be walking back to Natchitoches."

He glanced back. "Well, I'll still give you a ride even if you won't give me a second chance."

"That's all right. I think everyone deserves a second chance."

"Damned good thing, too."

"Why's that?"

"I don't give up easily."

"Kiss me again."

So he did.

"John Henry," she said afterwards.

"Mmm?"

She gritted her teeth. "About that vandalism to the sluice gates . . ."

John Henry laughed again.

10-02

FINES 10¢ PER DAY